Idle Hands

Michael A. Occhionero

Foreword

Hello, my name is…Marcus. I am a writer. Or, perhaps I've become a writer. Perhaps I was always slated to be a writer.

I am a victim of circumstance. Or, maybe I am a victim of design. Maybe those two- circumstance and design- are in fact one.

They say it is part of the healing process to come to terms with your past. And so, I've tried to document everything as accurately as I can remember it. The names have been changed, though. This is not some cute writer's device- a poetical patina, if you will- but is truly to protect the parties concerned. In light of the tale I will tell, I think it is understandable.

Looking back, I really don't know if what happened was my fault or if it was destiny. I suppose it is one of those unanswerable questions, one of the questions one is supposed to ignore.

Is existence just a continuum? Is life a chain of predestined, inalterable events set off at birth? Or are we a product of our decisions? Do we really shape ourselves through the actions that we take?

Does it really matter? Is human life, as Nabokov put it, 'but a series of footnotes to a vast obscure unfinished masterpiece'?

A chain of events led to me being here, whether it was predestined or not. I will recount the chain, in hopes of better understanding it, and what happened.

Besides, my current circumstances provide me with plenty of time to kill...

My reflection on the whole thing thus far has brought me to this dawning certainty: that the beginning of my chain wasn't even really an action so much as it was an idea. A dangerous idea permeated my mind and I could not get rid of it. I'm unsure when it got in. I just know that I felt it really profoundly for a long time.

The idea was simple: that there was no sense to life.

Life was absurd, a paradox, and thus devoid of meaning. Everything timeless was actually just a subjective human perspective, and so was false. My life was subjective and relative and individual and alone. Rules were only to be followed by those lacking the wherewithal to be truly free.

What I didn't anticipate, but how could I have, really? What I didn't anticipate was that to be truly free, to be free of any attachments and entirely alone, was to float freely through the atmosphere, without purpose, and often desperate to touch ground.

An inborn impulse bids us rise. And still, we crave desperately to feel grounded.

I don't know if what happened is good or bad because, despite the damage, it has opened my mind.

I expect it truly does depend on how one looks at it...

Part One

'The Bubble'

I really hate my car. I've had it for five years now and it's only gotten progressively junkier. It's too old, it's too plain, and it's too ugly. I really don't like it. I don't like the boring gray paint job. I don't like the bulky old-man-sedan feel it gives when I take those necessary extra wide turns. The old rust bucket angles worse than a beaten up school bus filled to the brim with screaming children and is just about as noisy. I hate it. I really, really hate it.

I'm ungrateful; most people don't even have cars, what the hell am I complaining about? Gas prices have taken a dip recently. The talking heads are saying that it could be devastating for the economy. I think of it as more of a blessing to morons still driving v-6 sedans.

It's snowing tonight, and the bar I'm headed to is in The Plateau near Ontario street, which is about a twenty to thirty minute drive from the east end suburbs where I live with my mother. The snow is coming down in heaps though, and it looks as though the ground will be thickly covered in white by morning. I'm twenty-two years old, it is January 20--, and Montreal has always been my home.

The radio waves are cluttered with bad music tonight. All this commercial stuff sounds the same. Manufactured for the masses, shaved of any real intellectual depth, to be ingested like candy. I really don't like Lady Gaga. Though maybe I should give her more of a chance; I mean people seem to like her. *Girls* really seem to like her. Some of her songs *are* catchy. Disco stick *did* initially strike me as a clever metaphor for a penis. But then, people are stupid. Why would I want to follow what people do?

I can really use a drink.

I tune the radio to 97.7, Montreal's classic rock station, and lean back in appreciation of the change from Lady Gaga to the Beatles. What's the difference between the two really? Why do I like the older stuff so much better? I mean, the Beatles are basically the Lady Gaga of the 60's aren't they? Maybe their sexual innuendo is a little subtler. Okay, a lot subtler. I guess it's just a universal principle that art, or whatever Lady Gaga makes, appreciates with time.

As the song ends, the radio DJ brings in the next:

"That was The Beatles with 'All You Need is Love' from 1969's Yellow Submarine. Great track, always puts things in perspective for me. Alright, we'll hook you up with another thirty-minute rock ride just after this."

I push the radio button off, just as the ads are about to begin. I try my best to avoid ads.

I hit a red light by an underpass of the metropolitan highway, and unsurprisingly a hobo comes up to my car. Normally I don't even acknowledge beggars' existence. It's not that I don't sympathize with their plight, it's just that, frankly, I like to repress things that don't make me happy. Thinking about negative things slows me down, and I don't want to be slowed down. I have places to go, I need to make something of myself. I'm going to be graduating soon. At the very least I'm aware of my hypocrisy. The awareness is soothing, in its own way.

Something about this particular hobo's dirty face and sunken look, or maybe the fact that I am pissed off at society, or maybe the fact that it is snowing pretty hard and the chump is in tatters, I don't know, something pulls on my heart strings and I open up the window and hand him a few dollars from the pile of change in my cup holder. "God bless you", he says, jingling the coins in his plastic cup. I roll up the window without replying or looking too long, and laugh maniacally.

'God bless you', that one really cracks me up.

I turn up De Lorimier Street, deciding to avoid the highway intersection the next street over. I can't help wondering if I'm still subconsciously drawn to the street.

The drive up De Lorimier, admittedly, still makes me think about Bella. We broke up three long months ago, but I still can't shake certain memories from my mind. I still have these moments of vague lingering desire that I can't quite rationalize yet. I guess it takes more than three months to get over a relationship with that level of intimacy, but it's so frustrating that I can't just wipe things clean. No matter how I may try, certain things linger longer than others. Her smell still envelops me from time to time, and her giggle still resonates in my inner ear. She used to wear this green Nirvana tank top that was really cute. She had really pretty hazel eyes that I'd lose myself in… until one day there was nothing left behind them but a reflection of myself.

I finally get to the bar about ten minutes later, and from the outside it looks to be a hipster spot in the mile-end. My windshield wipers are on at the highest level. The snow is coming down in thick fluffy flakes, creating a soft white blanket on the ground. It is the beautiful kind of snow that falls only in the early winter, before the Montreal landscape becomes drier, colder, and blunt.

I followed my phone's GPS, but had neglected to do any preliminary research about the bar. I guess I don't really care. I've been preoccupied with too much lately. From the outside, the place looks pretty laidback, like an informal college bar. The brick wall façade holds no sign. A lit up 'Stella Artois' neon juts out from above a black door.

As I get out of the car, I light a cigarette and check my

watch. I was supposed to meet my date at the bar an hour ago.

I'm hoping she's by now a little drunk, or this may get awkward. No, no, *put on your game face Marcus and stop being a baby.* It's about ten o'clock and the sky is a white-speckled purpled gloom bordered by black.

I parked right across the street from the place in a metered parking spot on Ontario Street. The snow is still coming down heavily. I smoke half my cigarette and run across the street, worrying that the snow might ruin the intricate gel-work in my hair. I spent about half an hour in front of the mirror placing every strand, working up the confidence to go through with this.

If I remember correctly, her name is Marie, or was it Martine? Marie-Anne?

The towering bouncer greets me in a black overcoat and holds the door for me. The coat-check girl smiles. The place is dim, with a chintzy black and gold color scheme. The glow of candlelight illuminates the tables, and dimmed spherical lanterns hang low from the ceiling.

The coat check girl's breasts are the clear focal point of her outfit, accentuated by the ol' open-buttons-and-push-up-bra combo, and when she turns, I notice her thin leggings also expertly highlight the contours of her shapely *derrière*. Her body language suggests I can leave with her tonight after her shift. But then, it may just be part of the whole coat check racket. Her leggings are black, and topped with a red plaid blouse opened at three buttons, exposing a black bra. I bet she's a dirty girl. I tip her a few dollars. She probably lives nearby.

Shut up and focus.

I turn away from the coat check, and walk nervously to the bar to order a gin tonic. The place is surprisingly full for a

Thursday night. It seems to me to be a mostly French-Canadian crowd. Most of the guys are dressed in jeans and clean simple blazers. I feel as though I stick out like a sore thumb, dressed in tight burgundy corduroys and a gray wool sweater. I thought the place would be more of a hip *student* bar. I scope the place out while I wait for the barmaid to bring me my drink. The crowd is a lot more posh than I thought it would be, and seems to be a spot for young professionals. Most of the cut-jaw men stand in groups, staring at the scantily dressed barmaids and smiling arrogantly. The gin tonic arrives and the barmaid tells me, with the help of her fingers, that it is fifteen dollars.

The music is a sort of upbeat electronic ambient, playing fairly loud. There's a girl right next to me at the bar in a tight red cocktail dress. I start chatting her up to rid myself of the unwanted nerves. I throw a few lame premixed lines at her and smile before the blank look on her face leads me to the conclusion that she doesn't speak English. I figure I just set a new personal best, a strikeout clocked in at fourteen seconds flat. That's probably not true. I've had girls reject me with their eyes. At least I spoke to this one. It's okay, she's cute and she smiled at me- I can feed off of that.

I look around the place again. The layout is very nice: high ceilings, urban décor, dimmed lights, bar smack in the middle of the place, tables out to the sides.

I notice a girl in the far corner staring at me with both hands wrapped around her drink, sipping shyly on a straw. She's a brunette with frizzy hair and glasses, which perfectly fits the profile. We met on a dating application and chatted a little while. It seemed understood that this would be a casual encounter. Her pictures had revealed the brown frizzy hair, the glasses, and the tight body. But more importantly, her bio assured me that she 'loves to have fun'. There was a pucker-up graphic by the description so I'd know it was legitimate.

She looks even better than she did on screen. But then, it is dark, and I am as starved for flesh as I've ever been.

I walk over to her casually. She's wearing a thin white blouse open at several buttons, and a tight black skirt. The red bra pops against the white, underscoring the anticipated passion.

"Martine?"

She smiles revealing great pearly-whites

"Marie-Eve. You must be Marcus. You don't know how to keep the time."

She offers me her hand with her nose up and I shake it with a sheepish smile.

"Sorry. I am Marcus, and it is lovely to meet you. Say, has anyone ever told you that you should work for Colgate?"

I smile at her, hoping for a laugh to ease the tension, but she stares at me stone-faced.

"Okay, I guess you're not a fan of my humor. I hate to have to reveal it this early, but I don't think I bring too much more to the table."

She leans into me, the arm holding her drink wraps around my neck, the other ever so lightly brushes my groin:

"I don't speak English very good. *Parlez-moi en français.*"

I guess the noise of the place masked it, but in close her heavy accent becomes audible. I've always had a thing for French accents, and her breath on my ear and strategically placed hands are only adding to the excitement.

"Well, in that case, you've got a great rack, and though I can't see your rear from this angle, I'm sure it's *beyond* satisfactory."

Blank expression. I grin. The liquor is kicking in, and I am enjoying the game.

"*Est-ce-que t'aimes le gin tonic?*"

I ask clumsily motioning to my drink.

She smiles drunkenly and feels up my arms and chest with surprising abandon.

She leans in unnecessarily close, pressing her cheek against mine, the welcome smell of gin accompanying the soft touch of her skin. An arm lingers on my chest. My free arm instinctively coils around her, and in her sexiest, she tells me:

"*J'aime tes bras*".

Loosely translated:

"I'm warmed up and just about ready for insertion."

The music in the place is picking up and I glance at my watch. It's just about eleven and the atmosphere is becoming more upbeat. Tables are being cleared away to free up space on the dance floor. Groups of girls move over to the dance floor and are soon followed by groups of men.

We move to the bar, keeping close. I order us two more gin tonics. I pay the barmaid in crumpled fives and tens instead of what seem to be the more customary little black, or platinum plastic squares. Martine whispers in my ear that she loves art. I tell her I'm an art student. Her favorite novel is Dumas' *Les Trois Mousquetaires*. We kiss. She tastes of gin and sugar. We touch. The warmth of her breath and body feels great. I run my arm down her back, and her skin quivers and submits with delight.

"*Je m'en vais à la toilette.*"

'I need to use the little girls' room.'

She smiles at me and I smile back.

Her canines are slightly longer than her molars. She has very nice teeth.

I watch her walk across the bar to two homosexuals aggressively making out.

She seems to be telling them something hilarious, or entertaining. They turn toward me and smile lewdly, then turn back to her and slap her arm playfully, like the overly theatrical homosexuals on television do. She walks away and their faces become one again. I watch them lap at each other a little while, considering what it must be like to be a homosexual. The easy promiscuity must be appealing.

Leaning against the bar, I wonder if Bella and I ever had this much fun. I wonder if maybe I had been too hasty, if maybe I could have worked harder, if maybe I was making a big mistake. Everywhere I go, I seem to bump into something or someone who reminds me of her. I wonder if the universe is trying to tell me something. And I tense up.

As if on cue, the DJ plays a sappy pop song. Taylor Swift. The girls on the dance floor scream and throw their hands up. The men edge closer.

Marie-Eve emerges from the bathroom and I relax. She looks super sexy in her skimpy ensemble. Her curves are just right. Her skirt is short, and her legs are long. I feel a rush of excitement as I envision her naked. She approaches, pulls me in by the belt, and eagerly kisses me square on the lips.

"Do you want to get out of here?"

I ask with just a hint of desperation.

She looks me in the eyes, though she is barely able to keep hers fully open. She lingers a moment, then melts in my arms and submits.

"Wow, you are fast."

The sexy French accent again. I look her up and down, waiting for the assent.

"Okay."

I smile at her and she smiles back. I hold her a while, enjoying the weightless feeling of momentum.

"Okay let's go."

The coat check girl flirts with me again as I get my coat, and as though in retaliation, Marie-Eve grabs my arm and clings to me. I can feel my testosterone levels surge. I feel incredibly virile. *You're petty and pathetic.* Am I pathetic, or just a victim of the human condition? I grin.

Behind the wheel I feel the effects of the liquor and know I shouldn't be driving.

We make small talk as I find a deserted lot a few blocks away, in an industrial sector just outside the city center. It's a dump spot for snowplows. I let my car idle behind a giant pile of snow isolating us from the street. The snowfall has lessened and now falls patiently, enjoying the descent.

She jumps over to me and bites my lower lip as she undresses. We move to the back seat.

She reaches back to unhook her bra and I struggle to focus, repressing the images of Bella flooding my mind. I kiss Marie-Eve and reach around to remove her bra myself. Her skin is soft, but it is cold out in the open. I feel goose bumps all over her, as I run my hands down her back and up her arms trying to warm her. I bite playfully at her breasts, bite her neck, shoulder, lower lip.

I slip a condom on and she gets on top of me. I bounce her a while and Marie-Eve is loud, safe behind the screen of the snowplows and snow banks. But I'm not there. In fact, I can barely hear her from how far I am. I'm weightless the entire time, somehow detached from the action. I think about hockey, and light waves, and how it's interesting that French girls moan 'Ah Oui' instead of 'Oh', and how that might make for an interesting detail in a novel. I satisfy Marie-Eve, more out of *courtoisie* than passion, and climax into the plastic receptacle. She holds me in the backseat, my car running and the heaters blasting, by the giant mountain of snow still protecting us from the eye of the world. The sweat between our bodies keeps us stuck together for just a few moments. Her hair is frizzier now than before. She looks better without her glasses on.

I get dressed and take the wheel. She tells me she lives in St. Henri. I drive, for the first time in a while, without a single thought in my head. The snowfall has stopped.

The drive is slow, and silent.

I approach her neighborhood and she reaches for my free hand. She lingers around my hand waiting hopefully for a scrap of affection. Her touch clouds my mind and I wriggle my hand away without looking at her. I think that I probably know how she feels, and so I don't want to see her face.

I drive slowly and pull up to her street, which is a *cul-de-sac* encased on either end by decrepit houses all pouring over into one another. The street looks as if a street of middle-class houses were put into a vice and torturously compressed.

Her house is in shambles, with a close-line out front, and visible electrical wires in the back. I see the screen door in front is broken, and that the steps are covered in snow. I finally turn to look at her. Her mascara is running and her lipstick is smudged.

Her eyes are charged with an emotion I refuse to recognize. She looks at me half-expectantly, half-dejectedly. I think to myself that she looked prettier in the club. The thought of the club makes me wince.

"Goodnight."

She looks down, and then back up at me with her best hopeful puppy eyes.

"Goodnight."

She lingers for a second, or two, hoping for some recognition, for a kiss, for anything.

I fish my lighter and carton out of my jacket pocket and light a cigarette.

Marie-Eve slowly gets out of the car and walks up the steps to the broken screen door.

She holds the railing the whole way up, needing something to lean on, and then disappears through the dreary doorway.

I let out a sigh, exhaling smoke. The streets are slippery, and I know it will be a long drive home, so I turn the radio on for some company.

They are in between songs again and the radio personality is bringing in the next one:

"That was 'Yesterday' from 1965's Help! Always gives me shudders. We'll hook you up with another thirty-minute rock ride in just a bit, but first a message from our sponsors."

***

I don't know why I decided to start this there, at that specific point in time. I mean, I think it's relevant. After all, I think it all is, but I had to start somewhere.

IDLE HANDS

I saw Marie-Eve a few more times before things imploded.

The last time I saw her, we went to a party one of her friends threw in St-Henri. I wasn't in a good mood, and I ignored her nearly the whole time. Driving her home that night after the party, we were both silent the entire way back until I pulled up to her house. She began sobbing for a while, and I just sat there confused, waiting for her to compose herself. She did before long, and then she told me very earnestly that she no longer wanted to see me, nor have me as part of her life. She couldn't look me in the eyes. When I halfheartedly asked her why, thinking naturally that this was some sort of joke, or some sort of female over-sensitive exaggeration to a crass comment I had made, or some emotional mine I had accidentally stepped on, she told me that I knew why, and that she had had enough. I told her that I did not understand, and she told me that that was exactly the problem. She said I was self-absorbed. She couldn't take it anymore, and she was done waiting for something that would never happen. She told me she had lost faith in me, and that it broke her heart but she could never see me again. I again insisted that I did not understand, and that we should just talk things out. I think it was plain though, that I really didn't care that much. She started bawling again and left the vehicle head in hands.

I felt strange in that moment. I was unable to grasp why things were suddenly becoming so dramatic. With the flick of an unseen switch, Marie-Eve and I were no longer. I rationalized that some people were just repressed- ticking time bombs. I thought to myself, at the time, that I simply didn't have the time for ticking time bombs. I decided long ago that anyone who wanted to leave, could, and should. I don't waste time repairing broken bridges.

On a brighter note, I did finally graduate from the university in the spring with a Bachelor of Arts. Many of my friends laughed at me for studying literature. Most of them studied business, the more pragmatic choice, nearly assuring themselves lofty desk jobs upon graduation, where they could sit for the next forty years and slowly, but painlessly waste away. I wonder, looking back, if the painless choice might have been easier...

'Existential Angst'

She and I are in the kitchen of a vacant apartment. Maybe vacant isn't the right word. No one lives here. In fact, the landlord, and host of this party told me the place is for rent. It's a great little flat on top of a successful Italian bakery in Mile End.

I got here about an hour ago, coming in alone through a narrow carpeted stairwell straight off the street. The stairs were steep and difficult to climb. Beyond the confines of the apartment, it's a fair May night.

I threw my leather coat in a side room with a big white water heater in it, figuring it would be safer there than plopped on the bed with the others. I'm in a plain white tee that's old and wrinkled, and my jeans are ripped. All in all, I think I look pretty shabby-chic.

There's a party going on with twenty, maybe thirty people at most. My buddy Steve invited me here, but otherwise, I don't think I know anyone else. There's some hip-hop radio trash playing, but thankfully it isn't too loud. It's a good atmosphere for conversation. Which is great, because I feel pretty laid back tonight. There are a couple of tables in the kitchen topped with candy -peach fuzz, cherry sours, Swedish berries- and a few plastic coolers on the deck filled with cheap liquor and cheap American beer. There are a few kinds, but people are drinking mostly the one with the blue ribbon.

In the other room there's a hideous couch. It's white leather, run-down, stained, and outdated. A few black guys sit around the couch smoking weed and hitting on some sleazy Asian girl. There's one more room around the corner that's been fitted with a long narrow table, and there are a few frat guys in there getting drunk over an animated game of beer pong.

We- she and I- ended up in the kitchen though, and I'm leaning on the fridge. It's white too, and was probably manufactured in the nineties. The furniture in here is really ugly, and dated. The door to the patio is open; the coolers are out there on the deck. The ice in them is starting to melt. A few people are lined up to use the bathroom behind us.

It's pretty tight in here. The apartment isn't big enough to accommodate all these people.

She's standing in front of me, legs crossed, hands folded. I didn't notice her earlier, but now that we're talking I notice she's got great teeth. They're white and straight, and the gums are healthy. Very nice teeth. And good style, too- denim on denim, a cute plastic choker, a Bowie tee, and classic white chucks. Her hair is chocolate brown and complements her milky complexion.

She was talking to my friend Steve when she mentioned something about drugs in Copenhagen. I believe it was the Christiania community. I, bored out of my mind, pounced. Steve seemed annoyed, but was too drunk to let my interjection bring him down. He's in the living room now, smoking with the black guys.

We're mid conversation. I don't remember how we got here from the Europe thing. She had been to Europe, I had been to Europe, then books maybe?

"Do you believe in the grand delusion then?"

I ask.

"Sorry, I'm unfamiliar."

She does her best to look me in the eye, does her best to

keep smiling.

The music is kicking a little louder and the people waiting for the washroom are bumping into her back.

"Fair enough, there are many delusions. *Haha.*"

I fidget a little, repositioning myself more suavely against the fridge.

"Let me be more specific. Do you consider yourself a romantic, I mean to ask?"

She scrunches her face a little and furrows her brow.

"Oh. Yes, I'd say so. Are you?"

I smile broadly, sip my beer.

"Yes, I think I am."

Traces of innocence in her eyes. I rub my beard and continue.

"So you believe in it? The happy ending? The white picket fence, the dandy kids, maybe a dog?"

I look at her, smile, sip my beer.

She laughs. It's cynical and bordering on sadistic. I look away disinterestedly, doing my best to cool the blood rushing to my groin.

She uncrosses her legs and stands straight. Her hands move nervously as she figures where to position them. Her nails aren't painted. She decides on folding her arms. Her speech is rigid, but educated- probably a private school girl.

I look away, sip on my beer. It's in a bottle. I prefer beer in bottles.

The party is loud and in full swing.

The black guys in the living room, now trash talking and waving their arms, have decided to rap battle. The music gets even louder. Across the room I see my buddy Steve cackling at them in the corner, egging them on. I smirk, bringing my attention back to her, and she's staring intently at the ceiling. She's about a half-foot shorter than me, no heels.

"If you don't believe in it, how can you call yourself a romantic?"

I half-scream, needing to project over the music.

She answers without taking her eyes off of the ceiling.

"Oh, but I am a romantic. I love it when a man brings me flowers. Especially roses. They smell so lovely."

She pauses, smiles at the ceiling.

"And I prefer the red ones. But, I absolutely refuse to see him buy them. It's just so vulgar."

She moves her eyes slowly, lining them up with my skeptical, smirking face. She smiles this really great smile, all her teeth show. The Cheshire cat? I can't tell if she's serious or full of shit. I don't know that I care.

I laugh a little, cough.

"I see. So how do you suppose he got them, when he gives them to you? The flowers, I mean."

There's no hesitation.

"Well, maybe he picked them, or grew them himself. I don't like to think about it, I just want to enjoy the pretty flowers."

She smiles and tilts her head slightly forward.

"That's absolutely ridiculous. I suppose you are a romantic after all."

We laugh.

She has soft brown eyes, though they lurk quietly behind lots of mascara and eye shadow. Her eyeballs are really glossy. She's wearing this really great, really *piercing* crimson lipstick highlighting her youthful pouty lips.

I start again.

"But really, you don't go for that whole soul mate deal, do you?"

She retorts quickly.

"Do you?"

Her look is playful, though slightly bashful. I rub my chin and stroke my beard.

"I guess I do, in a sort of reserved, guarded, doomed-to-fail kind of way."

I let my head hang a little.

She looks me dead in the eye.

She does her best 'poor baby' pout, sticking her lower lip out. With a southern Baptist accent, she lets out a convincing "precious angel" and puts a hand to my face in mock-motherly reassurance.

Meanwhile, the rap battle wages on in the other room. Backward Yankee Hat and Dr. N-Bomb have made it to the sudden death, winner-takes-all round of the rap battle. The girl they were fighting over is gyrating so that her ass fat jiggles up and down. *What a prize.*

Steve must be really drunk because somehow he's landed the honor of officiating. I smirk as I see him rubbing his ridiculous soul patch, and deliberating the artistic merit of their respective routines.

I turn back to her and look her up and down.

She raises an eyebrow, playfully.

"I want to ravish you."

I bare my teeth.

She plays it cool.

"Cool your jets honey, we just met."

I walk over to the cooler to grab another beer. She's not drinking anything. I get the impression she's on some sort of pills. She fishes her phone out of her little party purse. The purse is a glitzy gold color, and covered in rhinestones. So is her phone cover.

I walk back over and she puts her phone away.

I change the subject.

"So, let me ask you. Because I really must know, do you pronounce it gas or *gazz*?"

"What?"

"Petrol. Do you pronounce the word *gasssss* or *gaaaaaazzzzzzzz*?"

She frowns.

"Gas."

I smile.

"Me too."

Sip.

"But then, what do you think of bumper stickers? Or those chocolate bars that are marketed as 'healthy' protein bars for that matter?"

She grins amusedly, begins to answer. I watch her lips move, consciously licking mine, without picking up on the words.

I think she realizes I'm no longer listening, because she stops mid sentence and touches my arm.

She takes the lead:

"Say, hotshot, I've got one for you. Have you ever had an original thought?"

I squint at her.

"Of course not."

She smiles.

"Neither have I."

She moves toward me, slowly, hesitantly. I pull her in close by her jacket and kiss her passionately.

Her lipstick smudges. Her denim jacket is rough against my naked arms. I command her to take it off, but she refuses. It scratches against me as I go in for another kiss. She stands there motionless, her arms hanging limply by her sides. Her tongue doesn't move either. It feels like I'm kissing a shucked oyster.

I move away from her and we stand there for a minute, looking at each other, neither of us flinching.

There's a commotion in the other room. It appears Dr. N-Bomb has won the rap battle. His brilliant a-a-a-a-a-a-a rhyme scheme, expedited by the repeated N-word end word has taken the cake. I see Steve lifting his arm and drunkenly declaring him the victor.

The Asian girl is in the corner, now heavy petting with some other random guy.

I smile.

My little zombie yawns audibly and her voice drops an octave.

"Guess the party's over."

She backs off, goes to 'check on her friend'.

Steve is trying to escape the uproar in the other room.

Why the hell am I here?

I make my way over and slap Steve, telling him it's time to go. He's drunk himself to the border of control, and does not retaliate.

We grab our coats from the back room and head down the claustrophobic stairwell. It's too steep and a few of the more drunken partygoers take a tumble down the last few steps. Steve and I cackle at them. It seems everyone has decided to leave at the same time.

Outside, there's a mess out on the street. A sizeable hoard of drunken 'young adults' has spilled out onto the pavement, sending up plumes of cigarette and marijuana smoke merging into visible smog refracting the streetlights. It's dark out but it's a mild night. I'm comfortable in my leather jacket. The street is dim, there's minimal traffic, and the sounds of the city and the murmur of conversation are all I can hear. I light a cigarette and check my watch. It's about two in the morning.

Steve has gone to take a piss in the alleyway across the street, on one of those big blue dumpsters. I look around for the party girl and see her with her buddies, passing around a joint. Her friends look raunchy. They're an obnoxious gang; mostly guys dressed in ripped jeans and dirty t-shirts with obscure band logos- *Christ's Deception, Necrosis Oblivion.*

I shuffle over confidently, dragging on my cigarette.

"Hey."

"Hey."

She hands me the joint. I hit it once and pass it off.

"Thanks. So, um, I'm gonna get going."

She looks indifferent. Tries to remain part of the conversation going on in the circle.

"Oh, okay."

"You should give me your number."

She looks me square in the eye. There's a red mark going around her neck where her choker was.

"Why?"

"It'll make the image of you I conjure in the shower later more potent."

Not even a smile. Maybe she didn't hear me. I stand there feeling pretty dumb for a second.

"Look, you seem like a really nice guy. But what's the point? We'll text for a little while, have a pleasant back and forth. Nothing will arise from it. And we'll be back here doing this in a couple of weeks, give or take a few faces."

Steve's stumbling back from the alley screaming my name. He's in the middle of the street with his pants around his ankles.

"That's really cynical."

"Look, I don't want to be mean. You were fun, but I'm not that into dating."

She turns away coldly, deliberately massaging her hair into an up do.

"Just give me your number."

I do my best to smile.

She sighs and puts her number into my phone. I look at her contact information and put my phone away.

"I'll talk to you soon, Joanie."

My tone is a little sharp.

"Yeah."

She shrugs and turns her attention back to her friends.

I move to take care of Steve.

I slap Steve in the face a few times, venting a little frustration before giving him some water.

"Wake the fuck up you idiot, you're making a scene."

I let him zigzag in front of me on the way back to the car. From the way Steve's moving, I figure it must feel like the earth's tectonic plates are shifting beneath him.

In my car, he rests his head against the window and is quiet the whole way home. It is a ten-minute drive. The party wasn't too far from the suburbs. I listen to the radio. 97.7 Classic rock. I know every one of the songs they play.

It's when we get to his house and I drop him off that it happens.

"So are you gonna fuck that slut Marc?"

Steve slurs his words and his limbs are spaghetti.

"I guess not man. She didn't seem too enthusiastic. She's not a slut."

"What do you mean man! You see those guys she came with? Apparently she's fucked every single one."

"Alright Steve you're wasted, go sleep it off."

He turns to me, his eyes are glossy and in a squint.

"I don't understand man. You were hitting it off with her why don't you fuck her?"

"Dude, she's not like that."

"What do you mean dude! I don't get you, man. What do you want?"

I open my mouth to answer, and it happens. For the first time in a long while, I draw a complete blank.

'Styleman'

I walk into work that afternoon with a thumping headache and a mouth like the Sahara. I have been drinking heavily for the past three nights straight- a real lemon-lime nightmare. Vodka and I have never seen eye to eye. Though every time I tell myself that I'll never drink vodka again, I'll find myself, shortly thereafter, drinking vodka again.

I have been drinking for most of the month of August. There just isn't much else to do. Besides, this is probably going to be the last summer I have to screw around before the realities of life come down on me, and I have to begin taking on responsibilities and stuff.

Luckily, I only start work at two in the afternoon today, and so I arrive just fifteen minutes late and with only a slack case of the Monday blues. This is my third dead-end job so far this year. I'm twenty-three now and working at the mall nearest to my mother's. I guess it's fair to say that I'm not exactly what one would call a 'go-getter'.

I parked my car pretty deep in the parking lot, like I usually do, because 'I like to walk'. Really it's because my car is a piece of garbage and I really don't want any of my 'colleagues' to see me coming out of it.

I enter the mall from the side with the least amount of foot traffic- a calculated move- and make my way through the department store perfume section to get to the Stylefile-Styleman section of the store. You see, the store is actually owned by a European manufacturer that is making its debut in North America through a licensing agreement with a well-known chain of Canadian department stores called ABC. And so, it operates sort of like an independent store within a department store. ABC technically employs me, but I somehow technically work for Styleman, and so for bureaucratic reasons beyond my simple-minded understanding, I have, and more than that I *need,* four managers.

So anyway, I walk through the department store perfume section past all the crabby, bitter old hags that buy and sell in that department, and I have to pass through the dress section and be subjected to Joanie's pompous bitch smile. Joanie and I ended up dating for about three minutes and I sort of had an obvious raging crush on her and she sort of knew all along. Things flamed out really badly and so now she thinks I got the job at Stylefile as a ploy to get closer to her, and so she acts as though everything I do is directed at her, and for her benefit, and motivated by her, and for the most part avoids me like the plague. I told her the last time I spoke to her- I sort of cornered her at her cash for a minute while I was off to break- that she was just the forty lashes I needed to give myself as repentance for having treated Bella (my bitch ex) like I did. I thought that was clever, but Joanie still smiled at me like she had me in a box, and still does with that stupid face and her big nose every time I pass by her crummy little cash register.

The pre-Stylefile torture completed, I enter the store and have my headache immediately amplified tenfold by the blaring, and frankly horrible music they play every single day in the store. The manager, a flamboyant homosexual posing as otherwise named Keith, insists, and trust me I have complained adamantly, on playing a fourteen-track cd of electro-pop radio trash *on a loop for the entire day.* He says the local DJ- DJ Gino G- is a 'close' friend of his. The cd is awful, and it's enough to make me feel like I am actively losing IQ points as I idly 'serve' the customers. On top of that, it's somehow actually louder than a bloody club in here.

Today, my torture session begins with a little ditty called "I'm a Prostitute".

I walk in behind the Styleman register to punch into the dated computer system and take a look around the store. Being late, I came in ready for seven hours of Keith's passive-aggressive death stares. However, he seems to be in the back store for now, so I let out a sigh of relief and begin pacing the floor.

The store is laid out with two sections, one for Styleman, the other for Stylefile women's clothes, and this giant over-the-top portal separates the two. It's a black linoleum doorway with neon lights lining the sides, and a giant STYLEFILE sign seen from the men's side, and STYLEMAN seen from the women's. The Styleman side, where I am for the most part stationed, is laid out with a huge sales section and three smaller 'Suits', 'Casual', and 'Knits' sections. Our store has a huge sales section, largely because the mall caters primarily to a teenage clientele. Or at least that's what Keith says.

Unsurprisingly, there is a huge pile of discarded clothes to be folded, re-buttoned, and replaced on 'the floor' awaiting the new guy's (my) arrival. I grimace at the pile, and a stuffy customer- a turtle-necked, Andy Warhol look-alike- shoots me a funny look.

The only saving grace, really, is that Candy is working today. Candy is the new girl and this is my second shift with her. Candy's got great naturally wavy long brown hair, straight teeth, and a nose ring. Our first shift together, I saw her drinking a green liquid and asked her about it. She told me it was water and chlorophyll, which is apparently very good for one's immune system. She smiled when she had finished her explanation. They were lightly green-tinted because of the liquid, but she had perfectly straight teeth. She was wearing black tights with an oversized white tee and a sweat-stained black cap that looked to be carrying at least a decade of wear and tear. All in all, she looked like a stylish little vagabond.

That was last week, and today is the first time I am going to see her since. She works part-time as a student.

As I stand behind the register folding the pile of clothes Keith has left me, and daydreaming about Candy, Keith sneaks up behind me and starts berating me for my outfit. I'm wearing joggers and dirty Nike sneakers, which I admittedly wear just to piss him off, though I balance everything out with a fifty dollar pine green Styleman tee with contrasting white piping and pocket square.

"I told you already Marcus to get rid of those disgusting sneakers. I swear to God if you bring those to work one more time it'll be the last time. Boys, NO JOGGERS NO SNEAKERS, girls NO SLUTTY TOPS."

And with a flamboyant flick of the wrist, he dismisses me and struts aggressively into the back store, his bleached blonde ponytail swaying from side to side. I smirk and go back to my folding. Keith hates it when I laugh at his threats, but I really can't help it.

Looking wistfully through the portal to Stylefile, I see Candy snickering at me from behind a rack of blouses and I smile back playfully.

As "I'm a Prostitute" fades into "Sleep with Me", I walk over to the edge of the women's section to say hi to Candy. She slowly walks over and smiles at me. Today she is wearing white open-toe platform shoes at least five inches high, washed out black denim, a thin white see-through blouse paired with a white tube top, and of course her cute little golden nose ring. Her makeup today is fierce. She applies a bold red lipstick contrasted with a pale blush and a thick stroke of eyeliner that goes beyond her eyelid, so that with her hair styled in short bangs in the front and long and straight to the sides, she appears to me as a sexy Vampire-Cleopatra. Her most salient facial features though are her eyes. Beneath her gothic paint, she bats her soft eyelids to reveal oceans of blue marine so calm and indifferent, yet at the same time so wildly vast. I am so consumed by her, close up, that we stand there for a moment or two, lingering as she waits for me to break the ice.

"Hey", I say as coyly as I can, having to practically scream over the music.

"Hey", she replies shyly.

She smiles again revealing those absolutely dynamite teeth and I get the impression her canines are suddenly longer than her molars. Her long pointed nails are painted crimson red. She looks to me like she can claw my heart raw out of my chest at any moment, and I half want her to, just to put an end to this flat-line anesthesia.

"Do you have this in a forty-six?

A tap on the shoulder breaks my trance, and I turn to see a fat faced teenager wearing a black snap-back cap. He's holding up an awful black three-piece suit with a multicolor paint splatter design- one of our more 'fashion-forward' pieces...

"Hi!", I say as cheerfully as I possibly can, "Let me go check if we have some other sizes in the back", and smile widely.

I turn from Candy, who also smiles a grotesquely forced smile, and head toward the back store, catching a glimpse of my own stupid face in one of the store mirrors. In back, I pretend to look for the suit walking up and down the isles of lined up, faceless mannequins used for display in the store, killing some time before I'm finally released from this hell hole, and I take a long look at the life-size Cara Delavigne cutout we have lying in back of the store (we have three on 'the floor') and remember that I've been meaning to steal it, as it would be perfect for my bedroom. Cara, sporting a sexy and debonair itsy bitsy Stylefile bikini, stares me straight in the eye, mouth slightly agape and vague look in her squinty eyes, and I know that she feels my pain.

Analyzing the cutout, I think to myself how much sexier Candy's face looks painted with a scowl rather than a smile.

Back out on 'the floor', I catch a glimpse of myself again as I correct the scowl on my own face, replacing it with my Keith-approved 'floor face' and leave myself a mental note to suggest, on the next bi-weekly product feedback, that the company slice my 'floor face' off with a box cutter, mass reproduce it, and glue it to all the mannequins. You know, to give em' a little personality.

"Sorry *sir*, the models on the floor are all we have".

The kid looks confused and dejected.

"Oh. Can I order it in my size though? I have a party next week."

"Sorry *sir*, the ordering software is not working properly today."

I look at him stoically, daring him to try again, but he just sighs, turns to put the suit back on the rack and shuffles out of the store.

The rest of my shift consists primarily of folding and replacing clothes, repeating the phrase "How are you doing today? Do you have an ABC points card?", and watching the sexy high school girls shuffle in and out of the store in their innocent little plaid skirts and oozing their curious sexual charge. I walk around to Stylefile as often as I can to get a few seconds of face time with Candy, hoping that Keith won't badger me to 'get back to work'. That part really confuses me, because I essentially get paid, albeit very little, to show up looking pretty and pace around. Despite the joggers, I can't see how my interactions with Candy are in any way a violation of my job description…

A few high school kids shuffle into the store yelling obscenities at each other and make a beeline for the Styleman sales section. I pace around the store, measuring my slow, deliberate stroll to Candy's, and I bump into her, head down, causing her to drop a pair of jeans she was slowly going to replace. I slowly pick them up for her, smiling, and slowly ask "What time do you finish?", though I know she's closing tonight with me, and she replies, batting her eyelids, "At nine you?", though she knows too. The yelling high school kids walk by us out of the store, and I realize we're alone- except for Keith in the back store, and the dozen cameras lining the ceiling.

Candy shifts her weight onto her back leg and tilts her head a little to the left, still smiling:

"Ugh, this shift is so boring!"

I move a step closer to her looking her straight in the eyes:

"There's only about an hour left."

She slowly reaches over and takes the jeans from my hands, her pointed red nails lightly grazing my forearm:

"Do you know how to close the cash?"

I look her up and down slowly:

"I'll show you".

The light gleams on her nose ring, but she doesn't break eye contact, doesn't change that crooked smile. She opens her mouth, her red lips dancing:

"Okay, and maybe after..."

Keith interrupts her, running up to us wearing a navy blue seventy-five dollar Styleman button up shirt with preacher collar, and holding up another in pale powder blue.

"Which one guys? I really, *really* can't decide!"

'I really, *really* don't give a shit, get lost' is not a suitable answer, so I offer:

"The navy blue one looks great on you Keith, doesn't it Candy?"

She nods.

"Oh phooey, I'll just have to take them both I guess!"

He turns, absorbed for a minute in his shirt dilemma, then locates himself as manager and turns back to me:

"Oh, and get back to work. Marcus, your section is a mess, the fitting rooms need sweeping, you have a few items waiting to be placed back on the racks, and there are customers that I am certain I did not see you greet."

As the cd loops back to "I'm a Prostitute" for the twelfth or thirteenth time, I turn to see a few fresh high school kids play fighting in the 'Knits' section.

"Okay Keith, I'll get to it in a minute."

I turn back to Candy, hoping to pick up where we left off, but Keith taps me on the shoulder and I turn back to him.

"No, Marcus. Go do it now. It's a few shifts in a row now you show up to work unprepared. And now, on top of looking like shit and coasting, every time I come out on the floor I catch you flirting with Candy."

Candy looks down embarrassed and tries to move away, but Keith is determined to have it out.

"Don't move. I want you to hear this too. This is your last warning. I will not hesitate to make an example of you Marcus. Do you understand me?"

I stand there for a second, measuring Keith's threats, looking up at the ceiling and the cameras surveying every inch of the 'floor', at the huge posters of sexy girls and boys always staring at me, at the glossy-eyed perfumed customers twirling in front of the mirrors appraising the way they look in their prospective Stylefile-Styleman apparel, at Candy still staring at the floor, and from somewhere deep within me I am beckoned:

"I quit."

Keith just stands there, mouth slightly agape, looking like one of the posters on the wall. I look at Candy, half-expecting her to join me in revolution, but she too looks confused, and looks back at the floor. I pull the 'Styleman Personnel' badge from around my neck, drop it lightly at Keith's feet, and walk out of the store.

I have to pass by Joanie on my way out, but she doesn't see me. She's occupied with helping an old woman select a bathrobe, still nursing a visible limp and the cast on her arm. The sight of the cast brings back memories I've been trying hard to forget.

Back in my car, the sun's going down as I grind up some marijuana into a joint. I pull out my phone to see missed texts from Chelsea, Maria, Elsie, and Audrey. Annoyed, I throw my phone to the side and smoke the joint alone in the parking lot, calmly watching the magenta sky slowly fade to black. Finished, I throw the roach to the side and fish my cigarettes out of my back pocket. I light a cigarette and check my watch. It's now nearly nine o'clock. I move the car into drive and head home. Pulling out of the lot, I wonder how I will explain things to my mother. I know I will be in for a lecture, but I'll postpone it for as long as I can. Maybe I'll just lie. Besides, I am too old to work at the mall.

I pull out of the lot that night angry, and more confused than ever. Peering into the rearview mirror and contemplating the thousand fruitless and endless beginnings in my mind, I realize for the first time that my hair is beginning to thin.

'The Elusive Male'

It's a Tuesday morning, eight o'clock Montreal time and it's that time of year when the leaves begin to change colors and the Indian summer is winding down. It's still pretty warm out today, though, and so I made my way over to Cassidy's without a jacket.

We're walking down the stairs from the fifth floor, in the bleak stairwell of a red brick apartment building in Villeray. It's the kind of stairwell that has water pipes and safety valves and what-have-you's- the guts of the building- exposed, with those dreary steel rails that remind you of death and those concrete steps that seem to go on forever. Cassidy is leading the way, with a towel in her hair. She told me upstairs that she was just stepping out of the shower, and because of the considerable visual evidence substantiating her claim, I believed her. The blue towel in her hair is wrapped in a sort of bun, meshing perfectly with her blonde hair- she's the only real girl I've ever seen make this look sexy- and she's in short shorts with the word 'princess' across the buttocks, she calls them 'pyjamas', and a little loose-fitting old white v-neck tee. I can see through the shirt that her girly pink push up bra is keeping those supple little scoops of honey dipped vanilla perfection tightly in place. I came to visit her early this morning, before my day got hectic- I had plans to walk the park, watch a movie, and masturbate- with hopes of maybe perhaps for the first time getting a little glimpse of the aforementioned scoops of perfection and perhaps maybe alleviating myself of the need to masturbate later, or at least making it optional. But at the door, she, answering with towel in hair and toothbrush in mouth, seemed startled, and whisked me off hastily across the beige-carpeted floor to the stairwell, telling me her roommate and her boyfriend were in a vicious argument, and so we needed to move, and why hadn't I called, and that I looked like a mess. To the latter, I do concede. I am in skinny jeans- not because I am making a fashion statement, but because they are now the only pants in my closet with no holes in them- and a gray worn out cliché of a sweatshirt.

Girls love it when you visit them spontaneously like that.

But anyway, those skinny jeans are now very uncomfortably compressing my red hot blood-swelled groin, and cutie-pie Cassy, still brushing away at her pearly whites, is walking me down the stairs, quite hurriedly, her breasts gently bobbing with her every step, completely in her own world, which I imagine looks a lot like a blend of Candyland and a *Magic Mike* movie. I slow my pace a little, creating a nice overhead view for myself, watching those tits- breasts? can you call breasts you haven't fondled yet 'tits'? or is that more of a possessive term?- bounce ever so gently, and my groin a sweet masochistic double-churned mess of pleasure and pain. I perceive a subtle dew of perspiration on her breasts, those sweet beautiful tender breasts, and wonder what she had been doing before I arrived, and what she will be doing after I have gone, and why she hadn't invited me in... Had she been in bed with another, had I caught her in the midst of a post-coital cleanup? How could this sweet little thing ever treat me so bad? She's exactly that blue-eyed murder David Lee Roth was singing about all those years ago. Blonde hair, beautiful tanned brown honey dipped delicious skin. The best sex I'd ever have, if I just had enough patience. So petite, willingly submissive, dominant at times, slaps, bites, that ass so firm. But I can't trust the little minx as far as I can throw her.

We reach the bottom of the stairs and she has apparently been chattering the entire way down.

"Did you hear a word I said, Marcus?"

She leads me through a side door to the outside world.

"Sorry babe, I was just thinking about something the doctor told me yesterday."

"Doctor? You didn't tell me you went to the doctor?"

She looks at me concerned. So sweet. Daddy wants to pull little sweetheart's hair and give it to her hard from behind.

"Yeah, he gave me some bad news. I've got three months to live. Some sort of rare genetic muscle tissue degeneration. There is good news though, he told me that hanky panky with the woman of my dreams could cure me."

She giggles, her toothbrush now in her left hand, her perfectly manicured hands- she changes the color of her fake nails weekly, to match her mood she says- and I grab her around the waist, channeling my inner Marlon Brando, though I probably looked more like Jim Carrey in one of his fits of insanity, and kiss her passionately on the lips. The taste of fluoride and mint rushes into my mouth, and the sterile taste cools my loins a little. My little Cassy, playfully, oh so cutely and playfully, oh ! she belongs atop the pyramid of some high school cheer squad somewhere, slaps me in the face, still smiling, god she's so cute, and pushes me gently away.

"Marcus, you're so silly! Stop it silly bun! What are you doing today? I have to go to work, but how about later you take me to dinner?"

There it is again. Daddy's little angel beams at me and how could you expect me to say no to such a cutie pie! She works as a teller at the bank. It's got its perks- I mean she's financially independent, and thus so exhaustingly more difficult to get into bed, which is more than I can say for myself...

Alas, my Cassidy is not the brightest of bulbs. But her legs go on for miles and sprout from the firmest, shapeliest backside I've ever had the honor of admiring from afar and occasionally getting the chance to brush or graze whilst entwined in a consensual exchange of saliva, but no more, alas never more, my loins burning, always burning!

"Sure, babe. I've got a few things to do today. I'll come get you later."

She smiles, childish excitement, enchanted by my minimalist mystique, and kisses me twice on the lips, twice on the cheeks and gives me a hug.

"Have a good day cutie, I'll see you later."

She blows me a kiss and returns to the building and her life outside of my field of vision, her privacy, conniving, scheming, nymphomaniacal private life.

I light a cigarette and check my watch. The sun is really bright today, and strong, and I feel glad that it's mid October and I still don't need a jacket, but I'm sickened by this feeling all too familiar to Montrealers, of being on the cusp, with the long, cold, lonely winter just around the corner.

I told Steve I'd meet him at the bar at noon- it's only ten in the morning, as my encounter with Cassy was shorter than I had hoped- and I decide to swing by his place instead, remembering the bottle of Macallan 12 I have in the trunk of my car.

Lately, I've been carrying bottles of liquor in my trunk, because in moments like these, I'm always glad that I do.

The engine sputters to life as I turn the key in the ignition. I toss the old copy of *Lolita* I've been playing with into the back seat. As I drive, I slide an old R.E.M. cd- 1983's *Murmur*- into the cd slot, lowering the windows of my 98' chevy down. There's always been something about R.E.M.'s sound that has, for me, captured the melancholy of the changing seasons so well. I wonder why exactly that is as I slowly pass the trees down Belanger street, watching the countless leaves jumping from their branches, each one more gracefully than the last, down, down, in swirls, to their inevitable black paved death.

Chucking my cigarette butt, I quickly find myself thinking of Cassidy again. Cassidy and I have been dating for little under a month now, and although it is a little early, I really do think it may just be love. I've never desired a girl, physically that is but then what else is there, as much as I do Cassidy. The first time we met was so romantic! We locked eyes from across the bar. I tried to take her home that night, but she wouldn't let me...

It takes me about twenty minutes to get from Cassy's to Steve's, his parents' place in Anjou, eastwards. I pull up to his place and see a moving van, with a ramp leading to his front door, and a bevy of movers mechanically removing the furniture and other valuables from the house and into the van. Sliding past them into the duplex, bottle in hand, I see Steven sitting at the table in the kitchen, presumably the last thing the movers will be taking, head in hands, looking pretty dejected. Steven's parents have just divorced. He's taken to saying, 'as far as divorces go, it's not that ugly'. Which strikes me as somewhat of an equivalent to saying, 'as far as kicks in the groin go, it was mild'.

I slam the bottle of whiskey on the table and Steve looks up, not having heard me walk in. I move to the cabinet and fish out a couple of highball glasses, the rest I assume had already been packed away in boxes, and I gently place them on the table and sit down.

"Our appointment got moved up a couple hours buddy."

I pour us each a thumb of scotch as the movers continue to

move about, emptying the house from head to toe.

"Marcus. What's up? I'm sorry man I'm really mush today. My mom and dad just left actually. They argued the whole time, naturally. My mom broke a plate. It was dramatic."

Steve grabs his drink and downs it. I pour him another. Steve's eyes are bloodshot, and it looks like he hasn't been to bed in a while.

"Buddy don't worry about it, I completely understand. Listen, let's have a couple drinks and go for a walk, help you forget about it. It's a beautiful day, and it'll do me some good to get my mind off of things, too."

He looks as though he's too tired to argue, and nods meekly.

"Alright man, you're right. So how did things go with Cassy?"

"I'm here two hours early. How do you think they went?"

He smirks.

"Still a no-go, huh. Well bud, I think you and I both knew you were getting into this one for the long haul."

"Damn it dude. The girl's a genius. If she keeps turning down my sexual advances, I'll have no choice but to propose to her. It's all part of her master plan!"

Steve smiles at me, mocking my idiotic predicament.

"What's going on with you man? Moving day? Why do you look like haven't slept in a while? Do you need help with anything?"

Steve rubs his arm and looks around at the movers in blue jumpsuits, still coming and going, now emptying the furniture out of his sister's room.

"Naw man I'm okay, the movers will take care of everything."

Steve looks up from his drink. Pours another. We're both a couple in now, and the bottle is a quarter of the way down. He fingers the glass, spinning it, mulling something over. Then he sighs, lets his shoulders hang, and looks down into the dark brown scotch.

"I guess I'm a little depressed man. I guess, to be honest, I'm angry with my dad for not having tried harder, and I'm angry with my mom for having given up. My dad bought a mustang. I think that was the breaking point. A mustang! But I'm mostly just worried about my sister. She's younger than me, and girls always take these things harder. I just wish there was something I could do. It's a really shitty helpless feeling, you know. I guess I just need to be strong for her."

We pour even another scotch and already I feel that I'm drunk. I look at Steve and the familiar sadness and helplessness etched on his face. My parents had gotten divorced a few years prior, and so I felt as though I could sympathize in my own way with his pain. The movers are now clearing out Steve's room, and I see three of them in dirty blue jumpsuits carrying his mattress and bedframe across the tiled floor and into the truck. Steve puts an arm on my shoulder.

"I'm sorry, I don't mean to be a bummer. Don't worry about it Marc. There are worse things in life. People just need to do what makes them happy, right? At the end of the day, my parents weren't happy. And I couldn't ask them to keep up a charade, to have to put on a façade every day of their lives, could I?", he works himself up, and there's a knot in his throat, "I couldn't ask them to think of their kids before themselves could I? To think of my sister, and what it means to…"

He checks himself, standing and pacing the kitchen impatiently.

"It just sucks man. It just sucks. But it'll pass. Everything does right?"

I look at Steve and I'm completely at a lack. I have always been of the opinion that family issues are ones that should be dealt with internally. Besides, what would my two cents contribute to the situation?

"It's fresh Steve. It'll pass. It'll suck for a while, there is no doubt. But I promise it'll pass."

Composed once more, he lifts his glass.

"Everything will pass. Cheers to that."

We click our glasses and down the contents. The scotch burns my esophagus. I think to myself that it's funny how much better scotch tastes in small, measured sips.

"Did you hit the gym today Marc?"

"No, yesterday. And tomorrow. I worked out for an hour yesterday, curled forty-pound weights, and then ran on the treadmill for a good half hour. It's showing great results."

"That's nice Marcus. Keeping the body firm for the ladies."

Steve winks at me drunkenly and I smile.

"I don't have the funds to be a sugar daddy, so I guess that leaves vanity right? But you know what man, that's what it is Stevie, I've decided it's not the time to look for a place to go, but rather for something sweet to listen to on the way."

He throws his arms in the air emphatically:

"Marc shut the hell up. I can't understand the garbage coming out of your mouth when you start talking all cryptically."

We've polished off about half the bottle by now, and the

room is beginning to spin. I put my arm on Steve's shoulder, determined to get a smile out of him. His eyes are crinkled in a frown, and his beard is untidy.

"Stevie, I realized today that I have a talent that few others, the others being mostly journeymen like myself, can lay claim to."

I pause, dramatically raising a drunken eyebrow.

"Wanna hear what it is?"

"Yeah, out with it already man."

"I can tell a woman's age, rounded to the nearest half a decade, from just a quick glimpse of her backside. It's like looking at the rings on a tree trunk for me. A telltale sign, Skipper."

We laugh like drunken idiots.

"Speaking of backsides, Cassidy. Caaaa-sssi-deeeeee".

He exaggerates the syllables, making obscene gestures.

"Dude, no offence, but I have absolutely no idea how in the hell you landed her. She's a goddess."

We pour ourselves a fifth. I miss Steve's glass and we cackle even harder.

"Stevie, let me impart unto you a little kernel of wisdom. Women are attracted to men who don't give a damn about them. Men who are needy are just simply not going to cut it. So, when it comes to women, I become incredibly attractive to them by inhabiting a role… 'The Elusive Male'."

Steve rolls his eyes.

"You're unbelievably full of yourself, you know that?"

"The Elusive Male, my dopey friend, is the man who is inwardly focused, who has no interest in the needs of the woman, and who comfortably strides on, unhindered by his rich understanding of all his most lethal flaws."

"So an asshole? Really? That crap worked on that girl? God damn it, why are the pretty ones always so stupid?"

I raise an eyebrow, trying my best to repress the smirk forming on my lips.

"Stevie, it's not a question of intellect, and it's not a question of being an asshole! Women love a man with intrigue, with mystery. She likes me because I'm debonair, not because I'm dependable! She gets enough of that from her job."

I snatch the bottle, now nearly done, and pour the remnants equally- as equally as I could as drunk as I was- into our glasses. They're filled just about to the top, but neither us seem to mind, the whiskey by now tasting as familiar as water. We click our glasses once more.

"But Marcus, she doesn't know a thing about you."

"Exactly, my good Watson. She enjoys the persona because it's dependably two-dimensional."

"I thought the point was not to be dependable."

He smirks at me and I smile back, making a lewd gesture with my finger.

"You're oddly turned on by the impossible, Marc. The whole thing's a sham. It's a house of cards dude. It's shallow, superficial. It's just a matter of time before it all falls to pieces."

"When it inevitably falls to pieces, I'll simply build a new house."

"Jesus, a new house?"

"Yeah a new house, why not? It's not that difficult, once you get the hang of it. If you're really perceptive, you can even learn to draft blueprints."

"Why not just build something more sturdy? Don't you ever think about the future? It takes time for a house to become a home."

"A home? The future? The future is just a concept, a product of human thought. All that there is, really, is what is readily at hand. Who wants to live their lives dedicated to something they cannot see?"

"Aw, cmon Marc. That's just cynical."

And that was the last thing I remember Steve saying, or slurring actually. I was laughing, though I don't remember why.

I must have been out for hours, because when I woke up it was dark out, and I was lying on the floor of an empty house. Steve was gone, the movers were gone, the furniture was gone, and I was alone. It took me a couple of minutes to locate myself, and my neck and back ached from lying on the floor. My head was throbbing. I fished around in my pockets for my carton of cigarettes. I lit a cigarette and checked my watch. It was nine o'clock. I inhaled long and hard and the tobacco and nicotine calmed the spinning. I smoked half the cigarette lying flat on my back, unable to move.

It occurred to me that I had flaked on Cassidy, but I figured I could patch that up later, make it up to her by seeing her another time. What was the rush? Besides, my nonchalance would translate into greater desirability. If I looked at it that way, I had done myself a favor.

I finished the cigarette and got up. But as I got back to my feet I felt lightheaded, and overwhelmed, as though time, life, the world, were passing me by faster than I could process them. I stood there completely still for a while, leaning on the kitchen counter and staring at the simple, repetitive, tiled pattern on the floor- small black and white checkers.

It was a while before my head completely stopped spinning, as though I had just jumped off of a moving treadmill, having been going at full speed to nowhere, and the treadmill still whirring on just beside me, unchanged by my absence.

***

I guess I should offer some context to all of this. The thought occurred to me...

My father is an accountant. He was already an accountant when I was born, and I assume he continues to be to this day, wherever he is. He was always a very dependable one, too. His clients love him. It's my understanding that he hadn't missed a deadline since he decided to dedicate his life to the profession.

My mother is a very erudite accountant. She too, has been for as long as I've existed. She too, is a stickler for deadlines. My uncle, her brother, is an accountant. My other uncle, my father's brother, is also an accountant. My cousin, his son, has just become an accountant. My brother is in business school, studying to become an accountant. My aunt, who divorced my uncle who is an accountant, remarried last year. Her new husband is an accountant.

When I refer to 'east end guys', I generally refer to second and third generation Italian-Canadians, very much like myself, that I grew up with on the east side borough of St-Leonard, on the island of Montreal. St-Leonard is a primarily Italian suburb, now populated by second, third, and fourth generation Italian-Canadians. It's not quite the white-collar colony I make it out to be, but there are an awful lot of accountants in my social circles. St-Leonard has an Italian café bar at every corner. This is not an exaggeration. These bars are typically frequented by the types of people who do not believe in paying taxes. Not knocking them, just saying. The most popular of these bars is Café Gaetano, open since the seventies. Due to its popularity- Gaetano's Panini and Italian coffee have made it a Montreal landmark- it is easily the busiest and most outsider friendly.

I have been smoking marijuana for a few years now. I picked up the habit as a teenager, about the time my parents got divorced. There is no correlation between the two events beside their chronological overlap, I assure you. It started off as a cute recreational thing. I'd go out and meet my friends, and we'd smoke a joint every now and again, and laugh at one another in juvenile merriment. *Haha! Look how stoned Marc is. Pansy*. That kind of thing.

It's not like that anymore. The habit quickly grew to the point of being a daily thing. It's a disgusting word to use, but it feels as though it's become a *need*. It's not even necessarily weed. It's just a numbness I need to feel every day. I guess I enjoyed it more than I realized. I used to use the excuse that in the smoke I would find clarity. It was funny. It was ironic. It isn't anymore. I have smoked marijuana at least once a day every day for the past three years, among other things. I don't even know why anymore. It used to be an escape, a way to burrow myself neatly in the recesses of my mind, away from the judgment and guilt and responsibility of the world. Now, it no longer helps me run from the guilt. It is the guilt. But the numbness it brings is something I crave constantly. Numbness. Forgetting. A momentary clean slate- though the moments have been receding lately. Nothing is real when I'm high, and every time I emerge from the smoke, I feel a thicker haze shrouding my reality.

Then, of course, there are women. I know my love life is a

wreck. Is, was, I get confused sometimes with which verb tenses to use. It recalls the end of a solitary game. You know, the game on the computers. 'Would you like to quit and start a new puzzle, or would you like to undo some of your moves and restart the same puzzle?' I seem to change my mind every few minutes when it comes to women.

I have this silly correlation ingrained in my mind between satisfying a woman and possessing inane amounts of money. Here's the pseudo-rationale: women want a man who is in control and stable. Control and stability are one, and are facilitated by money. If I don't have a lot of money, I will be a letdown. I am a gamble, not a sure thing. Women are conservative, and do not like to gamble. I cannot take the rejection, thus I must stay away from women. I am not to be taken seriously.

I know it's completely ridiculous, and that this line of thought is fabricated. And yet, I *know* that it is true. I know it empirically as much as I know it instinctively. I know it as part of the fabric of my being that I will not turn out to be what a woman wants.

It may be an arbitrary detail, but my parents' wedding song was 'Moonlight Lady' by Julio Iglesias. It's a cheesy pop song sung in English, though colored by Julio's unmistakable Latino flair. It used to give me shivers as a child. Listening to it conjured vivid, though childish images of man and woman falling in love under the moonlight in a moment of unbridled passion and serendipitous powerless fortune. Forever in a passionate bliss, hearts tickling the verge of bursting and they, just sitting there, he in his tux and she in her moonlit sequent dress on the veranda of some lush careless garden. Hearts swollen, lovers lost in lovers eyes, in a bubble of romance and impenetrable aching for two, just for two.

Some of the greatest things you'll ever see or imagine will

exist only as these images of perfection running slowly away from you, never to return. And you need to be okay with that. You need to be tough, and know truthfully deep down that you are alone and you will always be alone and that that is okay. Because nothing lasts forever. Things and people come to an end. They just do. They perish, run their course. It is just simply fact that nothing can last forever. Nothing ever has. Life is long, and life is lonely. But what is the alternative?

My favorite line in that Julio Iglesias song is the end of the chorus, where he sings 'It's alright 'cause tonight's on me'. That brand of machismo has really stuck with me.

Besides, the lonely finding nourishment is just a trope that everyone loves because it creates this fuzzy feeling inside that's powerful enough to distract from the negative. 'Love is a drug'.

Sometimes I feel crushed by expectation. The feeling is of a crushing, overwhelming, jaw-locking, leg-paralyzing load sitting on my shoulders and keeping me completely static. The only way for me to cure myself of it is to knead into my brain the notion that I cannot please everyone. And trust me, I have tried to please everyone. But once you've learned that you can't, and I mean really learned that, learned it so that it adopts the state of ' unquestionable fact' in your mind, you're free. You're free from the bullshit shackles of expectation, and you can finally be yourself. And what you realize when you begin to be yourself, is that people often respect that. And suddenly, you find yourself comfortable in your own skin, and content. I equate that kind of comfort to immunity. Rock n roll music facilitates this sort of immunity for me.

A problem that I think I have with myself, and I'm only capable of locating these problems within the framework of my own psyche when my neuroses afford me a moment of clarity and I can take a glance at the internal wiring… A problem I have with myself is that I always venture south. Or at least, an overwhelming percentage of the time I do. I like to think of myself as an explorer, and yet, I always seem to venture in the same direction. I've been to the border of North and South, many times in fact, and I've looked over the fence. And yet I rarely, if ever, cross the median. It's my second-nature to excavate.

When I get high in the daytime I have this eerie feeling like a warm day in January. It's this strange out-of-time sensibility like something behind the scenes has stopped running correctly, and I am the only one who can see the glitch.

But then sometimes I think that the fact that I smoke every day suggests depression. Only depressed people take drugs every day, right? I'm 'depressed' because I'm broke, sure, but mostly I think I'm 'depressed' because even when I'm with other people, I'm always all alone.

Maybe I shouldn't use the word 'depressed'. It's a hot-button word these days, and tends to offend. Maybe I'll use 'melancholic'.

Sometimes I find myself in the deep end of the public pool and I think to myself that it's all luck. That it is all outside of my control. It's coincidence, and there's nothing I can do about it. When I'm sober, I think I realize that it's not exactly that it's all luck, it's that it's all *founded* on luck. It's not that there's no skill or effort involved, it's that the hand you're dealt is not up to you. It's difficult to see the difference sometimes. It's very slight, but it makes a world of difference.

And then sometimes I think to myself that it's insane that I would be lamenting the hand I'd been dealt. I was born in the first world, right?

I can't shake the notion that where you are has a profound effect on your reality. The geographical location in which you spawned as a human being, where you were plopped from the cosmos to begin this journey on planet earth plays such a critical role in how your journey unfolds. This fact makes me think of the whole world as a sort of show. And so, 'should be' and 'shouldn't be' are completely irrelevant. It's more like, in this part of the show, things work like so, shall we go see it?

I think about the meaning of life very frequently. I've come to various conclusions at different times in my life. Here's the latest, coming to fruition at the tail end of a bout of existential dread: we are not nothing. We are something. We are here. We exist. It has to mean something. *Has* to. And yet it doesn't. And even if it does mean anything, there's no way for us to know. So here we sit, on this plane of existence where nothing and everything are just spectral ends beyond our comprehension. Truth is a sphere. And we stand on that sphere.

But the tricky thing with spheres is that you can never see the whole thing from any one perspective.

I've had this fog clouding my mind for the longest time now. I don't know really how to explain it. It's like every decision, or rather excuse me. Every *stance* one can take, every position one can adopt when making a decision, is justifiable. I mean, I know. I put myself to the test in so many spots and I find myself able to see two, three, four sides to the same situation and all make sense and are feasible and are possible and are justifiable. And so, it simply comes down to something like, what rhetoric, or what logical framework backing each of these positions, these stances, these actions, is the one that I, as a person with morals, align myself with the most? Right? It comes down to values. Moral judgments. What do you stand for? Essentially.

Well, what if I told you that I didn't stand for anything? Nothing. Not a damn thing. What if I told you I could be convinced of anything? Would you think me an idiot? But then, what if someone else's rhetoric, a new rhetoric you had not been exposed to, makes more sense than what you were thinking before? And now that you have been exposed to this new way of thinking, it shatters the very ideological foundations you built your self-understanding upon? That would only be the case if you accepted this new way of thinking as truth, right? Would you accept something completely logical as truth if it shattered your perception of the world? Is it possible to go through life never changing your mind? But then, if you don't believe something is real, is it? And furthermore, if only what you believe is true, and there are seven billion of us roaming this earth, and each of us believes in our own unique, individual, distinct, unwavering, and never perfectly overlapping truths, then whose brand of truth is true? How is conflict avoidable?

That's why we're all self-interested. We only inhabit one mind, one shell of a body that houses said mind. And that's the only key we have to existence. So, at the end of the day, if existence is all we know for certain, and I think in their heart of hearts even the most fanatic of religiosi believe this, then it makes perfect sense to do everything in one's power to prolong this 'reality' we *know* is real. Right? It's our instinct. We can think critically, we can perceive through the senses, we can create languages through which to communicate. We can feel. Who wants to trade all of that away for the mystery behind the curtain of death?

I think it's a gamble *not* to do whatever you want, whenever you want, while you can.

So I guess to backtrack a little, how can it be that there is a truth, when knowledge only exists in minds? Well, if something is written on a piece of paper, and that paper exists outside of a mind as a physical entity, then there. Knowledge exists outside the mind. Wrong. Because the only way that language becomes ideas, and ideas become language is through the mind. And every idea ever was the product of a mind. And minds only exist in this world, that we know of for certain. And so truth must be existence, as we know it, and only as we know it, right? Truth is the human race. If that's the case, what good are morals? Morals are timeless, but reality is very much in time.

Very well then, I do believe we've made it to the crux of the argument: why believe anything when any idea is interchangeable with the last, should it serve my self-interest?

'Pretty Vacant'

It is a Saturday night, and I am out drinking with Steve. We came, as we so frequently do, to Carney's. Steve is mingling with a few of the other east end guys that like to hang around this spot. We've become pretty chummy with the 'regulars' since we're here nearly every Saturday. *These are the things you do when you're twenty-three and 'lacking direction'.* I love the place because they have the best rooftop terrace in the city, and they like to play a real eclectic mix of oldie classics and trendy electro beats. But most importantly, they're cool with us doing blow in the bathroom.

Carney's is on St. Laurent street- one of the more trendy nightlife streets in Montreal. It is a one-way street lined on both ends with bars, clubs, restaurants, and hip one-of-a-kind boutiques. The street is always jostling, but it really comes to life Friday and Saturday nights. The city refers to St. Laurent as 'the main'. This time of year, before the holidays, 'the main' is decked with beautiful lights hanging from lamppost to lamppost, illuminating the scantily clad young women and eager young men.

I invited Candy out tonight. I have been thinking about her quite a bit since the Stylefile fiasco, though I haven't gotten the chance to see her since. I had gotten her phone number while working with her, and so after a little bit of back and forth, she agreed to see me. It was simple enough, I guess. I'll admit, I was very excited when she agreed to meet me at Carney's tonight. I even went out and bought an extra-tight black haute couture t-shirt to wear over my raggedy jeans.

On the other hand, I still have Cassidy to worry about. I

eventually smoothed things over with a lot of sweet-talking and degrading apology after having stood her up last week, and she finally agreed to see me again. She told me she would be busy tonight with a family affair, and so we made plans to go for brunch tomorrow morning. Sunday morning brunch has always been an excellent way to appease an angry woman. But the question remained what to do on Saturday night, and so I messaged Candy.

Candy walks in up the stairs and onto the terrace, and she does her thing. The game has begun. She scans the place, very coyly making a point to look right through me. Then she and her clique, all dressed tomboy chic and wearing hats varying from bowlers to beanies, go to the bar to order drinks. They're all dressed in black. They look like a little gang of gothic scarecrows. I'm sitting in on a conversation between Steve and some mechanic friend of his, discussing the benefits of an air-intake valve. The mechanic tells Steve how he installed a muffler last week in his garage, drunk.

"So then I took a drunken piss in the bushes. You know what's the difference is between a piss and a drunken piss?"

"What?"

"Aim."

He's funny, but I have more important things to tend to.

"I hate taking pisses in the bushes. You're never more vulnerable in life than when you're taking a drunken piss with your back turned. It's awful. Almost as awful as peeing with an erection. Am I right?"

He and Steve start laughing.

I move over to the opposite end of the bar and lean over, waiting to order another gin. I'm a little hyped up, wondering if the impatience shows on my face. I'm doing my best not to sniffle, or to obsessively finger the little baggie in my pocket. Carney's terrace has a large circular bar in the middle of it, and palm tree tropical décor surrounding the outlying tables. It's mid-October, and so the setting is perhaps a little ironic, but the terrace is kept open thanks to the high-power heat lamps the employees have scattered about. Carney's is a bar that gets loud, and on the terrace, everyone is smoking. But, when the place is nearly full like it is on this particular night, the place becomes a party big enough to, if one has an eye for navigating crowds, create bubbles of intimacy.

I lean in on the bar and order two drinks. I ask the barmaid to invite the pretty lady across the bar to join me. The barmaid smiles and does as she is told, strolling across to Candy and whispering in her ear. Candy looks my way feigning surprise and excitement, and makes her way over to see me. She walks with a very distinct girlish gait, with almost a skip in her step. Her nose ring glistens in the haze as she makes her way through the crowded bar over to me. The DJ is playing a list of oldies that he has remixed to sound electronic and thus contemporary. He has just started playing his rehashing of "Who'll Be the Next in Line" by The Kinks.

"Hey, Marcus."

She smiles that great smile and the bartender brings us the drinks. Candy noisily takes her drink in hand, plastic gold colored bangles lining her forearm.

"Hey".

I begin sipping mine. It's weak and I notice, annoyed, that my shoelace is untied.

"Thanks for the drink. Haven't seen you in a while, how are you?"

She's of course dressed entirely in black, with the cherry on top being the ironic black sun hat she rocks in the dead of night.

"Yeah, I've been busy."

My response falls flat and we stand there a minute, sipping the drinks. I want to tie my shoe but there's no room for me to bend over. The bar is loud. Candy is wearing red lipstick again. The barmaid bends over and I can see a pink thong as her short skirt rides up. Candy's nails are also the same sharp red they were last time.

"How come you never text me anymore? You were so enthusiastic for a little while. You already got tired of me?"

She reopens the conversation coquettishly. She slowly reaches forward and lightly scratches my forearm with her nail. She looks at me pouty-faced, her take on the feminine come hither. I look down at her hand menacingly, causing her to recoil, and then back at her eyes. I stare at her big blue eyes with what I hope is a crazed look on my face. She holds her own.

In the haze of the bar, her eyes strike me more as fishbowls than seas of blue.

"Because you're a waste of time."

I say this viciously and Candy smirks, sips her drink daintily.

"That's not nice. Since when are you such a jerk?"

Something about her face annoys me. Her air of self-satisfaction and confidence is paper thin, so obviously a veneer. Steve comes over to say hi. I introduce them and Candy makes small talk with him for a minute or so. I look the other way. Steve eventually walks away and Candy turns her attention back to me, raising an eyebrow.

"Look, you're cool. Some would even say you've got a certain charm about you. But I'm simply not interested is all."

I say this flatly. She looks at me confused. I want to shatter her.

"I... I never assumed you were..."

"Look, you don't have to say anything. You know it, I know it: men want you. The thing is, sweetheart, you're great, but you and I are too much alike."

"Excuse me?"

She frowns a little. Her confusion amuses me. It's nice to see that you're rattling someone. It's so gratifying to say things to people that they'd never expect to hear. And to watch their faces contort in search of what to do, what to say, how to remain composed.

"You think you're some sort of prize, am I wrong?"

I smile and she snorts, uncertain whether to laugh or be offended, my theatrics toeing ever so gently the line between playful and sadistic.

"Honey, it's okay. I'm glad you think you're a prize. More people should for chrissakes. The only problem with that routine, sugar, is that you're face to face with the biggest prize of them all."

I sip my drink and wink at her, scanning the rest of the room. I wave across the bar at nobody in particular and smile a phony salesman's smile. I look back to the film unfolding before me, and Candy's face changes from frustrated to amused. She thinks she's in on the joke now. She even giggles. Maybe she thinks I'm ridiculous, maybe she thinks I'm hilarious, maybe she just thinks I'm an asshole. Either way, she hasn't thrown her drink in my face yet.

"You're weird."

She says this with a point of fact smile. This girl, and note I use the word girl and not woman, thinks that she can juxtapose offensive remarks with a pleasant demeanor and have the two cancel out. No, it's actually beyond that. She actually thinks it comes off as charming. Well, it sort of does, or at least it's distinct, but I'm in deep now and not about to break character. I smile back at her, accepting the challenge.

"Weird is such a plain and meaningless word. Did you mean extraordinary? It's okay honey; don't let your limited vocabulary get you down. I've seen people make it in life with a lot worse. And honey let me tell you, you've got assets. You've got a rocking physique and a real dazed look about you. Men love it. You don't have to tell me, I know. Your phone's lighting up day and night they can't get enough of you. You're beating them away with a stick, honey. I know, trust me, I know."

She tires of my act and decides to give up. Candy looks annoyed and rolls her eyes at me. She does this really theatrically. Gets her big blue irises to do a full revolution in their sockets. It's really pretty. And the mascara perfectly applied to those lashes. Gosh, is it ever pretty.

"Why are you talking that way? So do you have a job? Why did you quit Stylefile? That was so random."

She brushes her straightened hair back behind her ear, revealing pretty diamond studs. I do not have a job, and I quit Stylefile because...

"Don't change the subject. As I was saying, you and I we got something in common. We're selfish; we don't make time for other people. The only difference between the two of us, you see, is the nature of our charms."

Frustration is starting to build in her face, but she suppresses a frown. I assume because emotion is bad for one's complexion. Maybe it's bad for her look to be angry on the scene.

She's wearing black leather pants over black patent leather combat boots, with a sexy little black crop top, and a short black leather jacket. Her toned pale belly remains exposed, confidently sitting there for all to see. She's got a diamond stud in her belly button that I can't help but stare at for a while.

"You see… your charm is your aura. You're like a Venus flytrap for men. You got the smells, the looks, and the attitude all spot on. They take one look at you and they want you. You're… you're vice incarnate. You are the devil in the form of female desire. You're red hot and you look dangerous. And baby, you act it too. Me, on the other hand, I've got words. Some may say that beauty fades, and building intellect is a more effective way to spend one's time but I bet those idiots never had a look at you. You're a star. And you're going to be a star right up until your ass and tits start to sag and the crows start jogging on your face. I'm kidding, crows won't actually walk on your face, and you'll just get wrinkles and get old and ugly. But hey, youth is the belief that youth is infinite right?"

I finally get the rise I was looking for. Her face turns quickly from pretty and indifferent to nasty and wicked.

"You know what, fuck you Marcus."

I should stop speaking, but I won't.

"I was thinking the same thing. Your place or mine?"

I smile at her and wink. She flings her drink at me with full force. I jerk to the left to avoid it and it hits some chump behind me. I grab her violently by the arm and pull her in close, so that we're face to face. She resists but I look at her menacingly, increasing the strength of my grip on her arm. People are by now noticing the scene unfolding, but I don't take my eyes off of hers. She reflects my stare eyes wide open, unflinching. We stand there in the middle of the bar with people watching, neither of us backing down- alpha and alpha in a stare down.

This close to her face, I can see the imperfections in her makeup, the clump of mascara at the corner of her left eye, the uneven lines in her foundation. Her lips look dry. Her hands are soft, but frail. She has bags under her eyes from lack of sleep.

I loosen my grip on her arm. She must feel this because she tells me:

"Let go of me or I'm going to kick you in the groin."

I let go of her arm and my expression softens. She stares me down a few more seconds before composing herself. She adjusts her hat, and pulls a compact mirror from her purse, assuring herself that her makeup has not moved.

"You've got a clump near the left eye."

She looks at me over her mirror, then back into her reflection, and realizes I'm right. She corrects her makeup and puts her compact away.

"You're psychotic you piece of shit."

I stand there smiling.

"So you're saying I'm your type?"

I sip my drink. Things have settled down, people have returned to their bubbles of conversation, and we've blended back into the din of the bar. The wimp behind me is complaining to his friends about being wet without actually doing anything about it.

"Give me your phone."

I do as I'm told. She fiddles around with it and hands it back. I slip it back into my pocket.

"Look, I have another party to go to. One of my friends just launched his new place on Ste. Catherine near Crescent. It's an electro-lounge called *Orange*."

She says the name with a pretentious French accent.

"But, um, I put my address in there. I'll be alone later if you want to hang."

I put the glass, empty but for the ice, back on the bar. I fish the carton of cigarettes out of my back pocket and offer it to Candy. Thanks but no thanks. I shrug and spark a cigarette, glancing at my watch. It's about midnight.

She waits for me to give some sort of answer, but I just stand there smoking my cigarette.

She sighs and rolls her eyes, turns to fetch her minions and they shuffle down the stairs and out of the bar. I smoke my cigarette calmly, fiddling with the baggie in my pocket.

I show up to her place at three a.m., extremely drunk but wired. She lives in a rundown housing project near the gay village. Her apartment number is 6. The door is painted the same crimson red as her nails. I take a quick bump before knocking at it aggressively.

She opens in nothing but a black silk bathrobe. She smells musky and her apartment is a mess.

I move in without hesitation and kiss her passionately, sticking my tongue down her throat. She licks me, and I feel under her robe for the slit. I slide my finger in slowly, excited by the inviting moisture. She closes the door behind us.

We move to the couch and cut some lines.

It takes seven or eight to get us there.

It isn't long before she's on her knees. I pull her thick brown hair. I pick her up and throw her on the bed. Her robe is soft against my palm and the fabric slips away with ease. I kiss her bony frame all over, running my hands along her cool, thin skin. I flip her over and bite her backside. I lick her a while, flicking my tongue against her lips, my excitement rising with her moans. I put it in her unprotected and it slips in serene. She gasps. I flip her over again. I hold her legs up to my head and bite her red painted toes. I put a finger to her mouth and her cold lips quiver.

There are rave culture and DJ posters on the wall above the headrest.

She gets on top and I notice her ceiling is fitted with a funhouse mirror. The reflection makes us look grotesque, and deformed. The sight turns me on. From this angle, her skin looks almost translucent.

The walls of her bedroom are black, and swallow the moonlight filtering in through the lone window. I spank her hard and she pulls on her white silk sheets, writhing and squirming. I hold her arms back and put my face to hers, feeling her hot heaving breath moist against my chin. I put my arm around her and throw her down against the bed aggressively, getting back on top; thrusting and kissing hungrily, letting my animalistic groans fill the dead, humid echo of the empty room. The cool vitality of her lips eases the tension as I reach for her breasts. She pulls my head close, and whispers ever so gently:

"Come. Come for me baby. Come for me".

And I let myself go.

Everything outside of that moment melts away to nothing, as the moonlight is lost in all but the reflection of her big blue eyes. She clutches my back, digging her red pointed nails in, and orgasm comes easy.

***

After the whole Stylefile fiasco, I was sort of coasting for a little while. Several months went by and I did not look for a job. I guess I just didn't want to. I had a little money left from having worked at the store for three months, but that was very quickly dwindling. Furthermore, my love life was completely destroyed. After ditching Cassidy again for brunch the morning after, it was over. Cassidy cried on the phone and told me I had embarrassed her, that I had treated her horribly and neglected her, and that she'd never been so hurt by a guy before. I didn't see a reason to tell her I had cheated on her too.

Things with Candy were also over. I called her a few days after we slept together and she was blunt with me: she didn't see guys more than once and she had no interest in getting attached. That was all fine with me. She wasn't the type of girl I'd want to get attached to either way.

Things really changed in the early winter when I got kicked out of my mother's house.

My mother had begun seeing a new guy named Samson in the summer. She seldom dated after she and my father split, but I hated each new guy even more profoundly than the last. Samson was a cashier at the local market. He was seven years my mother's junior. He had brown curly hair very much like mine, and I hated him. It was nothing personal, I mean Samson was very sweet, very polite, and went out of his way to be nice to me. In fact, he had even tried to convince my mother that she was overreacting when she decided to kick me out.

I came home one night tweaked out. I had been out with

Steve and a few girls he worked with, and we had drunk, smoked some pot and balanced it out with a few lines of coke. Steve had wanted to get a hotel room for the night, but I backed out because I was getting to be really strapped for cash. When I got home, I still had some of the drugs left in a plastic bag, which I normally stashed in a sock at the back of my drawer. But coming home exhausted and extremely intoxicated, I had carelessly left the bag out in the open on the kitchen table.

My mother had no idea I did drugs. I think in her mind I still looked like an innocent five year old, but then my mother and I didn't talk much. Like I said, Samson was real sweet. By this time he had moved into my mother's place, and they were even sharing a bed. They had been dating for three months. He told my mother she was overreacting, that drugs were something that all young men tried. But she wouldn't have any of it. We had the most vicious screaming match I've ever taken part in. I said irredeemable things. She did too. And at the end of it, she told me I had twenty-four hours to get my things and leave.

So there it was: rock bottom. I had no money, no woman, no job, and no place to live. I guess it wasn't rock bottom, though. What I did have was a beat up car and a University education. It was definitely a lot more of a start than most people had.

I started by calling up a few old friends, high school buddies, acquaintances, the lot: anyone I thought might be able to help me out of a jam. Eventually Josh, a friend from high school, agreed to put me up on his couch for a few nights. I flushed my drugs, determined to have a fresh start, and I moved all my belongings into boxes. I headed over to Josh's without so much as a goodbye to my mother. Samson took me aside and told me it would all blow over, to be patient with her, and that she was very hurt. I told him to watch his back and to keep his hands to himself. Luckily, all of my things fit in five boxes. Movers are very expensive in the middle of the winter, and I certainly didn't have any money to spare.

I knew next thing I'd have to do was look for a job. I don't mean to paraphrase Bukowski, or Palahniuk, or whoever was the first to put this kind of stuff in print but, who the hell wants to wake up at five, or six, or even seven in the morning, every damn day, and sell eight hours of their time performing a monotonous, mechanized task? As a youth afflicted with this deviant ideology, what place did I have in society?

Josh's place was on St-Denis Street, near the metropolitan highway. The metropolitan is a major highway that cuts the city going east-west. Josh's place was considerably closer to the city center, a twenty-minute car ride west of my mother's suburban nest.

Driving up to his place, one of the things I noticed was the increase in small businesses around the area. One particular beautiful green sign caught my eye, as did the 'help wanted' board in the window. It was only a few blocks from Josh's, and I decided I would ask Josh about it when I got my things in order.

Josh's place was small, but clean for a bachelor. The front door opened into a corridor lined with one bedroom and one bathroom, and the corridor opened to a spacious living room and kitchen. There were wood floors and the walls were painted white and beige. In the living room, there was a sagging maroon polyester couch, a foot-high plywood coffee table that Josh later told me he had made himself, a very expensive sound system, and a decently furnished kitchen. There was no T.V., but a large freezer bag containing what looked to be over an ounce of marijuana lay on the coffee table.

I hadn't seen Josh in over a year, and I had forgotten how talkative he was. He began by telling me about his girlfriend, whom he had been dating for three years and loved very much, his job at the bank, which he hated, his rent, which was too expensive, and how difficult it was juggling all this responsibility. He told me all of this as he rolled a fat joint on the coffee table. Josh had shoulder length brown hair, a thin frame, and an earnest face. He was French Canadian, though perfectly bilingual, and I respected the way he wore his heart on his sleeve. I asked him about the green sign I had seen earlier and he told me, as he handed me the joint, that it was a bakery.

That Monday I walked over and found out that the bakery was named Bravia, and specialized in eastern European pastry-especially in polish donuts that they would drizzle with chocolate. There were only two employees. There was the baker, a middle-aged Haitian named Jean-Marie, and, after a brief chat with the owner, myself, the all-purpose bottom of command. The owner ran the front store every day. She was a thirty-something blond haired, second generation Polack named Dolly Jzòle, *prononcé Jole*. The first thing she told me was how she had grown up enduring the Billy Joel and Dolly Parton jokes, and that if I cracked one, I was fired. She laughed maniacally as she told me this, and I quickly took a liking to her. She was zany, and ran her business with a lackadaisical ease that suited me very much.

Dolly asked me to work six days a week, with Mondays off. My tasks included sweeping the floors of the small bakery, cleaning the glass display, dusting the various trinkets she had lining the shelves of the wood-panel walls, making runs to the corner store for milk or cream or sugar or eggs, and occasionally making deliveries nearby. It was an easy enough job, and Dolly was a great boss. The only downside was that Dolly would insist upon compulsively making terrible jokes that I'd be forced to laugh at, like, upon dropping a donut: "Oops. Haha. Good times. Mr. Donut is having a good time on the floor. Right? Mr. Donut didn't want to get eaten so he jumped to the floor. Haha. Where are you going Mr. Donut? Your home is on the display. Right? I can't sell you if you're on the floor Mr. Donut.

Haha."

Another one of Dolly's favorites was to guess, using the call display on the company telephone, what the customer would be like: "*Ring. Ring.* Oh, Martha's calling. She sounds fat, haha. Martha needs a dozen donuts probably, haha."

Jean-Marie the Haitian baker claimed not to speak a word of English. But after a week with both Jean-Marie and Dolly, I was convinced that Jean-Marie was a genius, and fluent around everyone but Dolly.

Jean-Marie always looked indifferent. He had a stern face, one that looked to me to have endured hardships. On the nights we'd close up together after Dolly had gone, we'd smoke pot by the dumpster behind the bakery. At first he was hesitant, but after seeing me do it several times alone, I guess he came to trust me. He told me about how he had come to Canada when he was fifteen years old. He had started working in an assembly line right away, fifteen hours a day, and got married when he was twenty. He had six kids between the ages of nine and twenty, and had been working seven days a week his whole life. He told me about how he had gotten desperate when he was younger, fed up with the way things were, and gambled his savings away on slot machines and blackjack. He warned me about the dangers of gambling but insisted he wasn't bitter about his losses.

"Restarting at the age of thirty does something to you as a person. Makes you appreciate the value of a dollar, makes you see what is important in life. I was lucky that my wife and kids stood by me, you know. Others, they might not be so lucky, and a mistake like that could lead to a lifetime of loneliness, my friend."

Jean-Marie had a thick creole accent, and a scar just below his left eye. The scar ran thickly down his cheekbone to his jaw. When he told his gambling stories, about his back alley meet-ups with bookies and shylocks, or his mental breakdowns after every big loss, he would rub the scar up and down its length. I came close a few times, but I never worked up the courage to ask him just how he got it.

Jean-Marie asked about me, and I told him about my scuffle with my mother.

"You must apologize. Right and wrong does not matter. She is your mother. And when she is gone you will miss her. Pride is the devil, my friend. Pride brings nothing but pain."

Deep down I knew Jean-Marie was right, but I shrugged it off.

I told him about my housing situation, and that after a couple of weeks on Josh's couch he was getting restless with me. Jean-Marie told me he had an old friend, Franz, who was looking for a roommate. I had Jean-Marie give me his number.

"He is a good man, but he has made many mistakes. You and him may learn from one another. I owe him much. He has a good heart. Call your mother my son, you will regret it otherwise."

When we finished smoking the joint, I lit a cigarette and walked back over to Josh's thinking about what Jean-Marie had told me. I saw Jean-Marie walk over to his car, the most rusted eye sore I had ever seen, and struggle to start it. It burdened me to think about how difficult the life of an immigrant had to be, and I pondered Jean-Marie's strength and resilience with admiration, as I lay on Josh's sagging couch and drifted to sleep.

While I worked at the bakery, I'd cross an intersection between Josh's and the bakery every single day. I'd encounter an old woman in the morning nearly every time. By the third time I'd seen her, I got the impression that she was waiting for someone. I offered to help her across the street, and this quickly became our little routine. I'd encounter the woman in the morning and help her across the street, and we'd exchange niceties about the weather. She'd tell me I was a lovely young man. It made me feel, for a while, as though I was washing away some of the karmic sludge I had been tracking.

I didn't, however, speak to my mother again.

'Always Crashing in the Same Car'

What can I say about Joanie? I really messed that one up.

Joanie, Joanie, Joanie. Joanie was fantastic. Joanie was fantastic and she had this obsession with lipstick- she thought it made her look sophisticated. And the way she'd wave away cigarette smoke with a dainty flick of the wrist, as though she were an aristocrat. What charm...

After I met her at the party in the spring, we spoke for a little while. We had great conversations for a little while over the phone. She turned out to be great. Everything she'd tell me was great. She liked the same books that I liked, she had decent taste in music, and she was really clever and funny. It was all very exciting for a little while.

But I soon discovered that Joanie was very guarded. She was very forthright about most things and spoke very earnestly her mind, but she was very guarded. She'd have moments where she'd close up on me without warning. Though she did not speak of it, and though I did not feel it my place to ask, I felt it obvious that she had endured much suffering. I could see the suffering in her eyes, whenever they weren't radiating. There was a very tender softness that would appear in them, but only in flashes. Most of the time it remained hidden beneath the gloss of indifference. In those flashes, I understood all too well Joanie's predicament: she could let the malleable soft substance beneath the shell through, but when she did it would only inevitably curdle, ultimately hardening the shell. So she kept it deep inside, locked in a protected room away from me, and anyone who might know it was there. It was a coping mechanism, I understood. But I wanted to give her all I could, to do something about it, to make it all right. I couldn't. I wasn't strong enough. Or there was nothing I could do. Or, it just wasn't meant to be.

It broke my heart that the most beautiful people were so often stowed away, and unreachable.
We only went on one date that summer. That was not my choice, but I understood. I regret immensely how I treated her on that date. Especially after all of the coaxing it took to get her to agree to it. I still think about her, a lot, all these months later.

I picked Joanie up at her house that night; it was in the east end, not too far from my mother's. It was a warm summer night, and the moon was big and strong in the clear night sky. The moon was incredible that night, crystalline. I had tickets to a show at Club Soda. We took our time getting there.

Club Soda is a popular small venue in downtown Montreal that fit maybe two or three hundred people. It is on the corner of two busy boulevards- St. Laurent, and Ste. Catherine. The tickets were for a local French-Canadian punk rock band called *Les Hip-Choquants*. I read good reviews and a few friends told me they put on a hell of a show. I thought she would like that.

***

We're both dressed really casual. I'm wearing an oversize royal blue t-shirt with a breast pocket, jeans, and my dirty Nike sneakers. She's wearing a dark green crop top, black jeans folded above the ankle, and slightly dirty low-cut white chucks. Her hair is up in a bun with chopsticks holding it in place, and she, I think because I told her I liked it, is wearing that same black plastic choker she had on at the party. She looks gorgeous. Her makeup is done just the way I like it, too. Minimalist: eyeliner, mascara, period. I told her she was gorgeous when she got in the car. She smirked, and without a word lit up a cigarette and looked out her window into the distance.

We don't talk much on the way over, which I don't mind. She tells me a few things about her week, and a story about how her friend fell off her bike the day before. We laugh. It's a nice moment.

I park a few streets down from Club Soda and we walk over. Someone at the door checks our tickets, and I lead Joanie by the hand, up the stairs to get a seat on the balcony. There are tables on the balcony with chairs, whereas the ground level has an open standing area before the stage.

The opening act is already performing. They're very loud. I keep holding Joanie's hand when we take our seats, but she wriggles hers away. A waitress comes over and I order us each a rum and coke. We watch the opening act without saying a word to each other, but every now and again I turn to look at Joanie and I notice her staring at me.

When the opening act finishes playing, there is a fifteen-minute intermission before *Les Hip-Choquants* take stage. Joanie whispers in my ear that she wants to go out for a cigarette. I know we'll lose our seats, but I don't mind. I want to satisfy her whimsy, and accompany her outside. I put my hand tenderly on her thigh and give it a little squeeze as we get up. We move down the stairs hand in hand, and out the front door. We move even just a little further away from the entrance, away from the crowd. People are smoking freely and conversing in the happy ways people do after a beer or two, especially in the satisfying heat of a beautiful summer night. And the moon still sits there, perched above the Montreal skyline, and I feel it watching us.

I have no cigarettes on me, but Joanie gives me one from her pack. I light the cigarette and check my watch. It is nine forty five.

"Why did you bring me here?"

She asks me this looking me straight in the eye. One of the things I liked the most about this girl, from the moment I met her, is the way that she looked me in the eye. She isn't afraid. She manages to be so vibrant in such an unimposing way.

"Because I thought you'd like it."

I exhale and smile at her. I hope that she sees my smile as genuine. I know that she is skeptical of the way I look at her. But I want her to know that she genuinely makes me smile.

"No, I mean why did you bring *me* here?"

I inhale and rub my chin.

"Oh. Because I thought I'd like it."

She smiles and shifts all her weight onto her right foot. She crosses her arm and looks at me over her cigarette.

"How did you like the opening act?"

I ask, pitching the cigarette butt into the street. I guess I'm nervous, because I smoke my entire cigarette in the time she takes to smoke a little over half of hers.

"They were okay."

She pitches her cigarette, three quarters of the way down, then lights another, and puts the pack away in her purse. She looks at me and raises an eyebrow. Under the flashing neon lights illuminating the club's sign, the color of her face changes from red, to green, to blue.

"I know we don't have much time before we need to go back in, but it's been eating me and I gotta know. We sort of got to the cusp last time we spoke, but I wonder. What's your take on truth?"

This is what I really like about Joanie: the way she can turn a conversation. She is not afraid to take the lead, and guide it places few others are willing, or even capable of going. I'll never be limited to talking about the weather when she is around.

"You shouldn't smoke so much Joanie. They say every cigarette is eleven minutes off your lifespan".

I shoot her a coy smirk and she raises an eyebrow.

"I think that's actually a bargain."

We laugh and her eyes take hold of me. Her eyes really twinkle with something that looks a lot like elation.

"You're buying too much into the 'live fast die young' rock n' roll lifestyle Joanie. You're a corrupt youth. Your parents need to take away your record player, the devil is in that music!"

She smiles wryly.

"Don't change the subject, Marcus. I'm serious. What do you think about truth?"

I furrow my brow a second, and look at my watch. We still have ten minutes before the band is set to take stage.

"I don't know, I guess it depends on the time of day. But one of my favorite ways of looking at it is a sphere. Everyone can look at the sphere, but no *one* person can ever see the *entire* sphere in any *one* moment, because a whole sphere cannot be captured from any single perspective."

She pulls hard on the cigarette, and a veil of smoke obscures her face. She replies smirking, her lungs filled with smoke:

"So you're a relativist?"

She exhales noisily, pursing her lips, and I squint at her.

"Don't do that. Don't do me like that."

"Don't do what?"

She looks amused, playing up her femininity by deliberately bringing the cigarette to the very tip of her lips, and puffing ever so gently at it. She holds the cigarette lightly, daintily, batting her eyelids as if she were Daisy Buchanan. I smile at her, enjoying the game.

"Don't reduce the profundity of my reflections on life to a single word like that. It's belittling."

She erupts into laughter.

"It's true, isn't it? You are a relativist are you not? You don't believe in a unified truth, in a God, in design of any sort. Am I misinterpreting your words?"

"No, I guess I don't believe in any of that."

"So then, smarty pants, if it's all a matter of perspective, then there's no such thing as truth? No such thing as right or wrong?"

She stands there with her arms folded, prodding me with my own rhetoric. *What a woman.*

"Well okay, I was thinking this the other day. Where you are, like geographically, for example, affects so profoundly how you see things, or for that matter, what things you see, right?"

She nods, eyes shrinking behind her veil of smoke, waiting to see where I go with this.

"Well, if that's the case, then how can I say something is right or wrong because I wasn't born into it? Like okay, okay, I know there's a line and female genital mutilation and whatever is unequivocally wrong. But I mean, what if it isn't? What if it's just a part of the show?"

"The show?"

"And then it sort of becomes not a question of is this part of the show right or wrong, because that's irrelevant, it *is*. It becomes a question of do I want to watch this part of the show? Do I agree with this element of the show is completely irrelevant to me."

She looks me up and down, sizing me up.

"So you are a bleak cynic who believes the world cannot, and should not be changed?"

I look at her angrily, baring my teeth.

"You are a strange individual, Marcus."

We exchange a smile. A small group of Asian tourists passes us by.

"Oh shut up. What do you know? You think you're profound all of a sudden because you've read Faulkner?"

I say this playfully. Joanie had recently told me that her favorite novel was *The Sound and the Fury* by William Faulkner. Personally, I thought it mediocre. My telling her this had inspired a spirited debate. She bites on my teasing:

"Hey! Don't make fun of Faulkner. He's one of the greats. And women love Faulkner. This is a fact. For that reason alone, you should give him a chance."

"What if I decide that I don't like women who love Faulkner?"

"God, you're so picky!"

"I'm not picky. So long as she's lovely, sweet, pretty,

genuine, tender, intelligent, and cooks, I'm happy."

She rolls her eyes.

"You should give Faulkner another chance."

"What if I don't want to? Will you stop talking to me?"

I nudge her playfully and she pushes back.

"Why don't you like him?"

"I don't know, I guess I'm just not a fan of stories set in the south. I guess I don't feel for the plight of the 'Southern code of honor'. They're just stories about a bunch of racists and idiots to me."

She looks at me as though I'm the idiot.

"But Marcus, the south is wonderful! The south is like this old drunken baggy whore on stage doing her dance, though no one is watching. She is in denial of how bloated she looks, but everyone in the club pities her too much to tell her she's ridiculous. So they just let her go on with her dance, so long as she doesn't get violent or hurt anyone. She's such a tragic figure!"

Frowning, I glance at my watch and notice that it's time to get back inside.

"Where the hell did you hear that? Is that a Robin Williams bit?"

She starts laughing.

"No, what do you mean where did I hear that, it came from my head you misogynistic jerk!"

I look at her skeptically and then grab her by the hand,

pulling her towards the door.

"Wait, hold on a second!"

Joanie frees herself from my grip and reaches into her purse. She pulls out an orange plastic vial and tosses it over to me. It's filled with a transparent liquid.

"Have you ever seen this before?"

I look at the vial. There is a pharmaceutical prescription sticker on the side.

"No, I haven't. What is this?"

"GHB."

I look at her, trying my best to mask my surprise and unease, though not doing a very good job.

"GHB? Isn't that the date rape drug?"

She chuckles and rolls her eyes.

"Relax, I got it from a doctor. It's prescribed for narcolepsy. But I've been reading up on it, and if we double the prescribed dosage, it's supposed to produce a euphoric feeling. It's totally safe. Bodybuilders use it for muscle growth, look it up! Relax. It's totally safe, I'm telling you! I'm going to try it."

She looks at me expectantly. I don't know what to say. I look back down at the vial, and then at my watch. The band is set to take stage in less than three minutes.

"I... uh."

She turns her head to the side and pitches her cigarette into the street. She turns to face me, arms folded, and taps her foot expectantly.

"Uh..."

She raises an eyebrow and scrutinizes my face. I know that I am driving and that I have never had an experience with this drug before, and that it would be irresponsible for me to try it for the first time under these circumstances. I have no idea what the drug will do, or how I'll react to it, but I figure I can trust her. I look at her face and I know that I can trust her. I feel like something, something monumental, hinges on me doing this with her. I don't want to disappoint her. I can't disappoint her.

"Okay, I'm in."

She smiles.

"Cool. You're supposed to take it with water. I'm going to go buy a bottle at the bar and mix it in the washroom. Wait for me at the back of the crowd."

***

Every now and then, another human being rouses in me a cathartic moment in which I glimpse a vision, and often it is the same vision give or take a few odd details. The other human being is female, and this vision is normally a domestic moment of comfort and happiness with that female. This feeling, though extremely rare- I have in fact only had this feeling on three or four occasions in my lifetime thus far, and each of them has crashed and burned more spectacularly than the last- has become familiar to me. I now relate to it as a woodland creature relates to a fresh block of cheese sitting atop an innocent looking pile of leaves in the forest- so obviously a trap, but much too alluring for a starving animal to simply walk away from. This is the feeling I felt very strongly with Joanie. I glimpsed the vision the first time I met her, the first time we spoke face to face. Her eyes burned an impression on me, as I like to think mine did on her. We both felt it. Her excitement was palpable, and my desire was instant.

With Joanie, it is sitting in a warm, cozy den on a winter's afternoon, reading silently side by side. That's it. This is my fantasy moment of serenity with Joanie by my side. Alone, together, in a bubble closed off from the world. It is funny, looking back at the first time we met, in the apartment above the bakery; I hadn't even thought to approach her. That night, something brought us together. And tonight, that very same something was bound to tear us apart.

***

We walk back into the theatre and head to the bar to purchase a water bottle. Joanie heads off to the washroom to mix the drug and I stand at the back of the crowd, hanging by the bar, looking around the full theatre anxiously, hoping she drops the stuff, hoping this is just a prank, trying to calm myself down. I lean in on the bar and order a Jack Daniels neat. The barmaid hands me my drink with a smile that seems to me to say 'calm down'. I pay her with a forced smile and down the whiskey. I look around and the crowd is getting restless. The place is full. The crowd is filled with leather jackets, and studs, and the occasional purple or pink colored hair. I stroll around to the corridor leading upstairs, letting the warmth of the alcohol circulate to my extremities. I breathe in through my nose, trying desperately to calm myself and wrap my head around what I am about to do.

The thing with drugs is that their effects are often caused by a chemical reaction in the brain. In other words, they mess with your mind. And as such, it is very important that one be in the best possible frame of mind when taking mind-altering substances. Look at it this way, if one were to be in a negative frame of mind, thinking about negative things, and then ingest mushrooms, it would only follow logically that this person would be predisposed to negative hallucinations, or a bad trip.

There's a big black man in a 'security' t-shirt blocking the stairs.

He calmly tells me the balcony is full, and to return to the standing area in the front. I walk back to the bar, still breathing heavily.

Joanie comes back from the bathroom smiling, with the bottle half full of a cloudy white liquid.

"Here drink this. I drank my half already. It's supposed to take effect pretty quickly."

I take the bottle and down it. The liquid is thicker than I had imagined. It slides awkwardly down my throat, leaving a slimy aftertaste.

The band is just getting on stage and the crowd is ramping up. The place is full to the brim. I take Joanie by the hand and lead us closer to the stage, nudging people out of the way. I look for a spot where we can both see the stage. Joanie is a lot shorter than I am, so we edge off to the side to get a better view. I put my arm around her and watch her face light up in a smile as the band takes stage.

The guys on stage salute the crowd in French.

"Bonsoir Montreal!"

The lead comes out carrying a fantastic lime green skull and crossbones guitar like I've never seen before, and the lot of them are wearing red and black plaid with black skull and crossbones bandanas. Fog rises over the stage and the lights go down.

I look at Joanie, smiling ear to ear, and I notice her pupils are super dilated. She looks almost like an anime cartoon, and I laugh out loud. She smiles back at me goofily, and starts laughing as well. The band starts suddenly, playing as loud and aggressively as they can. The adrenaline courses through my veins and Joanie's cheeks swell. I scream in her ear that she looks like a giant panda. She tells me, still with that goofy smile, that I look like an iguana. The band plays an aggressive punk rock cover of Bowie's "Heroes", and I lean in to kiss her. Her tongue sliding into my mouth feels like a slippery eel. I touch Joanie's ears and she starts giggling. Her ears feel incredibly soft and I rub them keenly. The lights coming from the stage look like cosmic strobes flashing on her face and I kiss her hands and cheek hungrily.

"Thank you, Montréal! Nous sommes *Les Hip-Choquants* and we're going to rock til your eardrums bleed!"

The band moves abruptly into a Sex Pistols cover, and Joanie punches me playfully in the chest. The crowd is pretty animated, and we start swaying with them from side to side, jumping up and down and bumping those around us. Small horns have grown out of Joanie's temples and I giggle at her, pointing. A mosh pit develops nearby and Joanie grabs me by the arm and pulls me in. I keep her towards the outskirts, with my arm around her waist, keeping her from moving into the eye of the hurricane. Studded, pierced lunatics jostle us aggressively from all directions, and I do my best to shield Joanie from the flying elbows and forearms. From the middle of the mosh pit, a pink haired punk with a bloodied nose emerges, rushing for the exit. The security guards begin to intervene, attempting to calm the crowd, so I take Joanie by the hand and lead her outside.

Outside, in the fresh air under the street lamps, I can see drops of perspiration on her brow. Her hands are clammy and she has a distorted look on her face. Feeling loose and happy to finally be alone with her, I grab her and start kissing her happily all over her face. Her arms hang limply by her side, and she doesn't move her lips. I move away and examine her face at arm's length. Her eyes are locked in a look of torment and fear, and her body has clammed up.

"Joanie, are you okay?"

"I don't know, I don't feel too good. I need water. I think I need water."

I turn to look around and the crowds of people passing by dizzy me. I try to focus, and I recognize a fuzzy corner store sign a block away. I take Joanie by the hand and lead her across the street, toward the corner store.

Crossing the street, it occurs to me to look down to see if there is a pedestrian crosswalk painted. There isn't.

A red Toyota swerves left. I see the red stain in my peripherals coupled with the horrible sound of tires screeching. I make it across the street, and realize that I no longer feel Joanie's hand in mine. I rub my eyes, feeling more and more dazed with every passing second. I turn around confused, and I see Joanie's limp body contorted in the middle of the boulevard, back grounded by the dissipating rumble of a speeding engine, and the whispering and shuffling of concerned onlookers. I run into the middle of the boulevard and put my arm under Joanie soft head, frantic.

"Joanie, Joanie, Joanie. Are you okay? Joanie. Talk to me. Joanie!"

Her eyes stay closed for a few seconds that seem an eternity before she comes back with a gasp. Her eyes open wide, as if suddenly emerging from deep, breathless waters. She inhales wildly, sucking in as much air as she possibly can. By now, the crowd is beginning to take more interest in us. I kiss Joanie's forehead and it brings me back into the moment. Panic sets in and I pick Joanie up and carry her out of the street. A passer-by asks me if I need help and I scream at him frenziedly to mind his own business.

Around the corner, I stumble and fall to the ground with Joanie in my arms. I do my best to shield her from the impact and I badly scrape the side of my arm falling to the pavement. I look at her head and notice a gash above her right ear. Joanie is in a daze, dancing off somewhere on the edge of consciousness. Blood spills out of her head and onto my arms and legs. I look back at my hands and they move uncontrollably, as I succumb to the sickening feeling of snakes crawling under my skin. The pavement feels like hot coals, and I shiver like a madman.

"Joanie, Joanie. Is anything broken? How do you feel? Joanie?"

There's no answer. I touch Joanie's blurring face and blink, suddenly transported to a faraway oasis. I see tall, still palm trees encircling a sparkling pool of equally still deep blue water, carved into a horizon of shifting sands. Lucid smells of sweet bread and baked meats waft into the air, and I am sensitive to the excitement of the forthcoming celebration.

I've happened upon a celebratory feast.

The realization sweeps me in a feeling of invulnerability lifting me light as air.

Euphoria.

The music of twelve angelic harps and an enchanted choir round the space, engulfing me in the joy of the anticipated merriment. Congregations of tiny homunculus swarm around a large erected idol in a swaying foreign song. Purple nymphs frolic by the water and call to me, and as I look up to the heavens, I feel the glimmer of the sun's most powerful ray puncture my pupil.

I blink and I am back in the street. I feel my knees scrape against the pavement, and I feel the weight of Joanie's limp body in my blood-covered arms as I keep squinting at the street light just above us. I blink again and again, but I cannot get back to the oasis.

Joanie's face is grotesquely contorted in an absolutely terrified look of unspeakable pain, and I put my forehead to hers, trying to penetrate her mind and help her fight the demons torturing her inside. I feel anxiousness rising from my bowels and it is difficult to breathe. I move away to have a look and her glossy lifeless eyes seem to say 'you did this'. I hear the echo of a cannon reverberate through my inner ear and I am suddenly conscious of the concept of the world again, of people across the street looking my way and the noises of a panicked fearful mumble. I begin to cry and scream incoherently. The plush feel of Joanie's cheek against my palm calms me, recalls the oasis. I kiss her forehead once more, willing her back into consciousness. Failure. The smudged makeup on her face is a blemish. I remove my shirt and begin wiping the blood and makeup off her face, cleansing her. I scream maniacally for help.

I'm suddenly overcome by a wave of pain from my feet rising to my throat and I begin to vomit violently and uncontrollably. I do my best to avoid Joanie with the vomit, turning to the bushes beside me, and my head is spinning faster than ever. Goblins run by me in the street, their faces disgusting and slimy, with tongues out and pointy teeth, pointing at me and laughing. I can't locate myself, and I feel the dread of helplessness seeping in.

I feel as though we are cooking under the intense heat of the streetlights.

I close my eyes and raise my head toward the sky, noticing for the first time the flaming boulders falling from the suddenly blood-red sky. I turn my head in a panic and am startled by the sight of black hooded horsemen galloping toward us. The shock forces my eyes open, and I am back under the intense heat of the streetlights. I put my shirt back on, smeared in blood and vomit. Blinding lights disorient me. Passers-by are crossing the street to avoid us on the curb, and I scream madly to them for help. The goblins, still pointing, laugh wickedly as they run away. A woman comes across the street and asks if I'm okay. I scream incoherently and she begins panicking, "Oh my God! Oh my God!", watching Joanie's head bleed all over my arms. I beg her to get us into a cab.

"Help us please, for the love of God help us!"

Some time elapses before we're finally in a cab. I'm crying like a madman desperate to keep a grip on reality. My head is throbbing. The lady helps me get Joanie in the cab.

"Go to the hospital! You must take this girl to the hospital! Her head is bleeding! Go to the hospital!"

I yell at the lady to leave us alone and I give the cabbie Joanie's address. The lady yells at the cab driver to bring us to the hospital. He nods, begins driving, and asks me again to repeat the address.

Joanie's head is limp in my lap. The cabbie notices she is bleeding but drives without any questioning. I notice a familiar reflection in the taxi window, though I can't place it. I lay Joanie's head in my lap and apply pressure to her head wound. The cabbie turns the radio up and a slow pop song saunters out of the car speakers. I open the windows. The air against my face and the feeling of motion calms me. There is vomit hardening on my chin, but I am calm.

Time elapses.

I give the cabbie all of my money. He cuts the engine and the string of pop songs cuts mid-chorus. The only soundtrack I hear is the sound of my own heavy breathing and the slow taunting tick of an unseen clock.

I take Joanie by the legs and the cabbie takes her by the arms and we carry her to her doorstep. I wobble and nearly fall again. There is a throbbing pain in my knee that makes no sense to me.

"Her parents! You have to tell her parents!"

I scream at the cabbie though he is right in front of me. He nods calmly. I can't tell if it is coherent, so I scream again, with more intent. Joanie's eyes are closed. Her face is ghostly white. An inhuman calm is etched on her soft eyelids and the curvature of her limp, motionless lips. The cabbie rings the doorbell, and I take one last look at her beautiful face before I drop Joanie's legs, covered in blood and vomit, and run as fast as I can.

'Holloween'

In the fall of 20--, while I was living on Josh's couch, my friend Blasé threw a Halloween party at his apartment in the plateau. He was living in a cozy three and a half on Mont-Royal at the time, just west of St-Hubert. The plateau area is rather posh, and Blasé's place was really very nice. He only had that place for maybe a year and a half; some extenuating circumstances were the only reason he had the opportunity to live there in the first place. It was something about a displaced brother-in-law; I don't quite remember the details. The story was rather convoluted, as Blasé's stories tended to be. But while he had the place, his entourage was treated to some of the most riotous parties they'd ever attend.

Blasé was the youngest of thirteen children in a rich Kenyan family moved to Montreal. He was a fun and generous person, though he wasn't without his special quirks. I had come to expect three things of Blasé's parties: that I would see people I didn't necessarily want to, that there would be lots and lots of drugs, and that Blasé would get overly familiar with all his guests after a few cocktails. Halloween of 20--did not disappoint.

***

I'm sitting in the green-lit smoke room, which I think was a good idea considering the rest of the apartment is fitted with red-lighting. Blasé thought that the red lights would be a nice touch, make his place feel more like a rave, he said. I think it makes the place look more like a strip club, or a sketchy European red light district, but either way I don't mind because a red light party on Halloween with scantily dressed females is more than likely going to be a good time. I'm sitting in the green-lit smoke room though, which is an office space, really, a tiny room now fitted with a table in the middle and a few chairs, my idea this space, and there are about fourteen conversations going on in here. I'm high as a kite, naturally, and the room is packed to the brim. Rebecca isn't high though, and she's sitting next to me with her hand firmly on my thigh, and her legs resting loosely on mine.

Rebecca is a real enterprising uppity snob of a girl, a high-class people handler and self-proclaimed philanthropic, a social worker or some bullshit of the sort, and for some reason she's latched herself on to me tonight. She's dressed as Spiderwoman, with a flashy red jumpsuit- unflatteringly tight- and generous bosom. Right now Rebecca is talking to Laura, Bill's girlfriend, who is dressed as a bunny, and the two of them are discussing the hilarious and timeless shortcomings of men, as if I'm not even there, me serving as the de facto male scapegoat, on trial for causing all of this comedic female angst. I've been trapped in this predicament for about five minutes, which feels like an eternity on a drunken house party clock, and I can't seem to muster the confidence required to just stand and leave. It seems every time my mind even approaches the idea of leaving, Rebecca's Spidey senses tingle and her hand moves further up my thigh, closer to my limp penis.

My mouth is severely pasting, and I can see Steve in classic form, hitting on the prettiest girl at the party. Steve's dressed in a white shirt that reads "LIFE", and is carrying a messenger bag full of lemons. He's smirking at something the girl said while rolling another joint at the smoking table. The one he just rolled is making its way around the room. I gave Blasé the idea for this Amsterdam café inspired smoke room, and it's a hit. The girl Steve's talking to is dressed as a pirate with generous bosom and a cute eye patch she doesn't wear because it'll mess up her mascara.

Izzy is in the room too, dressed inadvertently as Lenny Kravitz. He told me he was going for '70's guy' with his Afro and denim on denim. But with his brown complexion and aviators, he looked a spitting image of Lenny Kravitz. I'm dressed as a sexy latter years Mordecai Richler, with the glasses and the hair and the tweed, but after the first person to see my costume decides I look more like Einstein, I am henceforth an inadvertent Einstein.

Laura and Rebecca start laughing and Rebecca puts a hand to my face. I look at her coolly, and before I can say 'Get your fucking hand off my face', Laura interjects:

"So how long have you two been dating?"

We haven't been dating, and this question finally gives me the push I needed to leave.

Izzy hands me the joint and I take a long pull, filling my lungs. I pass the joint off and blow the smoke deliberately in Rebecca's direction.

"Excuse me, ladies."

I jump up from the chair, nearly causing Rebecca to fall over, and make my way over to the washroom. There's a three-person wait. The corridor walls have tile going half the way up to the ceiling and wood paneling the rest of the way.

The corridor connects the kitchen to the living room. The living room is where the sound system is, and there are some couches against the exposed-brick wall. Some of the sleazier girls at the party are in there, giving clothed lap dances to some of the sleazier guys.

From the red-lit corridor, I can see into the kitchen and notice that Johnny has just arrived. The party is really loud. When I arrived at around ten, I heard the music blaring from a block away. It's pretty surprising that there haven't been any police complaints thus far. Frankly, I'm surprised the place hasn't caved in.

I look over to Johnny again and cringe at his half hilarious, half depressing 'fat Mick Jagger' costume, complete with anachronistic Guns n' Roses t-shirt (deliberate, I'm sure...) and Elvis-style pompadour wig. Johnny is so stupid that it *offends* me. Johnny is twenty-five years old, broke or in debt depending on the season, and tied to a teenage girlfriend he impregnated *on purpose*. Otherwise, he's a good guy. I see him strutting through his greetings telling everyone that he's Mick Jagger, and his belly-bulging bride-to-be follows close behind, dressed as a groupie.

Steve emerges from the smoking room and leans on the wall beside me.

"Hey man, where's the sexy pirate?"

Steve's looking at his phone, seemingly annoyed. I don't say anything.

"Dude, I can't believe that slut. She must have gone up on the roof with the hot dog guy."

Blasé has a ladder on his balcony, leading up to the roof. The balcony has a sloped floor, curved from water damage, and looks to me to be a lawsuit in the making. There are four or five people out there smoking at any given moment. I don't dare hazard the risk.

"I think that guy is in med school, Steve."

I overheard that at some point earlier. The hot-dog guy's costume has a perfect squiggle of mustard running along the length of the dog.

There must be about fifty people at this party, filling Blasé's little three and a half nearly to the brim. I look at Steve's face. His eyes are in a squint from all the marijuana and alcohol. I laugh, figuring I must look about the same. There was supposed to be coke at this party, but Blasé wisely decided that the addition of coke to this cocktail might put things dangerously over the edge. His neighbors have complained before.

"Screw that. I got her on Instagram and she's obviously one of those three thousand followers, three hundred following girls."

"Well, she was pretty sexy man."

I'm used to Steve's drunken rants. I am subjected to them nearly every time a girl rejects him. To be fair, I rant about these things too. Steve listens to me or at least pretends to. A joker dressed up as a man in the shower walks by and his costume gets caught in the cotton webs Blasé hung from the ceiling. A few plastic spiders trickle into his shower and he starts jerking violently, obviously very drunk, and hilariously unaware that the spiders are made of plastic. I laugh out loud, but Steve is too wrapped up in his rant.

"I hate social media man. It builds these disgusting egos. What the hell makes that girl so special? She has three thousand fans that like to look at her half naked pictures on Instagram so she thinks she's too good for me?"

Steve looks in the mirror on the wall and starts fixing his hair. Two very sexy Asian girls in anime costumes walk by us and smile at me. Sailor Moon has a nice ass… Steve is still ranting into the mirror.

"That bitch. I'm really pissed. I want to get fifteen hundred followers on Instagram. Then these stupid Instagram bitches will see whose boss."

Steve is notorious for dating seven girls at any one time. He's good at it, though, and rarely has his network cave in on itself. He stretches himself so thin at times, I wonder if he is even present for his orgasms, or if he is, in the midst of coitus, already off somewhere else preparing the mental framework for his next…

"I think I'm going to rebrand my Instagram page. Maybe that's not the problem. I think I need to post more. And at peak hours. If I'm not getting at least one hundred likes on each of my pics… I need to post selfies actually. More selfies. And go to the gym."

He is a pretty sweet guy, though. A polygamous sweetheart. Makes sure to make the girl feel great while she's with him. A guilt-free screw is what he aspires to be, he told me so himself. Sometimes I wish I could be more like that. I have this obsession with wanting to change the girl. I want to get inside her and become a part of her fabric. I want to inhabit the air she breathes. Otherwise, what's the point?

"What do you think, Marc?"

The bathroom finally frees up and I move in without answering. I lock the door and begin to pee in the disgusting toilet, getting half the pee in and half on the floor. I laugh out loud at the image of girls squatting over this mess. Then I feel a little bad, thinking about Blasé having to clean this all up tomorrow. I zip up and the last few drops of urine wet my pants. I take my time washing my hands and I inspect my face in the mirror. I notice there is a crack forming in the plaster by the sink. It's a rounded crack, in the shape of a semi-circle, and I wonder what caused it. Did it start from the bottom or the top? Will it get bigger? Will it eventually take down the whole house? People start restlessly knocking at the door and I relocate myself in the apartment.

This party would be cool, if it weren't for the dynamic. It's a minefield of ex-flings, would-be hookups, and fizzled out flames. To be honest, it feels a bit like a bottom of the barrel desperate singles mixer.

I walk out of the bathroom and several people in line yell at me. I smirk and flip them off before casually making my way over to the kitchen for a glass of water. My mouth is still severely pasting. I nestle between two kissing couples to grab a plastic cup from the shelf, and then awkwardly move through them again to get some water from the sink. Sipping my water, I take stock of the kitchen.

The kitchen seems to have become the couples' zone.

Storzo, dressed as Salt, is eating the pumpkin cookies his girlfriend 'Cuddle Bug', dressed as Pepper, baked for the party. Colonel Jordan is arguing playfully with his girlfriend Private Connie. Johnny and his pregnant groupie are nuzzling by the window. Sandy is here, too. She's dressed as a mousetrap with generous bosom, and she's in the corner, on her boyfriend's lap, kissing him tenderly.

Watching Sandy gives me a sort of melancholic rush and I can't look away. I watch her lips touching his, gently, sweetly, and her arm brushing tenderly his cheek. It's very difficult to turn someone into a type when you've been given the privilege to see her as an individual. Just as difficult, I'd say, as overlooking a prejudice to see someone as an individual rather than a type, or a set of conventions. It's a different kind of prejudice. It's a bias: a bias in favor of someone you once cared for. I still hate running into her.

'Cuddle Bug' comes over to offer me a cookie from her plastic Tupperware.

"No thank you."

There are frosted pumpkin faces on top of the sugar cookie bases. Very artistic.

I finish my glass of water and head back into the singles' world of the living room. The sleazier partygoers are now dry humping on the couch and I languish the fact that I'm not one of them. Rebecca again latches herself on to me, still talking with Laura. Bill has joined the conversation, though only as a symbolic presence.

"Marcus!"

Rebecca wraps an arm around mine, pulling me in close.

"I was just telling Bill and Laura about how we met, do you remember?"

She's smiling a shitty rehearsed cocktail party smile and I feel so viscerally repulsed by her that my body trembles.

"No, Rebecca, I cannot say that I do. Probably at some party like this one, probably just as awful."

Her face turns to a theatrical frown, as if she were getting ready to scold a toddler.

"Markie, why are you being such a grump? Marcus and I go way back. My aunt was his kindergarten teacher, when he was just a cute little tike!"

That was true, though incidental. I only found that out later, much after we had met, as a sort of funny coincidence you happen upon in small talk, and that is usually immediately followed by awkward silence as both parties search for a follow-up...

"Oh, that's really sweet. Bill and I met at work. It seems that's where everyone meets these days, either at work or at school. It's just natural, being in proximity with those people day in and day out."

Rebecca watches Bill and Laura with pathetic envy.

"Yeah, that's really what it is these days. It's gotten so

difficult to meet people! You guys are such a cute couple though."

Rebecca tightens her grip on me as she says this, while Laura and Bill exchange a loving look. Rebecca leers at them, still clasping my arm tightly, and Laura takes the cue:

"So Markie", this playful jab angers me to the point of violence and I know this is not going to end well, "what are you waiting for to lock this beauty down? Catches like Rebecca don't stay single too long, you know".

Laura winks at me all in playful fun and I lose my mind.

"Oh. I was under the impression that Rebecca never had a serious boyfriend. Maybe that's my mistake."

It isn't.

"And generally speaking, I like to get more than fifteen minutes of face time, diluted over three meetings, diluted over a lifetime thus far, before I propose to a woman. But maybe that's just me. I'm a little bit kooky like that."

I wriggle my arm away from Rebecca, whose face is now amusingly contorted in a mix of embarrassment and extreme anger, and look over my shoulder to see Steve and the Hot Dog competing for the sexy pirate's attention. Sandy and her boyfriend approach looking for Rebecca, and Rebecca, reinforced by the presence of her friend, proclaims, "You're a prick Marcus", flings her drink in my face, and shuffles off angrily with Laura, Sandy, and her trophy boyfriend following close behind. I turn to look at Bill, and a few drops trickle into my mouth.

"Hmm… I wouldn't have taken her for a rum and coke person."

Bill laughs uncontrollably, as do several onlookers.

I head back toward the kitchen to dry myself off and I bump into Catherine, dressed as a sexy feline, blocking the way. She turns to me with a scowl and says:

"Hey, watch it jackass."

She's holding a red cup that I notice is nearly full and I slap it out of her hand at full force so that it explodes all over her.

"What the hell is your problem you jerk?"

"Relax, it's a party!"

Any chance of civilized dialogue is eradicated, and Catherine starts berating me with insults. I just stand there taunting her, pulling my cheeks and making cat noises.

"You better watch your back Marcus, you don't know who you're messing with."

"Oh yeah, what are you going to do?"

"I'll put you in the ground you peasant. Do you know who my boyfriend is?"

I don't.

So I grab my crotch like I'm Robert Deniro and tell her:

"Call your boyfriend."

I let go of my groin and start beating my chest like an ape.

"And tell him big daddy's right here waiting for him."

A few people are whispering by now, others laughing, and Blasé is making his way over to play peacekeeper. Catherine pulls out her phone to call her boyfriend and Blasé comes and give me a big hug.

"Marcus, calm down. I love you. You need to come to the kitchen and dry off. No fighting. There's no fighting at Blasé's parties."

Blasé's face is loosened by a lot of liquor and his well-to-do demeanor is infectious. I laugh and turn to apologize to Catherine, though Blasé pulls me aside and tells me that I really need to come to the kitchen.

And then everything goes black.

***

I was explained later that it was as we started walking to the kitchen that Catherine removed one of her ten-inch black suede pumps and threw it at me. It hit me in the back of the head, and the point of impact was the point of the heel. It knocked me immediately unconscious. I toppled like a sack of potatoes. Apparently, there was a lot of blood. An ambulance was called, and several of the women at the party got hysterical, thinking I had been killed. Everyone left even before the ambulance and police arrived. That was pretty much the end of the party, and the partying.

***

I awake the morning after to the sight of a slow-ticking clock behind a protective steel-cage. Noticing me stirring, a nurse comes over to explain what happened. I'm lying strapped to a cot, still in costume, in the corridor of a nearby hospital. I can't move. She explains with breath smelling of coffee and liquor that I suffered a minor concussion. The back of my head is bandaged where the shoe's impact has created a small gash. After checking my vital signs, and performing a series of cognitive tests, the kindly nurse tells me I can leave and releases me from the hospital.

I do not have my jacket and it is a cold fall day. I walk over to the bus stop with my wig in hand. I don't care to check when the next bus is coming. I just sit patiently, shivering in the bus shelter. My head is thumping and I feel woozy. There is a homeless man lying on the ground in a filthy sleeping bag. I can see a café across the street. Its sign reads 'Café des Isles'. It's decorated with painted palm trees, but it's covered in dead leaves. There is a stop sign at the corner with the first 'R' and the 'E' rouged into the background so that it reads 'ART' instead of 'ARRÊT'. I fish my carton out of my pocket and light a cigarette. The homeless man stands, startling me with a scream in a heavy French accent:

"Carry on the great struggle ahead! Carry on the great struggle ahead! Carry on the great struggle ahead! *Vive le Québec libre!*"

Finished, he yawns audibly, before lying down and returning to his sleeping bag.

I sit there for a while with my head pounding, taking in the sights for I don't know how long, shivering, watching an empty pack of cigarettes twirling in the wind, and in perfect synchronicity with the dead, crumbling leaves.

Part Two

'Franz'

The party at Blasé's house was yet another wake-up call. For a while, I felt that my life was moving laterally, and I knew that I was spending too much time dicking around with my friends. It began to get to the point where I no longer saw myself as a creature of purpose, and I needed a change.

So I stopped seeing them. All of them.

Just like that, I decided to be a loner. I lived out of my room for the entire winter of 20-- into 20--. I closed my world and focused on my work. It was difficult, living in such a small bubble, closing off my world to just the few people I needed to see, and the few places I absolutely needed to go.

I worked a lot.

And I spent a lot of time alone, reflecting.

The holidays were coming fast, and the manufactured cheer that came with them. I hated the holidays. Looking back, I think it was best that I spent some time alone around this time. I was spiraling out of control. Idle hands do the devil's work, as the old saying goes. In the end, I don't know if it did more good or harm, but it was inevitable, as I see now, because it was at this time that Franz would enter my world.

I moved into Franz's place about three days after I called him. I called him soon after Jean-Marie gave me his number, not more than a week later. I was pressed to move. Josh wanted me out. I had overstayed my welcome.

Franz took me in on a gloomy Sunday morning. The streets were wet. Church bells were tolling somewhere not too far off in the distance.

Franz told me over the phone that he was in serious need of a roommate, as he could no longer afford to pay the rent on his own. He quickly retracted that statement and said that he had tired of the loneliness of living alone. He retracted that statement too, and said that living alone was a lifestyle that didn't suit him. He sounded distracted for the length of the conversation, which wasn't very long at all, less than two minutes I'd say. Towards the end of it, he even threatened that if I didn't promise to move in soon he would give the place to one of the many others in the long line of suitors he had for the room. He actually used the word 'suitors'. His desperation betrayed him over the phone, and I felt very confident that his threats were empty. But I really did need to move out of Josh's, and Franz's place was cheap and available.

The apartment isn't exactly close to Josh's, though. It isn't anywhere near as nice either. Franz's place is a beat up three and a half in Hochelaga-Maisonneuve, a few blocks south of the Langelier Metro station. It is about twenty minutes back southeast of Josh's, away from the city center. The Hochelaga-Maisonneuve neighborhood is inhabited for the most part by immigrants, struggling minimum wage earners, and welfare collectors. Franz is of the latter persuasion.

The area is also abundant in drug dealers and crack fiends. After a few days in the area, I could easily pick out the addicts. They are noticeably pale. They roam the streets shabby-looking and with absolutely no intent, their lives unfolding in a reality devoid of time.

There are many low-income housing projects around, plain beige brick buildings simple in and out. Like many of the poorer areas around the city, the area is poorly lit at night. The darkness obscures the difficulty and desperation at every corner, and amplifies the feeling of unease.

Hochelaga-Maisonneuve does have a sense of community, in its own way. People are united in the struggle, if not by it. In Hochelaga-Maisonneuve, beat up couches or broken down furniture is left on the curb as a sort of pay it forward recycling project, and is often claimed within the day by passers-by in even more dire conditions. In many ways, this area is cut off from society. Police cars, garbage trucks, postmen and city workers of any kind are scarcely seen around these parts. Its inhabitants and their very real conditions are often neglected, and even more often ignored.

Franz turned out to be a very eccentric character.

It seemed evident in his stance that the man was a boxer. He always looked ready to pounce at a moment's notice. He was on his toes, sharp. He moved his arms with impressive dexterity, and was surprisingly nimble in spite of the limp he nursed on his left leg.

Our first encounter made an unforgettable impression on me.

Franz is a stout, five foot seven inch fifty-something, with salt and pepper hair. He speaks English fluently, though with a light German accent. He has a firm handshake that contrasts starkly his beady, watchful eyes. The look in those eyes, despite the sturdiness of the shake, gives me the impression that Franz is a calculating, slippery man. In fact, Franz's eyes remind me time and time again of Jean-Marie's warning to tread lightly. Jean-Marie warned that though Franz was a 'good man', I should never under any circumstances conduct business with him, or even discuss money for that matter.

I pulled up to his building noisily that fateful day, in my beater.

Franz meets me in the lobby, offering to help me with my boxes. His building is a shoddy twenty-four unit dimly lit beige brick complex with no elevator. It is a carbon copy of the building to the right of his, and of the building to the left. The lobby smells musty and lived in. There is a decorative painting of flowers hanging on the wall that has been vandalized with spray paint. The halls smell too, of grime meshed with the assorted scents of cooking, creole spices, and foul body odors. Every inch of the building has a very distinct and curious smell.

In the lobby, his handshake is firm. I imagine that this firm handshake has gotten him out of trouble at least a few times before, as the rest of his character seems to be on the verge of crumbling. His fingernails are bitten to the quick and sometimes bleeding. They are blackened with grime, and neglect. His hair is patchy and unkempt. He is balding heavily down the middle; his hair grows wiry and greasy to the sides. His eyes are quick and always in a squint, shrewd little eyes that seem to me to see everything and trust nothing. He has a lingering cough, the wheezing cough of a lifetime smoker, though his teeth are bleached a bright and unnatural white.

Franz has a nervous tick that compels him to look over his shoulder every now and again, without explanation or warning. He rarely bathes. This despite my eventual protests, though I imagine him at home all day, lounging in his filth. The apartment *is* fitted with a shower. He says his filthiness is a lifestyle choice. He says it frees him from the societal shackles of hygienic expectations. According to Franz, soap is an unnecessary expense. A corporate scam. He wears a five o'clock shadow for style and walks with a confrontational disposition and his chest puffed out.

The first thing he mentions after our first and only formal greeting in the lobby is how he was a boxer in his youth. He tells me his record was 19-1 as a German national. His eyes dart around madly as he says this. Though when I take interest in his boxing career, he forces a laugh, shrugs, and promptly changes the subject.

He talks often about sports. Franz says that sports are universal, and unite people from all walks of life. He enjoys keeping up to date on as many professional sporting leagues as he can. I'd often notice him scouring the sports sections of various newspapers, compulsively checking the scores and stats of several games.

He wears shabby stained sweatpants most of the time, and holed sneakers. He sports an expensive flashy royal blue winter jacket on top of his stained and holed clothing, though. It is a European designer jacket. Noticing the direction of my gaze, Franz explains that the jacket is a counterfeit, only to change his story a little later, claiming the jacket is real but stolen, and then a little later tries to sell me the jacket.

After we shake, he whisks me up the stairs and into the apartment, which is on the third floor. The lights in the hall are very dim, and the walls are covered with a tacky, peeling wallpaper with a subtle floral design: red tiny tulips over a white background. Well, it is supposed to be white, but with the grime and wear of poverty, and under the fluorescent light of the hall the walls look brown and disgusting.

Franz opens his door to a simple apartment with a closet in the entrance, a tiny bathroom off to the right, a bedroom off to the left, and a living area and kitchen just ahead, beyond a narrow corridor. Franz has a run down patio door with a little balcony, where he leaves his clothes to dry most of the year until the frost sets in. It is December, and Montreal has uncharacteristically still not received its first snowfall. Franz has no kitchen table, but makes do with two wooden stools pulled up to the counter separating the kitchen from the living room. The kitchen is fitted with an old yellow stove and a small white fridge, and the sink is full to the brim with dirty, mismatched dishes. Half of the grimy green cupboards have the doors barely hanging on their hinges, and the rest have no doors at all.

The apartment has only the one bedroom, but Franz insists with a sly smile that I am welcome to it... so long as I am willing to pay the lion's share of the rent. It is only fair. We quickly come to an agreement: I'll pay for two thirds of the rent.

I don't mind. Franz's place is so cheap that I can afford it. Besides, Franz's couch is ash-stained, as is the coffee table. There is an over-filled ashtray on the table, which he is too lazy to empty out. The apartment smells quite strongly of cigarette smoke.

The walls of the apartment are the same dirty white as those in the hall, though completely bare except for an amateur watercolor stencil of Aphrodite hung just above the couch. Again noticing the direction of my gaze, Franz tells me he painted it many years ago, when he and his ex-wife split. He winces as he tells me this. Aphrodite stands naked, her right arm covering her breasts, her left arm her genitals, on a seashell floating in the middle of the ocean.

The bedroom is tiny and barely fits the disheveled queen-sized mattress on the floor, going wall to wall. There is no nightstand, or any furniture at all in the room. There is no room for it. Some of Franz's dirty clothes are thrown haphazardly on the gray-carpeted floor.

I settle in, and move Franz's clothing to the hamper. Afterwards, I exit the bedroom into the living room intending to give Franz a piece of my mind, but something about the sight of him gives me shivers and I do not say a word. Franz lies on the couch fully extended, his dirty shoes mindlessly tracking dirt onto his stained white couch as he leisurely smokes a cigarette. I check up on him periodically throughout the day, as I unpack and settle in more comfortably. Franz just sits there all afternoon, facing the patio door and watching the sky. Aphrodite smiles just above him, while he smokes cigarette after cigarette and hardly moves an inch.

IDLE HANDS

***

The first two weeks living with Franz are very much the same as those with Josh, though I don't speak very much with Franz. I keep my job at the bakery, though my daily commute has become much more cumbersome. To save the money on gas, which I frankly can't afford under the circumstances, I walk to the Metro station nearest Franz's. It's a ten-minute walk to the Langelier Station. Then I take a twenty-minute metro ride west until the Berri-UQAM station, and then I take a bus down St-Denis the rest of the way to the bakery. Sometimes, when Jean-Marie is in a good mood, or when he takes pity on me, he gives me a lift back to Franz's after work. Otherwise, I repeat the commute. The times I get a lift, Jean-Marie plays his jazzy creole music, and asks me questions about Franz I can scarcely answer. Jean-Marie asks his questions obliquely, as though they have just occurred to him, but I'm skeptical. Jean-Marie seems fascinated by Franz, and is always curious about what is going on in Franz's life. He speaks about Franz in this weird, almost apologetic way, as though he owes him a great deal. Oddly enough, Jean-Marie never comes in to speak to Franz, though I invite him in every single time. And though Franz knows Jean-Marie drives me home, and that Jean-Marie suggested that I move in, he never seems in the least bit interested.

To make matters worse, I am experiencing car trouble. Time is taking its toll on my big old 98' Chevy, and the thing is shaking something awful when I drive it around the neighborhood to pick up weed for Franz and me, or to go do 'groceries'- which are mostly ramen and Kraft dinner. On the bright side, drugs have never been so easy to locate before. Franz knows a dealer nearly every second block.

Noticing his connections around the neighborhood, I tell Franz about my car, hoping he can hook me up with a decent mechanic. Franz sends me around the corner to the local mechanic he knows but no longer has a need for- Franz allegedly sold off his car to settle an undisclosed debt.

Hector, the burly Latino mechanic, takes a good long look at my car and tells me I need a new muffler, new tires, new brakes, and an oil change. All in all, he estimates approximately twelve hundred dollars for the work and used parts. I tell him I'll think about it, having a little over three thousand dollars to my name at this point. Really though, I immediately decide to forego the repairs, and no longer drive my car unless it is absolutely necessary.

Money is already incredibly tight living with Franz. Franz collects about eight hundred dollars a month from the government, which he spends almost exclusively on beer and cigarettes. I earn about double that working at the bakery, which is still peanuts. Rent is about four hundred a month, of which I pay two thirds. Franz and I agree cable is an unnecessary expense. Besides, Franz has an old record player at the apartment, and a sizeable vinyl collection that keeps us both entertained. We also play cards a lot. Franz insists we play Gin Rummy. To his credit, Franz *is* very generous with the very little he possesses. He is also a whiz with a deck of cards, and beats me nearly every time we play.

For mostly economic reasons, Franz and I eat Kraft Dinner on weekdays, and ramen or the occasional tomato sauce pasta on weekends. Franz only owns one pot and we use it daily. It is encrusted with a permanent film of powdered cheese residue. The bottom is rusted and scratched.

Franz has a limp in his left leg that he says was caused by an injury sustained in battle. He tells me he spent some time in the United States Navy, though he does not elaborate beyond that. However, from time to time, when Franz is stoned or when he thinks no one is watching, I notice him leap up from the couch with surprising athleticism, or skip to the fridge humming a tune, as though he is temporarily free from the physical limitations of his injury.

I come home from work sometimes, to the sight of Franz lying on that ash-stained couch with his shoes still on- in fact, he falls asleep in them more often than not- smoking cigarette after cigarette, and flicking his ashes into the half-eaten pot of Kraft Dinner he abandoned, while the ashtray on the coffee table remains forever overflowing. He does this as he peers through the patio door, watching the sky with unwavering focus, at times listening to his record player, at times simply enjoying the sounds of the world outside.

Franz loves show tunes and ballads. He has an extensive collection of records including what he considers to be each generation's finest balladeers. He has Bennett, Belmonte, Mathis, Humperdinck, Anka, Sinatra, and his personal favorite, Julio Iglesias.

Franz goes off on rants about Iglesias when we're smoking together:

"Iglesias sings 'Spanish Eyes' more beautifully than I've ever heard it sung. The man is a gem. I don't care what anyone thinks."

He tells me this defiantly, though I never disagree with him, and really couldn't care less. It is funny though, and it makes me think Franz has endured a lifetime of defending his love for Julio from people who want to denounce him, and tear their them apart. I nod and smile. And then, as he passes me back the joint:

"Your generation will never understand. Julio captured beauty in a way today's youth couldn't even begin to fathom. You kids have no patience. It's all about sex these days, no one takes the time for romance. Instant gratification or bust."

And again I laugh and smile, nodding in agreement.

Franz is the quirkiest man I have ever met. His defiance of the way things are reaches a new level, one I can hardly comprehend. Franz's defiance is perhaps best encapsulated in the way he tries to dodge the rain. It's true. I see him do it every time. We were out of noodles one night and we decide to walk to the corner store about a block away to get some more, and it begins to rain. I see Franz zig and zag, and bob his head forward and back in an attempt to escape the inevitable:

"Rain these days is toxic. It's very bad for your follicles."

That's his explanation.

My relationship with Franz develops through the simple fact of constant proximity. If we weren't roommates, I don't think I would have ever interacted with a man like Franz. We really get to know each other over the joints we smoke together every night. By the third or fourth week we're living together, I come home from the bakery, exhausted and sometimes already stoned, and he's waiting for me with a joint rolled and sitting on his ear, staring out the patio door at the moon.

One particular night, I come home to the sight of Franz sitting on the couch clipping his toenails. His feet smell and he's wet from walking in the rain. He doesn't take a shower of course, not even in these extreme circumstances, because "soap is expensive", and "I cant smell myself yet, so I know I don't need a shower". Franz is playing one of his Julio Iglesias records, and the record spins to Julio's duet with Willie Nelson, 'To All the Girls I've Loved Before'. Franz sings along, awfully out of tune. He lights the joint, still going at it with his goofy German accent, and then looks at me intently for a while before returning to his toenails.

"Say, kid, why do you work so much?"

Franz breaks the silence and looks up from his toenails, which are gnarled and a scaly yellow. He smiles at me over his toes. I'm already in a sour mood, having gotten caught in the rain myself after a long day's work, and frankly, the sight and smell of Franz is disgusting.

"How else would we pay the bills? It's not like your lazy ass does anything."

I pull a stool noisily across the floor and sit down. Franz clips his last pinky toe with a chuckle. The clipped nail pops up and falls into the cracks of the couch.

"I roll a better joint than you do, son. You can't place a dollar value on experience."

He winks at me with a grin and tosses a handful of his cut nails into the overflowing ashtray.

"That's a really great skill for an adult to have."

Franz throws the clipper to the side and grabs some matches from the table. He moves the joint from his ear to his cracked lips and lights it.

"I think it is a great skill to have at any age, really. Marcus, what do you think you will accomplish, exactly, by working hard?"

He begins his rhetorical with smoke filled lungs.

"What kind of question is that?"

Franz bears a relaxed, confident look that annoys me. His nonchalance and carelessness are really beginning to get on my nerves. I cannot fathom how this slob can be so egotistical. It makes no sense. He's disgusting. Every day I have to come home to him doing something disgusting, knowing in the back of my mind that he's had a leisurely day while I swept floors and made deliveries. And yet, here we both are at the end of the day, in the same position, smoking the same joint, in the same disheveled apartment, with bank accounts in similar states of disarray.

"Kiss ass while you bitch so you can get rich but your boss gets richer off you."

He taunts me with the Dead Kennedys line as he sucks on the joint.

"You know, I always thought that song would sound better sung with a German accent."

"Oh, so you know the song! I didn't take you for a punk rocker Marcus. I didn't think they swept floors."

He smiles his stupid smile at me and I want to punch him. But I just nod and smile ironically as he hands me the joint.

"Seems your generation is not entirely lost, Marcus. What does a person who can pick up on punk lyrics like that do with a job? Do you have a passion for sweeping floors, Marcus? What do you get out of that job, Marcus?"

He prods me deliberately, directing the rhetorical conversation like some delinquent professor.

"Money you nitwit. The thing we need to survive. The thing that keeps you sleeping on that disgusting couch in this disgusting apartment rather than outside in the rain, on the pavement."

I inhale long and hard and hold the smoke in my lungs as long as possible.

"Money, huh. Money is such an interesting concept."

Franz taps his chin with his forefinger.

"A platform, an arena, a medium through which material goods can be ascribed a universal value, and traded based on this value. Markets! And earning it is so interesting too, isn't it? A human being transforms himself into a useful tool for however many hours, in exchange for a set rate of capital. Do you enjoy being a tool for eight hours a day, Marcus? What's it like being a tool, Marcus?"

I look over at him and his stupid smiling face sets me off.

"Spare me the pseudo-Marxian bullshit, Franz. Can you even read?"

He takes the joint and leans back, still with that stupid smile, and crosses his legs.

"You sell your time, and then you buy a laptop. A laptop is worth, say, fifty hours of your life. And when you use this laptop, do you regain those lost hours in the form of pleasure? I never quite understood that rhetoric. And what are you building towards exactly? Or is it the fact that you get to numb your brain into submission for those eight hours? The consumerist worldview has always eluded me. But then I'm just an uneducated pauper. A taker. Can you explain it to me, Marcus? You seem to have a firmer grip on it than I do."

Franz is really getting on my nerves. His stupid accent makes everything he says sound cartoon. He passes me the joint and I take a last pull, before tossing it angrily on the table. Without a word, I get up to brush my teeth and go to bed without looking at him.

The sound of raindrops battering the window, and the wail of distant sirens keep me awake. It takes me several hours lying in bed staring at the spackle-drip ceiling and savoring the numbing taste of fluoride before I finally drift to sleep. I wonder what Candy is doing, and if Joanie is feeling better. Most of all I fantasize about a time when I can finally get away from this horrible apartment and its lunatic lodger.

***

The next day, still steaming about the stuff Franz said, I storm into work with a scowl on my face. It takes me a few hours of internal debate and building up confidence before I finally approach Dolly and ask for a raise. She seems slightly taken aback, as I have been working there less than three months, and generally, floor sweepers do not get raises. However, seeing as she is in a good mood, and that she likes me, and that I do my job well and laugh at her jokes, but mostly because it would be an inconvenience to find another employee, she smiles and offers me a thirty-five cent raise on the hour, which I grudgingly accept. I return to my tasks and work diligently, though still unsatisfied. Dolly's watchful eyes are more vigilant than ever today.

Later the same day, I have a delivery to an old folks home in Outremont. Driving there, I find myself a few blocks from the coffee shop where Marie-Eve works. It is a fancy artisan coffee shop, the kind that stresses the importance of the bean, and employs aproned baristas. I haven't spoken to Marie-Eve in months, and I have no idea if she even works here anymore. But I pull in, and idle in the parking lot smoking a cigarette for a while.

It takes me some time to muster the courage to enter the shop.

It's around three o'clock, and through the glass windows I can see there aren't too many customers inside. The place is decked out with holiday decorations- paper snowmen and ornaments hang from the ceiling, and the counter is covered in green and red shining garlands.

Marie-Eve is working. She sees me come in, and a smile of genuine surprise lights up her face. I move up to the register and we hug over the counter. She tells me I look great, I tell her likewise. She looks bigger though, and feels bigger when we hug. Her uniform is unflattering; though it *is* obvious she has put on weight. She asks me how I am. I lie and tell her I'm fantastic. She tells me she's in a relationship now, with a hardworking, honest man. An electrician. They've been together a few months now. I think to myself that it explains the weight. She asks if I am seeing anyone, insists we should double date. I tell her I'm not and she says she's sorry. I tell her that I'm happy for her. The small talk dries up and I order an espresso. I pay, though Marie-Eve insists it isn't necessary. I thank her. She smiles. And I leave the shop.

Outside I light a cigarette and check my watch again. I know Dolly will have questions for me, seeing as I'm taking longer than expected to make the delivery. Lucky for me, it has just begun pouring rain, and I know that the weather will provide me with a passable excuse.

That night, the streets are glistening a gloomy yellow when I come home to the sight of Franz masturbating on the living room couch. He has his pants down to his ankles and his face so deep in a smutty magazine that he does not realize I'm in the room until I slam the apartment door shut. The bastard isn't so much as startled. Franz calmly pulls his pants back up, and moves the joint on his ear into his mouth.

Franz lights the joint and I grab my stool from the kitchen. The magazine lies face up on the coffee table, open to the page he was enjoying.

"I found that in a thrift shop today. Can you believe it? On such a rainy ugly day I find this gem. It's the 1976 Hope Olson spread. I jerked it to that issue non-stop when it was first released. Non-stop kid. Today was a great day. I recaptured my youth through a string of nostalgic orgasms."

He chuckles and hands me the joint. Franz rises to open the patio door, in those disgusting sweats he always wears, ventilating the place of the lingering marijuana, tobacco, and masturbation smells.

"I'm glad you enjoyed yourself, Franz. While you were tugging it today, I got a raise."

I say this triumphantly, as Franz moves over to the record player and selects an Engelbert Humperdinck vinyl. The rain splatters noisily against the patio door and trickles in through the small opening. I grab a towel from the washroom and throw it by the door. The record spins to 'Release Me'.

"Marcus! That's fantastic news! All our troubles are behind us."

He walks over and puts his hands to my face. I slap them away aggressively and he laughs raucously. The smile on his face grows wider.

"How much are we talking baby? When do we move into the penthouse?"

He plucks the joint from my lips and plops himself down on the couch, crossing his legs, smiling ear to ear.

"Buzz off Franz. It was thirty-five cents. But it's still thirty five cents more than you got today jerking off."

He sits there, posturing in his pseudo-intellectual way, looking at me with that idiotic smile. He winks at me and licks his repulsive fingertips.

"So let me get this straight", he starts again with that wry smile, "You're going to make it to the top in thirty-five cent increments? You really have an unwavering faith in the system, don't you kid?"

"Listen, I got a raise. I sweep floors for chrissakes. How in the hell are you going to spin this off as a bad thing?"

He inhales again, his beady eyes going into their pensive squint, and he hands me back the joint.

"Marcus, I didn't think I'd have to explain to you that the game is not the game unless you're playing for something that matters."

I watch the cherry burn, listening to Humperdinck's smooth vocals bring in the chorus. *Pleaaaaase release me, leeeeet me goooo.* The song takes me out of the room, floods my mind with images of a car ride on the New York Interstate through the Appalachian Mountains. Images of lush foliage, and the sun shining through the windshield of my father's Pontiac. My brother and I are in the back seat, calmly enveloped in our handheld electronic games. My father drives, arguing with my mother who holds the map, about when to take the exit...

"Marcus. Listen to me. I don't get your game. If this is some attempt to move from the bottom ranks up to the petite bourgeoisie, then my friend you're going about it all wrong. The bourgeoisie remains the bourgeoisie by employing chumps like you and reaping the profits. You are human capital. There is no way that as human capital, you will make your way up to a position of any real stability or power. Do you really want to live the rest of your life slaving away in a standstill of mediocrity? Thirty-five cents is nothing. Thirty-five cents is absolutely nothing, Marcus. Do you understand that? They might as well have given you a raise of a gumball per hour. You have no prospects at that job. Do you think the proprietor is vetting you to take over? I mean, look at you for chrissakes. You have such potential. Such potential Marcus! Yet, you live with a washed up fifty something in a crummy apartment. You work six days a week. You have hardly any time for yourself. Don't you deserve more than that? Of course you do. You deserve more than this Marcus. Much more. You deserve much, much more."

I look Franz up and down as he sits there with his legs

crossed and I wonder where he fits into the car ride. I look at him, my own eyes narrowed in thought, and I say:

"If you don't take a shower right now, I'm moving out tomorrow."

He chuckles, but I stare him down as serious as I've ever been about anything in my life. We lock eyes for a second, two, three, then he shrugs and gets up to bathe. I finish the joint peacefully alone while he showers, listening to the sound of running water, watching the rainfall. In the light of the full moon in the remarkably clear night sky, I can make out the individually glistening drops as they race each other to the ground.

***

That Friday, I have a rendezvous with Bella after work. She called me out of the blue, and asked to meet up for a coffee. She sounded incredibly cheery over the phone, and insisted that she had a lot to talk to me about. So I agreed to meet her. It wasn't like I had anything else going on. We set a date for nine o'clock at Gaetano's, the famous coffee shop in the east end.

To be perfectly honest, I want nothing to do with her. The sound of her voice over the phone gave me an erection, and I impulsively agreed to see her in hopes that we would end up having sex. The truth is, I haven't slept with anyone since Candy. It is incredibly difficult in my circumstances. I have no car, no money to spare on extravagance of any kind, and no place to actually do the deed. I have a room and a bed, sure, but it's not possible to get Franz out of the apartment. And the man is not exactly the type I want to have around young women. I can't see him making any kind of effort to act normal for a night…

I take the bus to Gaetano's from the bakery. I brought a duffel bag with a change of clothes, so that I could head straight over after work. It's a cold crisp night. The air stings my skin as I walk from the bus stop to the café. I'm wearing jeans and a white t-shirt with black horizontal stripes.

Walking into Gaetano's through the terrace, I wave hello to the familiar faces behind the counter and in the kitchen. I move to the right of the establishment, the dining area, and look around for Bella. Gaetano's' granite-top tables and steel-frame chairs are well lit, and the bright dining room is noisy with groups of Italian-Canadians discussing business or sharing a laugh over a coffee and cannoli.

I catch sight of Bella in the corner of the dining room, by the window overlooking the terrace and the cars passing by on Jarry Street. I walk over to take the vacant seat across her.

"Hi, cutie."

She smiles as she says this in her flaky, familiar way. She reaches out and takes my hand in hers, still smiling. Her makeup is carefully applied, and her perfume is as strong as it is familiar.

"Hello, Bella."

I reply generically, treading carefully. Bella has striking hazel eyes. Her eyes are the feature that most attracts me. She knows this. She learned of the manipulative strength of her eyes early in our relationship, and used them to get the things she wanted from me. And here she is now, staring at me with those eyes once again, and acting quite naturally as though she saw me only yesterday, as though we haven't gone a year without talking, as though she could walk right back into my life without causing so much as a ripple.

"So, Mr. Groucho. How's everything? How's your mom? How are you liking graduate school?"

Bella has her blonde hair done in thick curls. Her nails have also been manicured; long, square-cut light pink plastic is glued to her fingertips. I get the impression all this artifice is supposed to show me her adult side; her mature society-approved side to contrast the side I have already seen and come to know- the side that is a confused, spoiled child. She looks to me like a little girl playing house.

"Graduate school is good. My mom is good. How about you?"

I glossed over a few details, and fabricated a little over the phone. I didn't want our encounter becoming too intimate. I also did not want to turn her off with the bleak truth that I am broke and living with a nutcase.

"Good, I'm glad everything is good. Everything is good with me too. Everything is good at the firm. It's hard work, but it's good. Teaching me discipline."

She smiles even wider than before, flashing her neat little teeth.

A waiter comes over to take our order and I recognize him from my childhood. His name is Joey. Awkward encounters with people from my past are a major reason I avoid Gaetano's. Joey and I played sports together when we were younger and were even friends, for a time. Somewhere down the line though, he decided that he'd put his head down and look right through me. Now he comes over and acts as though he's never seen me, with a face I could just slap. Bella orders an espresso and a cannoli, and without looking at Joey or acknowledging him, I order the same.

Bella babbles on about her day to day at the office and my erection slowly dissipates. Staring at the painting of coffee beans suspended on the wall behind her head, I wonder how she'd feel about me if she knew the truth about my life.

"So then Dave tells me that it must be the copier, and as it turned out, we had forgotten to refill the paper!"

She starts laughing and I space out for a while. A few minutes later Joey arrives with our coffees and desserts. I reach for my cannoli and bite into it hungrily. With my mouth full, I look at Bella and chew my food loudly. The neighboring table turns to look and I start laughing to myself.

"I see you're still a child, Marcus."

She says this with a scolding motherly frown. It isn't that I was incapable of having adult conversations with Bella; it's that I see no purpose in them. We have had them, and we don't see eye to eye. She is pragmatic, narrow-minded. She wants a husband, and a provider. I don't want to be that husband. It's simple enough.

"So, this Dave character, you fucking him?"

I ask with a smirk and she frowns at me, rolling her eyes.

"Yeah Marcus, every day at lunch. In the supply closet."

She nibbles at her cannoli daintily, trying to avoid getting her fancy blouse dirty. I stuff the rest of mine into my mouth.

"That's kind of slutty."

I say this with my mouth full and smile at her with cream and pastry bits wedged between my teeth.

"I was kidding you moron."

"Okay good, I guess that means I won't have to wear a condom later."

She looks at me with a stern adult face and I can't help but grin.

"I don't know what you think this encounter is about, but you're not going to be sleeping with me tonight Marcus."

"Okay, I'm sorry. So how long have you known this Dave?"

"Ugh, you're impossible."

She rolls her eyes.

"So why did you want to see me, Bella?"

I ask as I wipe my mouth clean, and Bella looks down, measuring her words:

"I don't know, I thought maybe the time apart might have changed things. I thought maybe we could meet as different people."

She sips her coffee. It's served in a red porcelain cup. The lip of the cup is nicked and a small surface crack runs down the length of the cup. The dining room is loud with conversation. The old men at the table beside us shout with urgency at the television, screaming at an Italian soccer game.

"Who's to say that's not the case?"

"Oh, Marcus, please. You're still the same old child you were when we were dating. Everything's a joke to you. You can't take anything seriously. I don't understand how you are getting by in grad school. How can you possibly have this attitude and get by in life? I really don't understand it. Unless you just act this way with me. Which would make me feel even worse!"

She looks at me, waiting for me to explain myself. I look at the wall and then back at her. She taps her fingernails on the tabletop.

I start:

"Okay, let's give this a shot. I was brushing my teeth the

other day and a thought occurred to me. It was a riff, a segment from a sad song. It just popped into my head and I started humming it while I brushed my teeth."

She squints at me and shakes her head. Her beautiful curls gently bounce with the motion of her head.

"What? What the hell are you talking about?"

I sip my coffee.

"And then I thought about it a little bit, and I wondered where it came from."

"Where what came from? What are you talking about?"

Bella frowns in frustration and erratically reaches across the table for the processed sugar. I pause, watching her measure the sugar to the spoon, and then quickly stir it into the coffee.

"Where what came from? Marcus?"

"Where did the song come from? Why did I start humming it? What began that strain of thought? Why that song? Why in that moment? Who the hell was behind the screen pushing the button that made that song pop into my head?"

She frowns at me, trying to understand but unable.

"What screen? What button? I'm incredibly confused. What the hell are you talking about? Can you speak like a normal person, please? You're freaking me out."

"I mean at the time I was hung-over and sort of luxuriating in loneliness and self-pitying, but there are plenty of songs I could do that to. Hundreds! Why that one? It came to me organically in a way I could not explain. I thought about it for a whole week and I couldn't come up with anything. I hadn't heard that song in months! Every action has a reaction, but who sets forth the chain? Where do things begin? Why can't we see the full breadth? Why can't we understand the machinations of the universe? We're so damn limited! It's frustrating. Don't you think?"

Bella's face changes from confusion to concern, and she softens her voice sweetly, as one does with an ailing child.

"Marcus, sweetheart, are you okay? Is something going on with you? Do you need me? Do you need someone to talk to? I'm listening, tell me what's wrong."

I turn my head and look at the old men sitting with their coffees, fixated on the television. I imagine they have been watching soccer their whole lives. I imagine they have always rooted for the same team.

"Does this shirt make me look like an escaped convict? Or worse? A fat escaped convict?"

Bella raises an eyebrow and takes a breath to answer but I cut her off:

"Oh, never mind. I'm going to go smoke a cigarette."

I knock back the rest of the espresso and it burns the roof of my mouth. Bella shakes her head and I rise and walk over to the terrace. I fish my carton out of my jacket pocket and light a cigarette. My breath is visible out in the cold. I check my watch and realize it's after ten and I work early tomorrow.

I see Bella inside settling the bill with the waiter.

I look across the street into the parking lot and I recognize her car.

Through the window, I see Bella making small talk with another waiter and a surge of jealousy rises through my body. I keep my eyes locked on them gritting my teeth.

Bella finally comes out to join me on the terrace for a cigarette, my duffel bag in hand.

"Thanks for taking my bag."

"Don't mention it. You got a light?"

I light her cigarette and pull another from my pack. We smoke quietly for a while. She wears a beautiful beige pea coat I've never seen before. Her purse is designer.

"Hey, Bella, do you mind driving me to a buddy's? My car is at the garage for an oil change and I don't want to take the bus. It's not too far. Please."

"Yeah, fine."

"Thanks."

We walk across the street to the parking lot in silence.

I tell her that she can drive me to the Langelier Metro station and that I will be fine on my own from there. She agrees.

Bella drives in silence, with the radio off. I chew gum, trying to erase the aftertaste of the cigarette. I listen to the sound of her tires turn on the wet pavement.

Half way over and without any warning, Bella veers into a deserted strip mall off the boulevard, and parks behind a building, out of sight. I don't say a word. She keeps the car running.

She turns and stares straight at me, her emerald eyes overcome with lust. Putting a soft hand to my face and stepping over the armrest, she takes a seat on top of me. She kisses me eagerly, though completely in control, making sure to lightly bite my lower lip and press her entire body against me. Her body is warm, and melts into the warmth of mine. I reach around to remove her jacket and feel for her breasts over her shirt. She leans in, moaning so that I can feel her hot breath on my ear. She bites and licks my earlobe playfully. I reach into her pants and feel for the familiar contours, grabbing at every fold of skin and pressing her closer to me. Our lips lock and our genitals line up in hot passionate thrusts. I pull my pants down and she slides into the leg space while I recline the chair. She puts it all in her wet mouth. Her tongue moves up and down, fueled by desire, and she makes slurping noises that set me off. I pull her by the hair, bringing her face up to mine and she reaches back to remove her pants. She sits herself back on top of me and I slip myself effortlessly into her with a gasp. She holds my face with both hands, kissing me tenderly on the cheek and neck and lips. I bounce her aggressively on my lap, in a primal rush releasing animal cries of desire. The sensation is maddening and hurried for that little while, before I surrender into the familiar welcoming warmth. And we hold each other for a while, I am still inside of her, while I stare at the ceiling of her Toyota and slowly become conscious of the heat.

We crack the windows and get dressed slowly, neither of us speaking. I chew on my gum calmly, as I clean myself off and put on my pants. Bella reaches over to touch my face and I very gently brush her arm away without looking at her. Her breathing becomes heavier, and makes me think she might shed a few silent tears as we drive on.

There's no way for me to know. I refuse to look at her.

She turns the radio on. I open the window wider and enjoy the indie rock song and the cold crisp air blowing through my hair, but unable to penetrate my thick beard.

I think about what has just happened and compulsively rationalize it.

Sleeping with Bella is a futile attempt at carving a pocket in the continuum. It is an attempt at a standstill, a defiance of time. We did, for a little while, turn back the clock. The few moments inside her were thoughtless, instinctual. But then I know on a primal level I am simply starved for intimacy, for human contact.

I'm lonely.

I have never felt it that much before, but I'm lonely. I craved her touch more than anything else. Her kisses. The feeling of knowing that another human being out there was connected to me in at least some way. Even if only for a moment. The feeling of knowing, even if only for a minute, that I was not all alone.

It was cowardice, I suppose. Running back into the safety of the past nestled in her arms. Running from the difficulty of the future into the safety of the past, the safety of her embrace, and the warmth of her acceptance. There is safety in the past, I suppose, because there can be no surprises in what has already happened. No matter how good or bad, it has already happened. The initial impact has passed, and the familiar can be counted on to offer the false promise of happiness and the false resistance of change.

Around the corner from the station, she turns off the radio and starts in on me again:

"Why do you insist on always playing this ultra guarded macho card? Why can't we just have a conversation like adults?"

"I don't know what you're talking about."

"You're like a caricature, Marcus. You know that I care about you, and I'm trying my best to understand what you're going through but you won't let me in. I can't help you from the outside Marcus. I need you to help me help you."

"I really, really don't know what you're talking about. I don't need your help lady."

"I guess you've always been like this, though. Even when we were dating I always had to steal my kisses from you, work for the affection."

"I think that says more about you than about me."

She parks the car in another strip mall. This one is much closer to the apartment.

"Why do you need to be like this? Why can't you see I care for you? Do you understand that I care for you? How can you be so coldhearted? I've spent the past year thinking about only you, Marcus. Do you understand how much you mean to me?"

She looks at me in exasperation, running one hand through her ruffled hair and the other one trembling. The tension of the moment makes me chew harder on my gum.

"I'm sorry."

Anger flares in her eyes.

"Sorry? What are you sorry about Marcus? Your words are so empty! You're full of shit Marcus. Answer my question! Why? Why? Why!?"

She works herself into a frenzy screaming at me. I look at her as calmly as I can, managing the tightness in my chest, doing my best to quash it with indifference. I look at her and her face is contorted- her upper lip is quivering, her mascara is running, her fists are clenched, and her eyes are aching with a desire that will never be realized. She whispers:

"Why?"

And I cannot hold it any longer.

"Because you don't exist! What don't you understand? You existed at some point in the past but now you don't. We can't recapture that moment. We can't recapture the past. And even if we could, the past is broken. It's lodged somewhere in our brains, scattered and shattered in a million little pieces that we'll never put back together. Can't you see how obvious that is? I know what you're feeling Bella, a nostalgic fond remembrance of times that were better because the times right now aren't so great but it's all a lie. The past was no better than the present, and the future will just be more of the same. What the hell do you want from me? You want to burrow yourself in me? You want to project all of your shortcomings and missed opportunities on me? Do you want to take refuge from the difficulties of the world in my affection? I can't help you, Bella. And God knows you can't help me."

I look her in the eye and she can't hold my gaze. She puts her head down and begins quietly sobbing. Streaks of black leak onto her fingertips as she no longer struggles to keep herself together. I had seen those hazel eyes weep many times before. Many times I had been the cause.

There was a time when they would pull on a heartstring, hard, and I'd end up with my arms around her begging for forgiveness, kissing her forehead asking what I could do to better my wrong. But those days had long gone, and they weren't coming back.

"Why are you so afraid of emotion!?"

She screams out, slamming her hands against the steering wheel and inadvertently honking the horn.

A man and a woman leaving a restaurant are startled by the blast of the horn. I take a deep breath and wander beyond the car, wondering if the couple had enjoyed their meal, and where they were off to now.

"I'm not afraid of emotion. It's only that, this stuff makes you old."

Her face is twisted in disbelief and confusion and anger and hatred and I say:

"Anyway, I have an early morning tomorrow. Thank you for the lift. I wish you well."

I reach for the door and her head shoots up and she reaches out for my hand, teary eyed and frantic.

"Marcus wait, please. I... I want to feel you one last time. Please. Make love to me again Marcus. You'll see, it'll change how you feel. Or maybe it won't. I guess I don't care. I'm okay with it being a lie. I just want you inside me. Please."

I teeter for a moment on the familiar seesaw notions that Bella is pathetic, or I am the worst human being on the planet. I look her in the eyes and they are filled with sadness, black-brimmed from the mascara. Her lips are trembling. Her face was reduced to desperation and sorrow that I did not want to acknowledge. Her pale face is tight and young. Though I know that with time, the plump curvature of her cheekbone will slowly recede like the jagged rocks of a wave-battered bluff. In her pupils, I see waves of black cresting and breaking, and turmoil at once familiar and distant. In her hazel irises, I see Joanie, Candy, Sandy, and countless nameless others standing in a row, upon that hazel canvas, an army beckoning me to do right by my woman, to do right by myself, to do right by humanity. And in this moment I feel quite strongly that I am pivoting on a decision that will define me. Am I going to do what is right, or am I going to do what is right for me?

"I'm sorry, I can't."

"What?"

"I said no."

Bella looks up at me and her face goes blank. She wipes her eyes and composes herself, running her hands through her hair and adjusting herself in her seat. She sighs, and then punches me with all her might.

"Thank you, Marcus, for reminding me what a prick you are."

Her face is flushed. She looks insane.

"You aren't equipped for a serious relationship either way", punches me again, "I mean look at you; you have the emotional stamina of a twelve year old. Go to hell. You know, there's a reason you have no friends. When I bump into them around they all talk shit about you. All of them do. They all think you're a piece of shit."

I light a cigarette and check my watch. It's just about eleven o'clock. The rain is starting up again, and I know I'll inevitably get wet walking back to the apartment.

"I mean how long are you going to milk the excuse that your parents split? Oh, boohoo your dad ran away. You're just messed up. You're a sad, pathetic little man and it's no one's fault but yours that you will end up sad and alone, Marcus."

Bella continues yelling at me and I grab my duffel bag, open the car door, and walk off into the night.

Entering the lobby, soaking wet, I realize that the gum I am chewing has long lost its flavor, and I toss it angrily into the street.

I walk up the stairs neurotically pondering several decisions I know I cannot reverse. As I approach the apartment door, though, I'm swept up by the music of tribal drums coming from within. I unlock the door and enter to see Franz in his underwear smoking a cigarette in my bed, and two dirty hippies sitting around the coffee table burning vanilla-scented incense. They seem to be meditating.

I walk in and slam the door shut. The hippies- one male and one female- rise and introduce themselves as our new neighbors from across the hall, Jim and Luna.

"They just came to make our acquaintance!"

Franz yells from the bedroom, over the tribal drums.

The bohemians have hands blackened by soot. They rise, telling me that they have to be going. They say they are professional chimney sweeps, and that they just moved in. If I know anyone who needs their chimney swept, I should refer them. Their hair is braided and dirty. Beads of sweat run down their foreheads, and they look stoned. They wear construction boots and overalls. They just stand there looking at me dumbly until I nod, and show them the door.

Rising from the bed, Franz moves to the couch and puts out the incense. He switches the CD player off and spins a Sinatra vinyl. The smell of vanilla at least masks, if only slightly, the smells of sex and marijuana.

"Rough go with the ex-girlfriend sugarplum?"

"Bite me."

Franz cackles like a hyena. I turn to lock the door and hop in the shower.

I stay in the shower for about twenty minutes, washing the smells and touch of Bella's skin from mine, and torturing myself with visions of her sleeping with one of my friends out of spite.

Out of the shower, I change the sheets on the bed before moving to my spot on the stool, ready for the nightly smoke with Franz.

I can see that he rolled three fat ones, and is smoking one in his usual position. He is lying shirtless on his dirty white couch, with his dirty shoes on, staring out at the night sky.

"I noticed black fingerprints on my sheets, and on the walls. The next time you have an orgy in here, you stay out of my bedroom. And you owe me for the sheets."

He moves to a sitting position and looks over at me with a seemingly repentant face.

"I'm sorry Marcus, really. It really did begin with just an innocent knock on the door."

He smiles like a child caught rummaging through his mother's purse.

"So why don't you tell me what happened sweetheart?"

"What do you mean?"

"Your ex-girlfriend called you up out of the blue. That can only mean one thing right?"

He winks at me.

"Yeah. In the end, she got too emotional."

Franz frowns.

"Of course she got emotional. What's wrong with you? Why are you so afraid of a little emotion? For chrissakes all you do is mope. Here let me show you something."

Franz reaches into his back pocket for his wallet.

"I'm not afraid of emotion, I just don't want to deal with all that crap man. She started in on me real bad at the end."

Franz empties out his wallet on the coffee table. There are

over twenty cards in his wallet, everything from library cards, to identification cards, to credit cards. How the hell he managed so many credit cards in his financial condition is beyond me.

"Ah, well, it is your ex-girlfriend. You knew that you were stepping into a minefield. Ah-ha here, look."

He pulls out an old pocket-sized polaroid photo and hands it over. The photo is of a beautiful woman with the big eighties style hair teased out for volume. On the back, it's captioned 'Mina, '87'. I flip it back over and stare at the woman. She wears a tight red over-the-shoulder dress and black heels, and poses with a confident smile. She has an enchanting gaze that welcomes the attention.

"Who is this?"

'That's Mina, can't you read? My ex-wife and the only woman I've ever loved, really. Though I don't think she ever loved me back. We were together for a few years, while I was heavily in the black. She was a fantastic lover. Really knew how to please a man. She left me right about the same time the money did, and like the money, she never came back."

Franz sighs.

I look back at the picture and the creases make me feel as though I hold one of Franz's most personal and coveted possessions. I look up from the photo, and for the first time I see Franz as something more than a bad joke.

"Franz, I think there's a story you need to tell me. Why are you here? How do you know Jean-Marie? Why don't you have a job? Who the hell are you?"

He puts out the first joint and lights another. He looks me up and down as he does so.

"I think so too. But we've got all night, right? Why don't you tell me more about your night?"

"Okay. We had sex. Then she lost her mind. What more is there?"

He pulls on the joint before passing it.

"Did it rekindle anything? Did you feel something you thought you couldn't ever feel again?"

He says this with a grin as he leans back on the couch. He sits directly beneath the watercolor so that it looks as though Aphrodite stands on his shoulders.

"I felt romantic about her for about twelve minutes and I had my dick in her for eleven and a half of them."

Franz chuckles and I hand him back the joint.

"My chest felt heavy after we had finished. I couldn't breathe. I don't think that's how you should feel in that situation. Your heart is supposed to be light as air isn't it? If anything makes you feel like you can fly, it's sex, right? It just wasn't like that."

"Alright, Marcus, so you know. Don't overthink it. That's the worst thing you can do."

He gets up to open the patio door a little, letting in a cool gust of air.

"I mean I guess I still melted little at her kitten eyes and that pretty little beauty mark on her left cheek. I made her smile. She smiled at me. It feels like I haven't had a woman smile at me in months. I don't know, Franz. It seems more and more everywhere I look I see people that are so uptight. I don't really have anything against that, but I feel like 'good for you'. I'm not. I don't see myself as a straight line. I think there was a time when I did, but that time has long past. Can you relate to that at all?"

Franz nods and crosses his legs.

"Marcus, you and I are very much alike though you may not realize it. The only difference is that I possess something that you do not, yet."

"Oh yeah, what's that?"

I can't help but laugh at the idea that Franz and I are the same. My laughter seems to peeve him, and he answers with a serious face.

"Wisdom. It is a character trait very rare in this day and age, and in fact, age alone no longer assures it. I remember when I was a young man, very much like yourself: uncertain, confused, mistrusting, lost in the ebb and flow of life."

He passes me the joint and I keep my eyes on his, though struggling to take him seriously.

"I, of course, had direction thrust upon me. I had a skill, and I had people around me who recognized this skill, and wanted to foster it, to cultivate me into a champion."

"You boxed."

He nods.

"And so, with all these well-meaning people surrounding me and always smiling and cheering me on, I acquiesced. I mean, of course I did. What's a young man to do in a position like that? Turn his back on what all those around him, all the people he loves and all those who love him insist must be his destiny? Just throw it all away? No. That's not something I had the strength to do as a child, though it may have crossed my mind a great many times. My father was an amateur boxer in his youth. So I boxed. And I boxed well, I assure you. I knocked fighters out with a head of height and twenty pounds on me. Right jab to the ribs, right fake to the head, left uppercut. That combination alone earned me nine knockouts. And I trained. Don't kid yourself, kid, you don't get to be razor sharp and lightning fast without training your goddamn ass off every day. But I lacked something. For all my hard work, I lacked the intangible required of any great sportsman. Call it heart, call it the desire to win, perseverance, I don't know. I lacked it. I would knock the other guys out because I was a tactician and a masterful mover. I would knock the other guys out because I could outsmart them, and outlast them. I would knock the other guys out because it was all that I knew, and it was all that anyone had ever wanted for me. I would knock them out because my father was watching. But I never knocked them out because *I* wanted to. And that is what I lacked. In my heart of hearts, I always knew that I did not care. To me, boxing was just a game."

"So what happened?"

"I only lost one fight, and it was my last. I was 19-0 in the late seventies and poised for big things. I was even beginning to garner media attention. I was one of the most promising junior boxers in the world. The pressure was immense. It got to the point where I would fill out two thousand person venues when I fought. Politicians and public figures would sometimes be in the stands. But anyway, the fight. I was fighting the twenty two year old French champion, in what was being hyped as a battle of national prodigies. I remember it like it was yesterday. His name was Richard Poulier. He was 13-1. He was a massive boxer, a heavy hitter. He had three inches on me. His natural weight was maybe thirty pounds heavier than mine, though he got it down for the weigh-in. That was the only reason we could fight in the same weight class. I gotta give it to him, the guy had incredible control over the fluctuations of his body. The promoters booked us a five thousand spectator venue and everyone I knew came out to see the fight. It was nineteen eighty, and boxing wasn't like it is today. It was a blood sport. It was one of the most popular sports in the world."

"So how did it go?"

He waves at me to pass the joint.

"Well…"

He sighs a heavy sigh and looks at the floor.

"I went down in the first round. Twenty seven seconds in. I took a barrage of punches and I hit the mat. My face was swollen to three times the size. Stung like nothing I had ever felt before."

He hits the joint and moves to the kitchen to fetch the carton of milk from the fridge. He sips the milk straight from the carton before putting it back in the fridge. He walks slowly back to the couch, mulling things over in his mind. He sits back down, and continues:

"I made fifty thousand dollars that night and I never boxed again."

"What?"

That one takes me by surprise, and I can't help the outburst.

Franz just looks at me and nods.

I frown.

"I don't understand."

"Think about it. What was the value of all that training, of all those broken bones? What was the value of all that constant dissatisfaction and hard work and striving? What was I striving toward? Greatness? I knew very well that was a concept I did not believe in. I was a lapdog. I was bred and trained to do one thing and one thing only. I took control of my fate that night."

I shake my head trying to put things together:

"So you're saying that you flopped?"

His eyes narrow, and his face becomes more serious than I have ever seen it.

"Don't be stupid. I took control of my life that night."

"This is crazy, you threw the fight? What happened to the money?"

"Didn't I say we've got all night? Relax."

He looks out the window and crosses his legs once more.

"Everyone was shocked, of course. Even though Poulier was a great boxer, I was supposed to beat him. My parents were crushed. Even more so when I joined the American Navy. I joined a month or so after. Everything happened pretty quickly after the fight. I did it so I could go live in the States. I wanted to start fresh. I wanted to be discharged somewhere in the U.S. after my stint in the armed forces. It was a means to an end. I was a physical specimen at the time, and I passed all their physical and psychological tests easily. It took a while to get all the paperwork in order, but eventually they let me in and deployed me overseas to Beirut. To make a long story short, I had to fake an injury to get discharged. It wasn't easy, believe me. They don't let you out of the army that easy, and I had to use all my cunning. Bribing doctors and constantly faking a limp. I even took a knife to my leg to create a believable scar."

He lifts his dirty pant leg to reveal the scar along his left calf.

"And then, I made it to the states, where I began my career as a gambler. I eventually made it to Vegas, where I could gamble every single day. I built what was left of that fifty thousand into nearly three million in just a few years."

I look at him incredulously.

"You what!? How?"

He puts out the joint, and without hesitation lights the third one on his ear. I am watching Franz with eyes wide open. I can hardly believe the things he is telling me, and yet his easy demeanor somehow assures me all of it is true.

"Well-timed bets. In retrospect, I can see I was blessed with lots of luck. You see kid, there's no logic to it all. There's no way of really knowing when things will go your way or when they won't. Never mind what anyone says, life is all about momentum and at that time, I had it. Every bet I placed was golden, it seemed. I would play a system of course, but I knew I was riding a wave that would eventually crest and fall. It had to. Life is cyclical, as is luck, but when you're riding as high as I was, as young as I was, it gets difficult to put perspective on anything. I felt invincible at the time. I should have stopped, certainly, but there was just no way I was going to. I could have been somewhere else right now. Maybe I could still have Mina by my side. God, I remember the feeling so well though. It was like nothing could touch me. I was a golden boy."

He chuckles and shakes his head.

"Would you believe it that people would stop me in the streets, as I was walking out of the casinos on Fremont. These nobody losers would pull at my pant legs begging me for my picks on a boxing match, on the football game, to throw out a roulette number. It was insanity."

He passes the joint and I say nothing, completely absorbed by his story, waiting for him to continue.

"I started off betting on boxing and boxing only. It started light, of course. I figured boxing was probably my field of expertise, and that with my experience I'd be a lot better at sorting out the contenders from the pretenders. Who the hell knows if that was the case, but it turned out that I was winning.

The first ever bet I placed was a gutsy twenty thousand dollar bet on a 1983 junior fight in Mobile, Alabama."

"Jesus, Franz, twenty grand? That's light?"

"Easy kid. It was about half my bankroll at the time. I bet the underdog, this big burly Dominican fighter with a face like a bulldog and a body like an ox. Rodriguez. I knew he would win. I saw it in his eyes that this guy was hungry; he was a fighter to the death. He pummeled the favorite, McIntyre, a flashy All-American type wearing red white and blue trousers. I remember the Dominican caught him with a straight shot to the nose. The American painted the canvas red as he dropped. That bet paid five to one."

He pauses, leaning back and running his hands through his thin greasy hair, struggling to recollect the events that led to his current state of affairs.

"And remember, this was the eighties! One hundred thousand then was a hell of a lot more than one hundred thousand nowadays… The next bet I played was in Vegas. I moved out there right after I won that first bet. Kid, if I can give you one little piece of advice, it's this: you always gotta win your first bet. Remember that. It sets the tone."

He pauses again to go take another swig of milk.

"It was when I moved to Vegas that things really began heating up for me. That's when I met Mina. She was a dancer at one of the cheaper bars, far off the Strip and Fremont. I was living in a discount inn not too far off from there. She was a midwestern girl, moved to Vegas to be a dancer. The first time I saw her she was on stage performing a strip tease that absolutely captivated me. She performed it just for me. The only other person in the bar was some older gentleman asleep in the corner. She was nineteen at the time. I must have been twenty-three or so. She moved her body in a way I had never seen. She had such a confidence, that woman. She was just about the sexiest thing I had ever seen."

Franz exhales and I notice the apartment is becoming hazy with all the smoke.

"I tell you, Marc, I never saw anything like that ever again. It was the greatest moment of my life. I mean moving to Vegas wasn't the most wholesome thing to do, but I was uninhibited. I didn't care. I wanted to marry Mina right away because I knew a girl as beautiful as her in a town as volatile as Vegas wouldn't be on the shelf for very long. Besides, my bank had nearly tripled to well over one hundred thousand dollars, and I knew I could always find more action in Vegas. I was confident I would win. I felt I was God sent. I bet thirty thousand on the 1984 Hagler v Hearns fight. I bet Hagler big and he won despite getting cut up real bad in the first round."

He passes me the joint. It's about halfway through, and I can barely think anymore, but Franz takes it upon himself to roll another one. He empties the remnants of the baggie into the grinder and continues his story.

"Mina and I moved into a condo. Condos were all the hype back then, starting to come up all over, and we were young newlyweds, what did we need with a house? Besides, all the houses in Vegas are removed from the action and have no view. Our place was fully furnished and on the fifteenth floor of our building. We could see the lights clearly from our condo. It was incredible. Really, it was something."

He looks regretfully around the apartment, sighs, and sprinkles the ground cannabis onto the table.

"Then, I started to play other things on the side. Our condo was walking distance from all of the casino floors. At first, I told myself I would avoid the casino floors. I knew they were risky, and that the odds were stacked against me. But, like I said, I was riding a wave, Marcus. Not even the casino floors could stop me. Roulette became a favorite of mine. And more specifically, the roulette room at the Nugget. It was very nice, as were the rest of them, but it was more of a superstitious thing. I won my first five bets on that table, and so it became my table."

He pauses, focusing for a moment on his task. He carefully places the ground cannabis onto the paper.

"In my opinion, roulette is the rawest form of gambling."

"How so?"

"What I mean is that there is the least amount of human involvement in the game. It is just you against the wheel of fate. I developed my own system for roulette, of course. In retrospect, I think more to give myself a sense of security than anything. It was a good system, though. It was so simple, yet it was always effective."

He pauses to lick the papers and finish up the joint. I am almost too stoned to think. I put out the joint in my hand, though there was probably enough left to go around one more time. I rub my temples and go to the kitchen for a glass of water. The tap water is murky, but I guzzle down two cupfuls.

"What was the system, Franz?"

He lights the fourth joint as I retake my seat.

"It was like this: I would bet a thousand on red, and if I won, great. I'd bet a thousand on red again. But if I lost, well, then I'd bet two thousand on red. And if I lost again, I'd bet four thousand on red. And so on and so forth, until I recuperated the original bet, and I'd start again at one thousand. It is a sure-fire way of winning, you see, because by doubling your bets consistently, all you need is one single win to erase all your prior losses. And with a bankroll as large as mine was at the time, I could afford to double my bets very liberally. It was almost impossible to lose, as long as I had patience, and stuck to my bet sizing."

I frown and rub my temples, trying to understand the system.

"But you did lose, didn't you? I'm sorry to be so blunt, but you wouldn't be here if you still had that money? What happened?"

He passes me the joint and I get up to open the patio door. The opening clears some of the smoke out of the apartment.

"What happened was that human nature took over. I was young and foolish, and I got greedy. After I ran my bank up to almost three million, I was living life like a king. Partying nearly every night, eating at the finest restaurants, sleeping with a different beautiful woman every single night. I was still taking care of Mina, and so I think she chose to turn a blind eye to my behavior. In retrospect, I wish I had treated her better. She was an angel, that woman. But like I said, I thought myself invincible. The money and the success and the drugs and the attention all elevated me to the point where I actually thought I was infallible. I began placing arrogant bets. *Big* arrogant bets. And I began to lose. I bet stupid amounts on underdogs that I had no business betting on. I bet twenty thousand dollars a spin on the roulette wheels. Sometimes on a single number! I would go to parties with some of the other gamblers who were riding high at the time, and we'd get hopped up on coke then go for a gambling session on the casino floor at four or five in the morning. We gambled away hundreds of thousands of dollars completely impaired. It was all fun and games until suddenly it wasn't. I spiraled out, but I couldn't stop. I got heavily addicted to cocaine, and I drank all day long. Then suddenly, I didn't have any more money for coke. I lost the condo, and moved back into the sleazy motel. Towards the end, I would bum out on the penny slots just so I could squeeze enough liquor out of the casinos to get a buzz going. On the way down I bought extravagant gifts for my lady friends. I bought a fifty thousand dollar pearl necklace for this one stripper- Ivy- who I'd begun seeing regularly. Mina found out. She checked my credit card bills. God, I was such an idiot. She lost her mind. But it was all part of the blur, you know. And before I knew it, the money, the women, the drugs, the attention, it was all gone."

Franz lowers his head into his arms for a moment, then lifts his head, shakes it into a look of indifference, and rises to take another sip of milk from the fridge. When he sits back down, I hand him the joint, almost too stoned to talk, and he goes on:

"Marcus, I came crashing down from such a great height that it's a wonder it didn't kill me. I was living under an overpass in Vegas for about two months with a bunch of vagabonds and drug dealers. I became addicted for a time to crack. I begged for money every day. Creditors repossessed everything I had, and they were still out for me. Not only was I broke, but I owed a few bookies and shylocks around four hundred thousand. It was as though I had been erased from existence. I don't quite know how to describe it, but I remember it occurring to me at one point that I didn't own anything. I was wearing a shirt, but it was not mine. If given the opportunity, someone would rip the shirt straight off my back because I no longer had any right to it. I became paranoid, and took drugs every chance I could get. Harder drugs. The hardest drugs I could find. I looked over my back constantly, and I stayed as far away as possible from the strip."

He crinkles his eyes as he reawakens the dark, dormant pain.

"So then what? How did you get here?"

He puts out the joint and I sigh in relief. I fish out my carton and we both light a cigarette. I check my watch- it is after midnight.

"My family saved me. They really did. I hadn't spoken to anyone in my family since I had lost the fight and run away. I had turned my back on them completely. Well, eventually I summoned the courage to call them. And I came clean. I told them about my debts, I told them about my drug addiction, I told them that my life was in danger. My mother and father were in their old age and God bless them, they still wanted to see me do well. They flew to Vegas in the early nineties and helped me clear my name. It was heartbreaking to see the disappointment and sadness in their eyes. They cleaned me up and put me into rehab, also out of pocket. They bought my debts at the expense of their financial stability. They mortgaged their home; they sacrificed their retirement funds. Both of them went back to work to pay off my debts. My mom as a secretary, and my father as a bookkeeper. They were modest people and they kept their promises. They had me cleared within a decade, somehow."

He inhales hard on the cigarette, looking down and contemplating the overflowing white porcelain ashtray with a look of deep regret. I inhale on mine. The familiar feeling of the tobacco and nicotine gently burning my lungs calms me, and refocuses me.

"But that still doesn't explain how you got here."

Franz looks up at me and presses his lips together, as though begging me to let him off the hook. Then he shakes his head, decides that he must see it through to the end, sighs once more, and continues:

"I fled. The horrible ugly truth is, I simply fled. I took the little bit of money my parents had given me, and I fled to Canada. They thought I was still going to the rehab center. I don't even know when they found out I had lied. They must have, I guess. Luckily, I did stop the drugs. I guess it had finally gotten to me, the realization of what I had done, what I had lost, how deep I had dug myself in. I was broken, and I had a long way to go to put myself back together. I had a lot of climbing to do before I got out of the hole. I got into the system and claimed disability on my leg. I've been collecting cheques from the government and laying low for the past twenty years."

He rubs his eyelids as though reawakening from a vivid dream, confused and rejecting the contrast of his lackluster reality.

"That's absolutely crazy. Franz, I almost don't believe it."

I look him up and down and the realization sets in that I had typecast Franz before I really knew anything about him. Everybody comes from somewhere. I just never took the time to look.

"But wait, where does Jean-Marie fit into the story?"

He sighs again.

"After a couple of years laying low, I got involved with some bad people again. It's hard adjusting to a modest living after being filthy rich. It was all too easy to dip my feet in, with my reputation. We're all creatures of habit, right?"

He looks at me as though seeking absolution. I nod.

"I met some guy at this sleazy bar I would go to every now and again, and I got involved with a biker gang doing some shylock work. I'll spare you the details, but I lent Jean-Marie some money. He was a degenerate gambler and he couldn't pay. The bikers would have had me kill him over a few thousand dollars he owed. I bought out his debt and dealt with it personally. He was grateful, and did eventually pay me back, but I couldn't let him get away scot-free. You never learn until you feel pain that's strong enough to change you. It's a very sad truth, but there it is."

Franz keeps his head down as I piece it all together.

"You gave him that scar?"

He has a hand over his mouth, and his words come out slightly muffled:

"And another on his back. It's the price he had to pay for his life. And as far as I know, the man hasn't gambled another dime since."

Franz looks up at me. His face is charged with emotion. I see the struggle in his eyes, as he labors to convince himself he has done nothing wrong.

"Jesus."

Franz's tone becomes didactic:

"Listen, kid, all this to say one thing. Gambling is not for everyone. It takes nerves of steel and discipline. The thing that no one seems to understand is the discipline part. That night, the night of the fight, the night that changed my life forever: that night I took control. I took things, my own destiny, into my own hands. And despite it all, I have never regretted it."

He looks me in the eye, amplifying the importance of his words.

"You know, I used to wash my face after every fight. I would come barging back into the locker room after being out there, sometimes covered in blood, always dripping sweat and I would hastily remove my gloves and undo the tape and throw everything to the side. Then I'd rush to the sink. And every time, in my hurry, I would rush to the sink and open the hot water tap to the fullest, and throw the scalding hot water into my face. It would burn me and I would feel the heat and I would know that

I was alive, that it wasn't all just some game. But that night, the night of the fight, when I got back into the locker room I removed my gloves and went to the sink. And I saw in the mirror that my face was bloodied and cut, probably worse than it had ever been. But that night I played with the water, the hot and cold, until I got the temperature just right. I cleaned my wounds calmly, slowly, and deliberately. That night I felt perfectly in control."

Franz looks at me with an intensity that scares me. I look at his hands and see for the first time the hands of a powerful God, hands that have purposely cut another man, hands that had experienced life's greatest luxuries and riches only to have everything taken away. Hands that clawed their way out of an abyss. Somehow he had escaped. His were hands that had been worthless, and all powerful, that had held human life in their palms, and that had doled out punishment, and mercy.

"I don't know that I fully understand Franz."

His dark eyes preserve the intensity of his gaze, as his will penetrates deeply through the eyes. I feel as though he means to transpose some understanding, some truth, to bypass the limitations of language, to circumvent my mind and leap directly into my soul. He barely moves, as he utters his next words:

"Human hands never break bread evenly, kid. But don't ever feel bad for that. It's important that you *never* feel bad for that. Otherwise, you might let it stop you from going for the piece you want. And then you're dead."

He pauses, looks out at the moon, and watches the light filtering in through the window. The moonlight illuminates his face, and the mystical portrait hanging just behind him.

"You eat until you're no longer hungry, and then you eat some more. There is no such thing as too big a piece."

He seems to be talking to the moon until he turns his gaze back on me. I feel his eyes piercing some threshold within me, forcing a door open at a crack to be flung wide open, never to be closed again. He narrows his eyes, seeing the change taking place within me, undergoing it by my side, and leading me gently to the place I was scared to go alone. We linger there a while together.

And then his expression suddenly lightens, and he smiles. He leans back in his familiar position on the couch, crossing his legs and lifting his arms to rest them against the back of the couch. He helps himself to another cigarette and slaps my knee amicably.

"Relax!"

His face is back to its regular setting, conveying the familiar jovial disposition I have come to know. The intensity returned to its resting place beneath the surface. I swallow and take a deep breath, still wide-eyed, as the adrenaline coursing through me slowly dissipates.

"How are you still alive?"

Franz snorts.

"What can you do kid? You run until you fall on your face. Then you get up, lick your wounds, and you run some more."

He laughs, fingering his cigarette like a child's toy, enjoying himself.

"You know what they used to call me back in my heyday? *Glücklich*. The lucky German. I always hated that. It made it sound as though I had nothing to do with the whole thing. But then, maybe that was true."

I can barely keep my eyelids open anymore, and I rub them to make sure this hasn't all been a dream.

"What do you mean Franz?"

Franz springs up from the couch and flexes his arm. The cigarette still burns between his lips, and smoke rushes out of his nostrils as he speaks:

"I mean I had balls of steel. And they called me lucky. It was belittling of my talents! What about you kid, how did you get here?"

He transitions with a smile, still lightening the mood, changing the subject, and leading the conversation to a space where I can feel at ease.

"I got kicked out of my mom's because she found out I was doing drugs."

He raises his eyebrows.

"That's rough. So she kicked you out? Just like that?"

"It was pretty damn repressed in that place."

He chuckles. His laugh eases my nerves and I am able to relax. It looks like we will return to the dynamic we settled on before I knew anything about Franz's past.

"I might have guessed. You're a little neurotic kid. You think too much."

He winks at me playfully. I rub my eyelids again.

"I don't know Franz, I mean how are you supposed to make sense of things without thinking? I mean how do you know what's important? Like what you choose to have for breakfast in the morning. It can affect your entire day. What if you make the wrong decision and it sets off a chain that ends with you in a ditch that could have all been avoided if you had only chosen the pancakes instead of the scrambled eggs?"

Franz finds this absolutely hysterical, and laughs himself silly. He even slaps his knees. It takes him a few moments to compose himself, and his eyes are tearing in laughter. He responds ironically:

"You can't see the future kid, you're overthinking things. Besides, you don't decide how things will unfold. All you have to do is make sure you win your first bet and hope all goes well. The way I see it, life is like a record. And when you look back at it, only the major moments make the soundtrack. Breakfast would never make it, unless that breakfast was in the company of someone like the pope, or maybe a woman that you loved."

He looks up at the ceiling and lets out an audible yawn. He stretches his head all the way back, scrutinizing the painting still hanging above his head. In the final minutes of the afterglow, Aphrodite is illuminated from head to toe, and the brilliant purples and blues coloring her backdrop sparkle in the moonlight.

"Mina's favorite used to be French toast. With the outsides burnt ever so slightly. She was so finicky about it, too. She used to have me make it again if I didn't get it right the first time. But I did it gladly because the smile that would light up her face when I did get it right… well, it was priceless. That's what life is about kid. Not the filler."

He looks down from the painting and back into my eyes.

"You've got to get your head out of the gutter."

Another yawn.

"Goodnight."

And with that, he sprawls out on the couch in his dirty clothes and within seconds is snoring. I sit there on the stool, alone, pondering everything we discussed, staring at the sky out the patio door. Then I watch Franz sleep a while and wonder about the inner-workings of his mind.

What does this madman see when he stares at the sky?

It was a while before I shut the lights and got to sleep.

***

The next day, I wake up to the coldest day of the year. There is a light a mist falling from the sky, swirling through the air and quickly freezing, covering the ground in a fine frozen film. I nearly slip as I walk over from my car that morning, fighting a lingering craving for Bella, into Marie-Eve's café.

Marie-Eve greets me with less excitement this time, as there are many more customers to serve at this peak hour. Most of them are dressed in suits and carrying attaché cases. I figure that the novelty of my presence has also worn a little.

I get my coffee with minimal small talk and quick half-forced smiles, then grab a seat by the window facing the street.

The café, and the rest of the city for that matter has been decked in Christmas cheer overnight. The streetlights are decorated with illuminated sleighs, bells, and mistletoe, and the businesses dress their windows with holly, blow-up Santa's, and dancing plastic snowmen.

As I look out into the snowy street, I watch the passersby and think about what Franz told me last night. I think about it with a moral imperative. Is Franz a good or bad person? Am I a good or bad person? Would it even be a relevant question if we were successful? Can one find paradise without first stepping through hell? Besides, what are heaven and hell, good and evil, but concepts created by an artist long, long ago?

The last few months, whenever I've looked into the mirror, all I've seen is a question mark. And sitting here in the café, watching the people go by, I wonder if every single one of them sees the same thing. Or maybe putting on that suit, or uniform, or maybe gelling their hair for work in the morning gives them a true sense of purpose. A role. A part to play in the show.

I turn toward the counter and watch Marie-Eve force a smile for every customer. She fills the orders out one after another, mindlessly. I wonder if *that* is happiness.

I imagine her leaving the café after her shift and returning home to her lover, he also tired from his job, and the two of them quashing their feelings of loneliness and desperation through lust, and gluttony. I see them sitting on the couch, crunching potato chips, and forgetting, if only for a moment, that their next day will be the same as their last was, and the day after that all the more the same, and the next, and the next. Maybe the day has already come, and they no longer even have sex. Maybe the potato chips are more fulfilling.

I think again about Franz and his confidence. He walked away from a path carved out for him, a path that many indeed would have killed for, to carve out a path of his own. A path no one could see but himself. A path that was crazy, by most standards. Could it be possible, given the current state of things, that he truly did not regret his actions? Or is he simply a maniac, recklessly speeding toward a steep precipice? Do I want to get into the car with this man? Am I already in? Can I do anything to stop it?

No.

Because acknowledging that you're great, or could be great, or self-assessing one's potential for greatness, I would assume, is the first step to achieving greatness. Daring to dare, so to speak. But others, pessimists perhaps, fearful people striving fearfully for the fearful comfort of mediocrity, would have me believe that this confidence is not the first step to greatness, but rather the first step to self-indulgence, excess, vanity, and lethargy. *Entitlement.*

Toeing the line between the two so vaguely defined worlds of confidence and cocky over-certainty is so riddled with nuance that I've decided to stop listening. It's noise. Doubt, that is. And noise never inspires, it only distracts.

***

I knew that Franz was a madman. I knew it in that moment. I knew it while we were on the rise, and I knew it while we were falling. And I still know it now. I know it now more clearly than ever, as I sit here looking back at things. But he was driving the car, and I was in the passenger seat, tired of hitchhiking and waiting by the road, and tired of being limited by fear.

Maybe loving yourself is arrogant. But I'd rather toe the line between cocky and confident, than the line between realistic and insecure.

I wondered a lot that afternoon in the café. I sat there thinking the entire afternoon. I wondered if Franz was using me, but then I realized that he had never really asked me to do anything.

In many ways, Franz did not turn out to be the madman behind the wheel.

I did.

In many ways, Franz was merely the passenger in my madman's vehicle, wielding the map, arguing with me over when to take the exit.

Yes, I think that makes more sense.

I was behind the wheel.

I am behind the wheel.

I never let go of it.

I took it firmly in my hands for the first time that afternoon, when I walked out of Marie-Eve's café and drove slowly over to the bakery to quit my job.

'Venus De Milo'

I'm lying in bed, smoking a cigarette. It's not my bed- it's Jenna's.

I'm naked.

She's in the kitchen fetching me a glass of water.

Miles Davis' 'Kind of Blue' is playing from the speakers on her laptop.

I've gotten accustomed to Jenna's bed, to her apartment, to the peculiar way she walks and talks, to her high pitched moans and her delicate little frame, to her smile, and to her frowns.

I've been coming here quite often, when I or she or both of us have the whim. We drink, listen to music, discuss likes and dislikes, which very often pleasantly overlap, and have passionate sex. The sex is normally followed by a cigarette pause, and then we usually repeat the process. It's all very mellow. Miles often accompanies us throughout. It's great stress release.

This all happened very organically. We met through a mutual friend, intrigued by intriguing dialogue, facilitated by a mutual sharp-tongued indifference. From the onset the sexual tension built, the sexual tension boiled over, and the lonely filled the void in each other's company, drowning out the noises of the world for a few hours at a time. It was all I could ask for.

Jenna came into my life at just the right time. The holidays are tough for me. I feel like shit throughout. My head doesn't function properly. There is a fog over things.

I snap at people, and push them away. They can't understand, and I don't quite understand either. I want nothing more than to be absolutely alone, and at the same time I need more desperately than ever the solace of another human being. I need someone who can understand, at least partially, the turmoil going on in my head.

Jenna came into my life at just the right time.

Jenna lives a few blocks down from Franz and I. She's thirty-seven years old, and works at a department store in the appliances section. She's been working there for twenty years or so, unquestioningly. She says it's a very easy and very steady job, so long as she turns off her brain for eight hours at a time. She says this without sarcasm or malice; it is simply a matter of fact.

"It's nearly impossible for me to lose my job, so long as my brain is turned off for the eight hours a day I'm forced to work it."

I don't nitpick, probably because I like her. Certainly that is why. We don't talk about that hardly at all, it's just an incidental detail. She can be a neurosurgeon for all I care. It's incidental.

Her apartment sits just above a dry cleaner, with fuzzy neon lighting and a decrepit sign- an immigrant's small business no doubt. *Nettoyage Jacques* is what the sign reads, though I'd bet a lot of money that no one actually named Jacques works in that little hole in the wall.

Jenna's apartment is located just beside one of Hochelaga-Maisonneuve's most prominent drug dens. It's just next-door, actually. Across the street, there's a crummy used car lot adjacent a poorly lit and dingy park. It's all very dim.

The walk to Jenna's apartment is almost apocalyptic with the zombie-like drug addicts walking around, the clacking of high heels against the pavement, and the dull buzz of fluorescent neon lights. As I walk by, I occasionally catch a glimpse of the little white door, the door to the den, sometimes open to a view down a long dim corridor. Beyond the dim corridor, I've never seen. I can't see any further without entering. I've seen people exit at all times of the day, though I scarcely see anyone enter. I think there's an unseen back or side door somewhere.

I'm too often accosted by disgusting prostitutes with rotting teeth as I walk up St-Catherine to Jenna's door. They look like soulless ghouls, grabbing at me and practically begging me to screw them for a few dollars, which I assume will send them promptly through the white door. I've had to get used to them living in this area. They litter almost every street in the neighborhood. I just swat them away like flies.

I glossed over a few things. Jenna and I actually met through Franz. He introduced me to her when we bumped into her at the corner store, out for ramen. Charmed, I withheld from asking any further questions.

Jenna is petite, with a face much younger than her years. She's got a very laidback demeanor. She is of mixed ethnicity, a mixture of African and Oriental by the looks of it, and has a great smile. She takes great care of herself, and has a clean face and silky smooth hair. She's an anomaly around these parts- a sheltered tulip in the eye of a hurricane.

Her apartment is beautiful. Walking in is like entering a protected, even protracted world somehow contained amidst the desolate conditions just beyond her front door. It is very modern, long and wide, open, spacious, with two large bedrooms and a living area, a granite-top island separating the kitchen from the living space, and oak floors. She has a sectional couch and a beautiful large flat screen television, and her entire apartment adheres to a burnished oak and rich dark cocoa color scheme that contrasts tastefully.

Her room is very much an extension of the rest of the apartment. Her bed frame is dark cocoa and rests on the light oak hardwood. The walls and ceiling are white, and a patio door to the right opens to a little balcony. She's also got a large walk-in closet off to the left. Her nightstand is cocoa as well.

I lean over to ash my cigarette in the ashtray sitting on the nightstand. There's an alarm clock, an ashtray, some magenta orchids, a nail clipper, and a green and yellow lava lamp bubbling very slowly on the nightstand.

Jenna is in the doorway, leaning casually in nothing but an oversized white t-shirt and her pink lace, watching me smoke my cigarette with a glass of water in her hand. She was a dancer, in her youth. An elegant artist, not an exotic tramp. The moonlight filtering in through the patio door shades her sensual silhouette, and obscures her face. I smile at her invitingly, and she steps forward into the light of the room with a smile of her own. I put out my cigarette, lift the covers to welcome her back into bed, and begin kissing her all over.

We make love for an hour or so, sinking deeper into each other and deeper into the night without a woe between us. We forsake our obligations, and the only inkling of the world outside this bedroom is the noise fighting its way in through the crack in the patio door. The prostitutes walk along, their high heels still mimicking the clack of cloven hooves against the pavement. We hear the banter of the insane, and the minimal traffic and ubiquitous cry of a far away siren.

Jenna's room is a sanctuary. It's the fifth time she's invited me over- we always meet here and never at my place because of Franz's stifling presence- and each and every time we have found a way to maintain an air of ease and comfort. We have found a wonderful way to temper our conversation and curiosities, never letting ourselves stray beyond the complacent bubble of Miles and our momentary moods.

I ponder a lot lying in her bed, with the warmth of Jenna's body comforting me. I am graced with the breathtaking sight of her rising in her panties and her oversized Garfield t-shirt, her toned buttocks dancing with her every step. I stare at the walls and smoke cigarettes, and look deep into the lava lamp for stretches of what seem hours. I have always been intrigued by lava lamps and the way they operate on a loop, perpetually bubbling and yet no bubble the same as the last, each a different size, and shape, and shade.

I heard through the grapevine this week that Bella has returned to the scumbag she was screwing before me, and this angers me. 'The grapevine'! Who am I kidding? I found this out through a morbid compulsion to check her social media profiles on the daily. She hadn't exactly made it difficult to observe. It sunk me into a self-loathing anger, the type of anger one can only bring upon one's self. It mostly angers me because I feel alone, which is ironic because I have made a great effort to push everyone away. I haven't received a phone call in months from any of my so-called friends. I can only pretend for so long that they're busy and legitimately preoccupied with other things. The truth is simply that they have forgotten me, that they have no idea whether I am thriving or struggling, whether I am alive or dead, and they don't care to inquire.

'Growing up': Glossing over the inconsistencies and paradoxes and inherent moral lapses necessary for the functioning of a modern-day capitalist society. Furthermore, getting a job sitting at a desk pushing paper, crunching numbers, luxuriating in the self-importance of a leather-seated vehicle and an ergonomic swivel chair.

He lives best who best deceives himself!

This is something I'm not going to do. And so I am labeled a cynic by the lot of them, who are hustling every day for their chance at mediocrity. And I am cast aside like some impediment, some unfortunate road kill. A man who preaches modesty must be ridiculed and labeled a cynic. Progress is consumerism. It has to be.

I don't need them.

I don't need anyone.

And then I have to run into her with him. Bella and her new boyfriend, as she is calling him. And not only that, I have to see them lip-locked. It was disgusting. In the lobby of my dentist's office, no less. I was getting a cavity filled, if you can believe it.

The funny thing is, I lost her *in that moment*. We haven't been together for well over a year, but I only really lost her in that moment. And what is even funnier is how even I see her as the hero of this story, and I as the villain. She overcomes her darkness and her better judgment prevails. She is happy. Without me. That hits home profoundly, I think. That I am getting just what I deserve: nothing. And as if God himself took the time to drive home how awful I was meant to feel, I smelt her in the elevator. I don't know how, but the elevator smelt of her perfume. I'm not ashamed to say that I wanted to cry. For the first time in a long damn while I wanted to cry. But the elevator dinged too quickly and I was on my floor. So I postponed it until later, or preferably, not at all.

So yes, Jenna's room means a lot to me.

After we make love tenderly that night for probably the third or fourth time, I hold her in my arms gently and there is a lot of kissing. While we are kissing, Jenna's mobile begins to vibrate. The first time, she ignores it. The second time she does the same, though by the third time it becomes quite clear that someone is intent on reaching her right here and now. She withdraws from me to glance at her phone, and a look of burdensome concern flushes her normally statuesque face. Worry is an ugly look on her.

"What's the matter?"

I ask casually, lighting another cigarette and still enjoying the smooth neutrality of Davis' instrumentals.

"Byron left his clarinet here last night. Shit. You have to leave."

I look at Jenna with complete indifference but understand everything in an instant. I have never heard of Byron before, though I presume then and confirm later, he is her long-time boyfriend. It is the middle of the night, slightly after midnight, and this is obviously some ploy. I never think of Jenna with other men, or with a boyfriend, but frankly, I never let my mind wander that far. It is dangerous, for just this reason. In this instant, I understand all too well: another bubble is unfortunately, though inevitably, bursting.

I find out that Byron is part of a symphony set to play a big show at Place des Arts next week. Jenna answers my questions frantically, hoping to get me out of the apartment quicker. Apparently playing Place des Arts is a career-altering milestone for a clarinetist.

"You have to leave, now. He's coming. Please! Get dressed."

Hints of desperation resonate repulsively in her words. I rise from the sheets to dress, resting my cigarette on the ashtray lip, but it is too late. There's a hard knock on the front door, and through the patio window I can see Byron in a leather studded jacket and a felt bowler hat. He's standing at the front door, peeking back at me through the patio window, and his agitation is rapidly rising.

"Open the door, Jenna!"

He bangs on the front door even louder, and Jenna paces around the room with one hand on her hip, and the other on her forehead.

"Shit, shit, shit!"

She screams as though this will help her calculate her next move. Byron is in his forties it looks like, and puny, frankly, so that I am really not too worried about a physical confrontation. The only thing I have to worry about, I figure, is the off chance that he's packing a weapon. I put on one of Jenna's t-shirts while she goes to open the door. It seems she has decided to take this inevitable confrontation head on. I stand in the bedroom in my underwear, startlingly calm as Byron barges into the apartment and pushes Jenna aside. He moves straight into the bedroom where he knows I am waiting.

I guess he doesn't expect me to receive him with such nonchalance because he stops short mid-stride, and sizes me up. Jenna shuffles into the corner of the room. Jenna's face is blank, as though her fear, excitement, and indifference are somehow canceling each other out. She looks as though she is thinking of nothing. Or, at least, her mind seems to be producing scraps of thought that will not connect. Haphazard thoughts, confused thoughts that are discarded as quickly as they are generated. It is a little bit funny.

Byron has a strong chin. It is his most prominent feature and looks as though it were carved from marble. I decide that he's a good-looking guy. I've got nothing against him.

I take my cigarette from the ashtray and smoke patiently. I even take a seat on the bed, waiting for the show to begin. I hear the clock on the wall tick audibly, as Byron gathers himself to speak. His words come out slow, methodical, deliberate, in almost military sentences, coherent and crisp.

He looks at Jenna.

"Who is this?"

Jenna's words, on the other hand, gallop out in a rush, tripping comically over one another.

"Marc, I mean Byron it doesn't, Byron baby, you don't understand, it's not how it looks…"

He turns and looks at me with disgust. I pull on my cigarette.

"I can't believe you. I really cannot believe you, Jenna. After all I've done for you, you cheat on me with this, with this child. We had plans, Jenna. We had plans and you ruined them. You threw it all away. And for what? A few nights of cheap sex? I thought we were past this. How could you sleep with, with this *scumbag*?"

He looks at me as he utters the word 'scumbag' with extra verve, trying to spur me into action. I just look at him with the beginnings of a grin on my lips, and I wonder if I should clap. I can't help smiling. I light another cigarette. Jenna whimpers in the corner like a worthless doe. She clutches her chest as though she is undergoing the most painful pang to the heart. It is a pretty good performance, I think.

"And you. Who are you? Who the hell do you think you are?"

He inches closer to me. He's really angry now, and he points his index finger violently at me. I stay quiet and continue to smoke my cigarette. His confidence seems to be surging, so I decide to have a little bit of fun with him.

"Hello! I am Marcus, but I do not know who you are. In fact, I have never even heard of you By-ron. But you're sort of ruining the moment, and now look, you've gotten poor Jenna all frazzled. What do you say you go get some air and come back in just a little bit?"

His anger washes away, and is replaced with a look of utter incredulity.

"Are you insane?"

He turns to Jenna.

"Is he insane?"

Then back to me.

"Do you understand what you are saying?"

Then back to Jenna.

"Is this idiot insane?"

Then back to me.

"You just slept with my girlfriend, I ought to kill you!"

That's the buzzword. 'Kill'. Something in my head clicks on, or clicks off, I'm not sure, but something changes. He pushed it too far. I was looking for a fight, and as it turns out the fight comes to me. I look at him, still with a smile, still sucking on the cigarette, and the confidence radiating in my eyes pushes him to the brink of madness.

"You smile? You smile after having slept with my girlfriend, after having defiled my relationship? After having ruined my life?"

He works himself into a frenzy and starts pulling his hair. I laugh. I laugh pretty loud. I laugh in his face in a moment that would shatter any human being. I laugh in complete and utter disregard, insolently, begging him to unleash his fury on me, to reclaim his manhood, to…

Byron rushes at me. We're only a few paces apart, but he springs into movement pretty quick, very suddenly, and in less than a second it is over. He lunges forward and I spring up from the bed, grab the lava lamp in hand, and bring it down with full force on his temple, yanking it from the outlet in the wall, shattering the glass, cutting his head open, covering his face in heated wax and god knows what else, and penetrating his skin. He cries out in agony, and falls to the floor with his forehead gushing blood. Jenna shrieks and rushes to his side, trying desperately to clean the wax off his face as he writhes in pain and hollers, clutching his face and trying to shield his eyes.

Davis is still casually playing from Jenna's laptop while I put my pants on, one leg at a time, and step out of the room.

I parked my car in front of the apartment, recklessly by the white door, but I walk right by it, favoring a stroll and a calm cigarette in the crisp night air before I'm inevitably picked up. It is a very dry kind of cold air filling the dead space tonight- the winter sting. It is the January kind of cold that makes the streets slushy, though the sidewalks remain somehow strangely dry. I walk along Ste. Catherine for about fifteen minutes, smoking one cigarette after another until I run out. My eyes smart from the cold, and I think very calmly about what happened, and what I would have to do next. Just about fifteen minutes pass before the sirens blare behind me, and the cops pick me up- I do not resist in the least- in front of a bar's large neon sign reading 'Le Savoir'. The smokers outside and the drunkards inside lucky enough to have a seat by the windows are treated to some entertainment.

The cops bring me to Station 22 on Papineau, in a slightly less dingy part of town. They escort me- I really am being quite civil about the whole thing, and am not resisting or inconveniencing the officers in the least- to a holding cell. There is only one other person in the cell, and he looks considerably hopped up on drugs. It must be morphine, or something of the sort, because the man hardly notices and hardly stirs when the cell is opened and I am chucked in right beside him. I sit on a very uncomfortable bench with my back to the blue concrete wall for a good little while- I don't have any sense of time or any desire to measure time at the moment- it may be an hour.

I think about the word 'mint'. In the sense of gum, like how it masks bad breath. But also in the sense of the sleazy used car salesman trying to sell you a junky Chrysler. Mint feels fresh for a while. Mint is refurbished. Mint masks imperfection.

They finally tell me I can make a phone call. I was thinking about this too while sitting in the cell, and even earlier walking down Ste. Catherine. The officers set my bail at one thousand dollars. So I call Storzo.

Storzo will have my back, I hope, and more importantly, he should have the funds to get me out of here pronto. The phone call is short. He seems surprised, startled, even, by my calling. I haven't spoken to him in over a month. I haven't spoken to him in over three months, really. I saw him at Blasé's party, but we didn't speak too much. And that was months ago now, too. I explain to him the situation, and he laughs, thinking it's a joke. I explain it again, dead serious, and he comes to the realization that this is real and I need his help.

He shows up a little while later, with the funds in cash to post my bail. The officers look at him skeptically but can do nothing but let us go. Storzo is wearing one of those fur-rimmed hooded jackets, and boots over his sweats and torn t-shirt. He looks like he just jumped out of bed. It is the middle of the night.

He doesn't say a word to me until we're outside. Outside, now accompanied by the night sounds of the city and the cold sting, Storzo gains the confidence required to confront me, and does so with a light tap on my shoulder.

"Marcus, you mind telling me what happened?"

He lights a cigarette and offers me one, which I accept.

"Disagreement over a woman. It won't happen again, don't worry. I appreciate you coming man, I really do. Goodnight."

I pick up my pace and try to walk away, but Storzo runs after me and pulls me by the arm beneath a streetlight.

"Are you serious man? What are you doing with your life? You were in jail man. Jail! Do you realize how serious this is? This is not a joke man. Why are you throwing it all away?"

It's been a long night, and I am exhausted. I answer him theatrically:

"Oh judge, judge away if you must. You haven't the faintest idea what the hell is going on in my life, you don't even care. You think you're so safe in your closed little world unfolding in black and white. Things get a little more complicated when you let color into your world bud, you should try it sometime."

I turn again to walk away, but he pulls my arm stronger than before. Anger burns hot in his eyes.

"Black and white? Color? What the hell are you talking about Marc? Are you crazy? Have you gone insane? You got yourself thrown in jail! This is not a game, Marc! Wake up!"

He furrows his bushy brows, half scolding, half pleading with me.

"What do you care Storzo? Really, what do you care? Seems like yesterday we were discussing what we were going to do over the weekend and now all of a sudden the interest rates on your credit card are your highest priority. It's the same bullshit with all of you. Money, stocks, suits! It's bullshit man, and I refuse to care."

Storzo's face softens, and he looks at me compassionately.

"Marc, it's life! We grow up. We're getting older. Why do you resist the inevitable?"

"The inevitable!"

I'm shouting by now, and that angers me. It angers me that Storzo can rouse me to anger. And it angers me that anger is now consuming me.

"The only inevitable is death, you clown. Life is what you, or I, or anyone will make it. Nothing more, nothing less. The inevitable. What a joke. You're just scared, the lot of you. All of you are just scared little chickens running back to the coop. It's warm, sure, but nothing worthwhile ever happens in there. Life is what *I* make it. Nobody, and sure as hell not you, is going to tell me what's important and what isn't."

He looks at me confused, wide-eyed and searching, unable to understand my rationale, my motives, bargaining with what he deems to be insanity.

"But, Marc, why do you have to be this way? Why do you insist..."

"Your girlfriends all hate me, Storzo. All of them. Your girlfriends all hate me because they know that I remind you of the world that exists outside of them, beyond the little bubble you've all for some reason agreed to step into and never leave. The world is a big place Storzo. You're twenty-three and your entire world is summed up in a girl and the vague desire and prospect of eventually landing some mediocre desk job. That's all you see. And I feel bad for you, really."

"Marcus, are you serious? You can't mean that!"

He looks at me with a similar degree of incredulity as Byron had earlier. I guess he has a hard time believing that, having just given me a thousand dollars and essentially having purchased my freedom, I would still speak so freely, and with such disregard. The anger returns to his face.

"Marcus, you can't mean that. It's simply not true, Marcus. Look, I'm happy, can't you just be a good friend for once in your petty life and be happy for me?"

"I'm happy for you Storzo. Friggin' ecstatic. Thanks for bailing me out, really. I'll send you a cheque in the mail, sooner rather than later. Thanks again. See you around."

I turn and walk to the bus stop. This time he doesn't stop me.

I look back and see Storzo return to his car shaking his head. He doesn't look my way as drives off.

I light a cigarette in the bus shelter and check my wrist, but I'm not wearing a watch.

It's not that dark out anymore- the sun is fighting with the darkness for control of the sky. It must be nearly dawn, and the next bus shouldn't be too long.

'Four Day Dividend'

Forgive me for taking a moment to break the consistency of the story. It is just that, this part of the story is going to be the most difficult to tell. I try not to think about gambling anymore. I don't know if it's healthy- deliberately ignoring a large part of my past to keep level- but then, there it is. I am very aware how much gambling has impacted my life. In fact, I'd say I'm sitting here now, writing this story in large part because of my experiences with the burning coals of chance. When I speak of gambling, I refer of course to wagering money on games of luck. However, I no longer see gambling as just an isolated event, a game to be played in a casino- it is inextricably part of every decision I make, every second of every single day.

The *Casino de Montréal- de* because we are in Québec, where English translations are the devil's work... The *Casino de Montréal*, built in the early nineties and still boasting the title of biggest casino in Canada is where we, Franz and me, took our big shot.

The *Casino de Montréal* is an architectural marvel. The façade of the main pavilion is surrounded on both sides by converging white rectangular segments, slightly overlapping, giving the impression of a giant trap, or clamp, or mouth slowly closing. The drive up to the casino, from the small waterfront road on Île des Soeurs with the forested area of Parc Jean Drapeau to the right, and the moonlit water foregrounding the beautiful illuminated white casino to the left, is an absolute revelation. The building's beauty really amplifies the anticipation of magic, and thrills, and instant life-changing gratification that lays waiting within.

As far as Casino floors go, the *Casino de Montréal* has the regular variety of table games, over three thousand blinking, beeping, buzzing slot machines, and a bevy of electronic games including Keno. The casino has several floors, and several restaurants, a lounge, and a theatre. Franz and I were never there for any of that, though. We covered nearly the exact same square footage every day, from the way we entered, to the table we played, right down to occupying the same parking spot day in and day out (fate permitting, otherwise Franz's superstitious streak would oblige us to wait). We walked in through the same entrance every time. We greeted the doorman with the same words (an enthusiastic *Howdy, partner!* according to Franz's instruction). We took the same elevator, to the same set of stairs, and climbed up to the same table, every time. And once we got there, we'd make the same bet and ride the fluctuations, day in, day out.

I guess I never *really* expected it to work. I mean, come on. Casinos are businesses open to make money. They sell fun, and thrills, much in the same way an amusement park does. I don't think there is any *real* chance of winning, of beating them at their own racket. Not long-term, anyway. The casino uses all the lights, and the sounds, and the images of smiling exhilaration on the faces of unsuspecting average people just like you and me, to obscure the truth, and to divert attention from behind the curtain of chance: the ever-so-slight but ever-present subtle sound and sensation of suction, sucking away at your billfold, sucking away at your hope, and sucking away at your soul.

The only chance anyone has is to get really lucky, really fast, and get the hell out while on top. Metaphorically speaking, the only chance anyone has is to ride the wave right until it is cresting, and to jump off right before it breaks.

The whole thing seemed, and still does seem pretty obvious. Though I can't stress enough how simplicity quickly gets convoluted when one suddenly has thousands of dollars of unearned plastic currency in his palm.

We are only human, after all.

Humans often forget to ask questions when things are going their way.

The main pavilion of the Casino has lux red-carpeted floors and very high ceilings with lots of windows in the atrium. A large ritzy chandelier hangs high in the center of the atrium. It scintillates, and really livens the busiest area of the casino. Glass staircases and escalators run up and down in the atrium, flowing elegantly and invitingly into the other more lucrative wings of the building...

Even the bathrooms are glamorous.

The bathrooms have gray vinyl flooring with big mirrors along the walls, large automated marble top sinks, polished steel paper towel dispensers, and beautiful glass backsplash tiling that made me feel more profoundly than anything else in the casino that I was enveloped in a billow of money, and the promise of *infinite* luxury.

Franz scoffed of course, and said: "It's nothing compared to Vegas". Still, it was the swankiest Casino (and only Casino) I'd ever been to, and it overwhelmed me.

There are so many games to choose from. Franz said most of them, like Keno and slots, are left entirely to mind-numbing chance.

Our game was roulette, though, and Franz had his system and his subtle knowledge of the nuance of the game. Franz had his system and according to him, it was bulletproof.

The thing is though, retrospectively, that I can say now with complete confidence that numbers are entirely fictitious. I see now that numbers and mathematics are simply a language, invented by human minds, in many ways just like the English language, to help make sense of the chaos of experience by ascribing subjective numerical 'values', and using these 'values' in a foolhardy attempt to organize the *infinite* complexity of the universe. I will admit that to a degree, they are useful in this last endeavor. They are useful insofar as one says 'there are two chairs there' and can affirm this claim through the help of the human senses of sight or touch. This conceptual association of 'two' with 'two' physical objects can help a human being navigate the world with a little more confidence, and lessen everyday confusion. For this type of math, I am grateful. This type of math is retroactive and keeps humanity sane, and I have no problem with it. Very much like the calculation of the height of a building- ascribing values to real things. Blueprints. Mankind has erected countless structures and has gotten better at its calculations of materials required to build, and the organization of these materials. I concede of course that this math is all very practical, and reasonable, and useful.

The math I find ludicrous and am taking issue with, really, is the math that now runs the world. The incalculable math that 'moves things forward'. Math that invokes Faith without ever admitting it. What I mean to say is, predictive math, the skewed presumptive math of insurance companies, of stock markets, of marketers, of brokers and businessmen of all kinds- the math of *gamblers*- the math that pumps humans with this completely unjustified pretense that they somehow, through data and mathematics and subjective statistical probabilities, possess the power to predict the future. This math, the math that runs the world, is *complete bullshit*. As though numbers on a graph could accurately capture the *world* they assert to represent. As though one could correlate eye color and the likelihood of contracting colon cancer. As though this invented correlation is not going to be manipulated to *exploit idiots*, or to put it in corporate terms- to *turn a profit*.

There are an infinite number of variables that come into play and effect what goes on in the world, and outside of the world, and in the universe at any given moment, and math can boil this down to an equation? Math can calculate what will happen in real time? Well, no. Math can predict what one mathematician believes *might* happen. Right. What one algorithm, designed by one human mind suggests *should* happen.

What is *should*, though? Is it not a human mind's judgment call? Is *should* not calculated on subjective assumptions? Are not all theories subjective human assumptions? 'Logical' and 'speculative' are not mutually exclusive.

To invent a juvenile example, let's say that there have been five hurricanes this year in Louisiana (I'm making this up, but bear with me). There have been five hurricanes in Louisiana, and there were only four on record last year, and five on record for each of the last five years prior. So, *mathematically* speaking, there should be no more hurricanes this year in Louisiana. Our data shows that there is but a mere 3.7% chance of another hurricane occurring this year in Louisiana.

According to what sample size of data? Who *interpreted* these statistics?

And then if there is no subsequent hurricane, humanity is genius and God-like and has predictive powers. And if there is another hurricane, well, we just add that to our database of information so that we can get the next prediction right. Trial and error. A wash. As if mistakes cannot be made. Data can only be collected. As if what happened yesterday could in any way help you confirm what will happen today. As if there are no limitations to human knowledge. It's arrogance, and ignorance, and it angers me so how the world is blind to the inconsistencies at the foundation of its societies.

But I digress...

I don't mean to say that humanity shouldn't try. I mean

mathematics is just an attempt to organize things, and what is the alternative? Just to let the ebbs and flows of life dictate an individual or society's fate? To leave things to the powers that be, and acknowledge our limitations as humans, and simply love the earth and be humble? Why, that's insanity! That's tree-hugging hippie rhetoric. There is no right answer, but to quit is negative. Don't call things what they are, that's negative. Taxonomy is necessary for sanity. Organize to understand, and understand to control.

Well, I say no.

Life is just a continuum of decay, and humanity just generations passing a baton, though no one can really tell why.

And not that He was the answer, but God is dead. There's no room for him in the first world because it's more difficult for a rich man to enter the kingdom of heaven than for a camel to pass through the eye of a needle. And until the first world figures out how to profitably pass a camel through the eye of a needle, then God will have to take a back seat to reason.

But, now I really digress.

The math behind Franz's system is simple. As it turns out, his system is just about as old as the game of roulette itself.

The system, I found out with help of the Internet, was something called the Martingale system. It originated in eighteenth century France. It was just about as old as the game itself. Franz tried to sell me the fact that he had 'come up' with it, but I saw right through that. I knew it was all fabricated. I knew he hadn't unlocked some hidden loophole in the game. I knew his system was just hot air. We were walking into a temple and praying to be named the chosen ones.

Casinos are built to make money. You can win money at any given moment, sure, but you cannot beat the casino consistently. No matter the system.

The Martingale system is a simple double up system, in which an original wager is placed, and then doubled, and doubled, and doubled, until a bet is won, which will net the gambler a profit in the amount of the original wager. In other words, if I bet twenty-five dollars on red and win, well, superb. I'll bet another twenty-five on red. But if I lose, then I bet fifty on red, and then one hundred, and then two hundred and so on and so forth until I win a bet, net a twenty five dollar profit, and restart the chain of bets at twenty five. Here's the proof: if I win a two hundred dollar bet, the fourth bet in the chain, then I'll have four hundred dollars in hand after wagers of twenty five, fifty, one hundred, and two hundred. This totals three hundred and seventy five in wagers to four hundred in winnings, or a twenty-five dollar profit (the original bet). We always bet red, so every time it comes up red, we win twenty-five dollars.

Simple.

Foolproof.

The roulette table proved to be more complicated than I thought, though we never deviated from out bet system. Still, I took it upon myself to learn the table inside and out in preparation.

Roulette can be bet on the 'inside', or the 'outside'. 'Inside' bets are high-margin low percentage bets made on single numbers, clusters of two or four numbers, or 'streets' of three numbers, and pay thirty-five to one, seventeen to one, eight to one, and eleven to one respectively at the Montreal Casino. 'Inside' bets are placed with special chips that are specific to the roulette table, as opposed to the regular chips that are valid as currency throughout the casino. 'Outside' bets are lower margin bets, which give the gambler higher odds, and require a higher minimum bet (at the *Casino de Montréal* the smallest stakes table has a minimum outside bet of 25$ to a minimum inside bet of 2.50$). 'Outside' bets can be wagered on the first twelve, second twelve, and third twelve, which all pay 2 to 1, or on the first or second 18, even or odd, or red or black, which all pay even money 1 to 1.

A roulette wheel has thirty-eight numbers: eighteen red, eighteen black, and two green numbers- zero and double zero. The zeroes are the casino's leverage because they aren't taken into account when calculating the payouts.

Franz's system was to play the simplest bet, to leave everything to the ebbs and flows of the wheel, and always, always, bet red. I had no idea if Franz knew any of the math behind the game, or if he was just completely winging it. I don't know if I really cared at the time.

The first night at the Casino was one of the most memorable nights of my life. It was late on a Wednesday night, the last Wednesday in January,

20--. I drove.

***

We finally get to the casino around eleven o'clock at night. It's snowing heavy and the drive is slow, though I am bursting with anticipation. I cashed my entire bank account yesterday, and we're walking in with three thousand one hundred and seventy five dollars in cash wrapped tight in a rubber band. I parked in P4, two spots to the left of the second concrete support beam to the left of the door. Franz breaks my balls about it, says it's his lucky spot. I don't ask questions.

Franz is dressed for the occasion. He showered for once, and shaved. He wears lots of strong perfume. His nails are scrubbed and polished. He even styled his hair with pomade and slicked it back, so that the tooth marks of the comb show. He actually looks good for once. He's wearing jeans and a swanky patterned shirt open at several buttons.

The whole way here he looked out the window, out into the distance. I tried asking him a few questions, but his mind was everywhere and anywhere but in the car with me. So we stayed quiet, and I watched the silent snowfall as I carefully navigated the snowy streets. I'm dressed almost the same way he is, and I'm wearing the same cologne though my collared shirt is solid black.

Franz insisted adamantly that we 'dress for success'.

There's some newfangled electricity about him tonight. There's focus and determination I'm unaccustomed to seeing there, tightening Franz's face. He's like someone else, someone I've never met before. It's like he changed overnight- into someone determined, driven, shrewd, and steely. He's all business. Even the way he's talking tonight is different. The tone. He's more decisive, I think. I am witnessing the resurrection of his former self. This new old Franz excites me.

It doesn't matter who's driving now, we're in the same car.

'Life is a greater gamble than the wheel'- that's probably the only thing Franz mumbled on the way over here. He whispered some barely audible little rant under his breath, something about there being winners and losers, and the wheel being just the tool that decides which we are. 'Life stripped of all the variables you cannot see'.

I can tell for sure there is something special about him as soon as we walk in. After we greet the doorman *Howdy, partner!* I follow Franz to the roulette tables. I notice people staring at him. It isn't anything too pronounced, and he doesn't cause any sort of commotion, but eyes linger just long enough for me to notice. People stare the type of skeptical stare that one stares when seeing something very familiar suddenly return after a long absence. People on the slots stare, croupiers stare, and some of the floor managers in black suits stare as well. A casino employee pushing a coffee and refreshments cart even greets him, a generic *Hello, sir* that seems to me somehow more familiar than it might normally be.

I follow Franz as he weaves his way through the blinking lights of the rows upon rows of slots. All these lights strike me as a maze, but Franz is confident in the direction he takes. He's cool as a cucumber, as comfortable as if we were at home sitting on his couch. He climbs one of the glass staircases and I follow close behind, taking in the sights of lucky sevens and various themed slots everywhere. The sights and sounds of my first time in the casino bewilder me, but Franz doesn't care to notice. His gaze is fixed directly ahead. His eyes are an image of deadly focus.

Franz walks onto the red carpet toward a cluster of tables, and I catch a glimpse of the roulette tables for the first time. My head is in the clouds as I'm trying to acclimate myself to these new surroundings and I bump into Franz, who has stopped short about twenty feet from the tables.

"Listen, kid, we didn't discuss this so I'm just going to make everything clear. We're going fifty-fifty on this. On everything."

He turns and puts an arm firmly on my shoulder. The look in his eyes is uncompromising.

"Fifty-fifty? How you figure Franz? I put up one hundred percent of the bank."

He clenches his fist and looks over my shoulder. I turn to look too, but there's nothing but a group of smiling retirees coming up the escalator. His jaw tightens and the veins in his neck become pronounced. His eyes narrow as he refocuses his cold gaze on me. His slow words congeal like freezing ice:

"Listen, kid, don't mess around. Now's not the time. I said

we're going fifty-fifty. You have no idea what you're doing and I do. It's inconsequential who put up the dough."

His hand is still on my shoulder, and he squeezes it firmly.

"And what's more, you're going to follow my lead. You aren't going to place a single bet without me telling you to, got that? In fact give me all the cash, now."

I laugh, uncertain how to react to his sudden change in demeanor. Franz looks at me stoically, waiting for me to do as I am told. I shrug and reach into my pocket, pulling out the lump of cash. The substantial stack of twenties is tied with a rubber band, and I toss it over to him.

"Okay, bandito. You're in charge. Don't drop the ball."

The bravado is meant to conceal my nerves. Truthfully though, I don't mind Franz placing the bets. The more I think about it, the more I realize that I prefer it. I crunched the numbers of his system, and I figure whoever places the bets is inconsequential. The bets will never change, and the math is simple. But there is something intangible, experience I suppose, that gives me greater confidence in Franz's bets. He has run a bank up to millions of dollars, and I haven't. Maybe *that* is inconsequential, but maybe it isn't.

Three thousand one hundred and seventy five dollars gives us precisely seven bets. Twenty five, fifty, one hundred, two hundred, four hundred, eight hundred, and sixteen hundred. Seven bets total three thousand one hundred and seventy five.

That's all I'm worth.

The only way we can lose is if the wheel turns seven consecutive black spins. The odds of seven consecutive black spins are 0.535%, or approximately one in one hundred and eighty seven. In other words, only one sequence out of the one hundred and eighty seven sequences of seven spins will come out black, black, black, black, black, black, black, and that's the only way we sink.

I think our odds are pretty good.

If the casino tables play twelve spins per hour, a rough estimate, and statistically speaking half of them come out red, then we will average one hundred and fifty dollars an hour in profit. If all goes well, and Franz eventually makes thirty two hundred in profit, then we'll have enough money for a chain of seven bets starting with a fifty dollar bet, which will up our margins to three hundred an hour. And if that works out, and he makes another sixty four hundred, then we can start with one hundred dollar bets and make six hundred per hour. And so on and so forth, the growth potential is unlimited.

Franz catches the money and walks confidently over to the table, in between spins, and spreads it all down on the felt to be exchanged for chips. The table he chooses is in the middle of a cluster of four roulette tables with varying stakes. We start with the lowest stake table in the casino.

The tables are green felt, soft to the touch but solid wood beneath, with the lines and numbers painted in the middle for all to bet on. The tables are rimmed with a teal colored leather armrest, decked with gold-colored cup holders. The tables are a lot larger and grander than I pictured them being. There are black upholstered chairs all around the tables, though no one sits. Up to eight people can bet any single table on any given spin.

The croupier, dressed all in black under the mandatory red vest, calls the floor manager over to verify Franz's exchange of cash to chips:

"Changing three thousand one hundred and seventy five!"

The wheel itself is a thing of beauty. It's perched up at the front of the table, also surprisingly large, and is separated from the betting area by the croupier. Its shining façade is visible to all. It's made primarily of beautiful varnished rosewood, though the initial point where the ball is put into action is made of waxed plastic. Everyone playing cannot help but fix eyes upon it.

The croupier plays the ball and it spins, in a suspension of a dozen seconds or so, slowly making its way toward the center of the wheel- the bowl- where the colored numbers each designate a pocket. The ball eventually loses momentum, or hits one of the plastic stoppers placed horizontally and vertically, and bounces into a pocket, designating the winning number.

There are digital screens by each table, indicating the results of the last five spins of the wheel. The one by our table reads 5 red, 8 black, 26 black, 12 black, 26 black.

Franz very shrewdly requests that he be given one yellow thousand-dollar chip, two pink five hundred dollar chips, ten black hundred dollar chips, and seven green twenty-five dollar chips. After the floor manager's verification, the croupier hands Franz our currency. His nametag reads 'Jéremie'. He smiles as he slides the chips over. His teeth make out a crooked, yellowing smile.

Franz thanks him, and moves a single green chip onto the outside betting area to bet red. There is only one other person betting the wheel, an old lady in a knitted sweater betting like a madwoman on the inside.

Franz's quick calculation of the chips makes me even more confident in him. It seems evident to me that someone as well versed as he is in the ways of gambling is certain to find success. This is his element.

The croupier puts the ball into action. After the ball makes a few spins, he announces 'no more bets'.

Franz whispers to me over his shoulder, as the ball is suspended in its slow revolutions around the wheel:

"We win this bet kid, or we leave."

He doesn't even turn back to look at me as he says this, but standing right behind him I am smothered by his strong musky smell.

"What are you talking about, it took thirty minutes to get here. We're not going anywhere. It's just one bet."

He answers me in a gruff whisper that feels tailored for the occasion:

"I told you. You always need to win your first bet. The first bet always sets the mood."

The ball lands on 1 red.

"Hey, hey, that's the way!"

Franz raises his hands in the air and turns to slap me on the back. I feel the rush of adrenaline course through to my extremities, making me feel lighter for a second. The old lady bet various numbers and lost. The croupier extends a long arm to shovel all of the old woman's lost bets into a hole at the back of the table, hidden by the wheel.

"We are the chosen ones, kid! Mark this moment, it's the beginning of big things!"

Franz's face is comically jovial and I laugh at him. Franz pays no mind though, as he happily collects the green chip we won and adds it to the chip pile. He leaves the original green chip in play, still on red.

"You know, one thing that youth will never understand is

that there are forces in the universe at play that are grander than the self."

His tone shifts so erratically to seriousness that I cannot help but laugh even harder.

"Really, Franz?"

He looks at me with a frown.

"Some are chosen and some are not. Simple as that."

I chuckle happily; watching the croupier help the old lady spread her next wave of forsaken bets.

"Really, Franz? And all of this came to you with the spin of a wheel, huh?"

"Some are chosen, some are not. What is life, but a spin of the wheel of fortune?"

He grins now, as the ball is again put into play.

"So you and I are the chosen ones then?"

He's still grinning, but his voice is steady:

"Life is cyclical. I was propelled from nothing to everything, and back to nothing again. I know we only just placed one bet, but I haven't felt this alive in years, Marcus! Perhaps this time we will both be propelled to everything for good. I don't think it's bad to hope for good things, Marcus."

"I think it's cynical to think that any human effort is devoid of meaning, Franz."

The ball lands on 19 red.

"Of course you do."

Franz does a little dance and smiles again, as he adds the newest green chip to our stack and leaves the original wager in play.

"Of course you would, Marcus. You are young. And the young must work, so that humanity may progress. It is required of you that you think nothing of chance, and everything of human toil."

"So you had nothing to do with your downfall last time. It was just fate?"

I say this sardonically but his answer is blunt:

"Yes."

The old lady loses again and the croupier shovels her lost chips into the hole at the back of the table. Again, he smiles his sickly smile at her as he helps her place still another wave of bets. I watch this as I digest the boldness of Franz's words:

"Marcus, it is easy for you to judge and pin everything on me. It reflects your worldview that everything is in your control. And if everything is in your control, then it only follows logically that everything must be in mine. He who admits to himself that he is powerless will not toil."

The croupier puts the ball into play once more. I am at a loss for words.

"Rationalizations are easier on the soul than the mourning of what might be, Marcus."

I can see that Franz is enjoying the effect his words are having on me.

"But Franz, you left Germany, you moved to the States. How can you say that there is no sense in trying? *You* did that. *You* made those choices."

"Yes, but did I really? Did *I* choose to be who I am, or did it just happen to me? The world shapes you, Marcus, more than anyone wants to admit. It was inevitable that I would leave Germany. I can see that now. I hated my life as a boxer, and that was not because I chose to. My circumstances pushed me to desperation, and the way I acted was a visceral response, that I did not control, to circumstances, that I did not control."

The ball spins and lands on 7 red. Franz throws his arms into the air once more, before collecting his bounty. His smile slowly fades though, as his face returns to determination and focus. The novelty of a win has already lessened by the third bet.

"Reason does not run the world, Marcus. Judgment does. And all the numbers and reason and analytics in the world can't measure judgment. It's the riskiest proposition there is."

I look around at the retirees in their knitted sweaters and cardigans, sitting nearby at the slot machines, staring mindlessly at the screens and waiting for cherries, or sevens, or whatever it might be to line up. I look at the croupier still smiling his rotten smile, and at the screen by the wheel, now displaying the three consecutive reds we just profited from. And I wonder what the odds might be of all of this happening at once, the reds, the conversation, the musky smell of Franz's perfume, the croupier's beady eyes meeting my stare and the profound realization in that very moment that Franz is right.

Franz must notice the change revealing itself in my face, and reacts to it:

"Here, take these three green chips. Go change them for some reds and play some blackjack or slots or something. Take your time. I'll run the table here alone, don't worry. Just come check up on me every now and again."

He smiles and places the chips in my hands. I look at them for a while, before walking away from the table. The old lady is cursing under her breath.

I walk around a while, strolling aimlessly, still acclimating myself to these new surroundings, before I decide to find the cashier's cage. The white-collared smiling woman behind the counter opens her hands, revealing her empty palms for the cameras before and after counting the three twenty-five dollar chips, and hands me fifteen red five-dollar chips as change. The chips have a hologram of the casino on them, and mark the 20th anniversary of the institution.

I walk down a flight of stairs to the blackjack tables and take a seat. I pay no attention and sit haphazardly at a table with a twenty-dollar minimum bet. I lean over the table, resting my elbows on the teal leather cushion, and wait for the hand underway to be completed. The dealer turns over a twenty; with the king of diamonds and the queen of spades, and all five players groan in unison as they lose their money. An oriental man in a fine silk suit was sitting on an eighteen. He complains that the table is rigged. The dealer, a plump French Canadian with a copper beard, adamantly argues with him. They go at it for a little while and I watch them patiently, bewildered by the futility of the silk man's protests.

I remember what Franz told me about setting the mood, and I lay my fifteen red chips all in the bet zone. The dealer kindly greets me and opens a new hand. He deals across the table, dealing me a two and a queen, twelve, though he has a six showing.

I read up a little on a few casino games before we made the trip.

In blackjack, the simple point of the game is to get a number as close to twenty-one as possible without going over. The way you do so is by being dealt two cards, and then deciding from there on out if you would like another card or not, by hitting or staying. In this particular spot, arguments could be made for either of the actions. This is because the dealer is forced to hit until he reaches a number of at least seventeen, at which point he must automatically stay. And so, with a twelve and a dealer six showing, an argument can be made for hitting, because a twelve is very low and cannot defeat any dealer result but a bust (going over twenty-one). But the risk of hitting is that a ten or face card (also valued ten) be turned over and the player then sits on twenty-two, or a bust, and loses outright without even putting the dealer to the test.

What is interesting about a spot like this is that there really is no right answer until after the fact.

I decide to stay with my twelve and the dealer reveals a king, giving him sixteen, forcing him to hit. The next card is a ten, and the dealer busts. The dealer pays me my winnings.

I finger the chips, feeling the electricity of their *infinite* potential. But I decide not to place another bet.

I walk over to cashier to cash my chips and wait for Franz in the parking lot by the car, smoking a joint by myself and smelling the plaster and drywall and concrete and rubber and moisture of the bustling parking garage in P4, two spots to the left of the second concrete beam to the left of the casino entrance.

I wait for Franz, smoking cigarette after cigarette until very early in the morning, almost six in fact, before we finally go home. He comes waltzing to the car with a big smile on his face, and tells me, when we are safely off the premises, that he, well we, made twenty five hundred today.

***

The next day I lend Franz my car and he goes to the Casino alone. I'm simply not in the mood. Franz insists he is on a hot streak, and can't miss a day. We'd be losing money. He wakes me up at ten in the morning, agitated and in a rush, and I throw the keys over to get rid of him.

I sleep in until about three in the afternoon. I make myself some Kraft Dinner and smoke a few cigarettes when I finally wake up. Yesterday's melancholy lingers, so I take a bus over to the east end around six o'clock, to sit at Gaetano's and have a coffee. I'm really just hoping to bump into an old friend or a familiar face. It has been a while since I have spoken to anyone other than Franz.

It's dark out by the time I get around to leaving the apartment. It takes a few buses to get to Gaetano's. The bus up Jarry Street passes by the old church near the bar. It is a familiar sight- Bella and I used to walk by it often in the summer. I can see through the heavy condensation of the bus window that the large tree in front of the church is still fitted with Christmas lights, illuminated to the top beautiful and bright. The sight of the sparkling tree, all the more dazzling against the blackened backdrop of the night sky, recalls the sensation of some far away lost childish wonder that makes me feel empty. And the memory- the way that Bella had put her arms around me one sunny summer afternoon under the shade of that tree and told me that she would love me forever and how I looked her in the eyes and knew that she had meant it and that I had thrown it all away for what reason I still didn't know. And the image of her patient face and my constantly troubled heart and her attempts to soothe and my impulsive rebuttals and pushing her further away.

'I love you okay.'

That was what she had told me with desperation in her eyes.

'I love you okay.'

And I nodded though inwardly I knew she had just signed

her soul over to the devil.

I arrive at Gaetano's and order an espresso before going to sit by the window. No one I know is here this evening, but I stay by the window, watching the cars go by and wondering how Franz is faring at the casino. I watch the sky darken as the night slowly deepens, and I look down into the black coffee. The lights of the dining room just above are reflected in the still liquid, and I wonder how that's possible. I watch the old men, their eyes forever glued to the screen on the wall projecting some soccer game or other. After a while, I get fed up, and I bring my cup up to the counter to pay and leave.

I look over my shoulder one last time, into the dining room empty but for the old men now screaming at the television screen. The only other people in the place are the losers who come in every day to throw their money away on the slot machines in the back area of the café.

I walk out of the café and to the bus stop.

I don't think about anything the whole way home.

Back at the apartment, Franz is waiting for me with a big grin. As I step in, he begins to roll a joint on the coffee table.

"Twelve thousand today Marcus."

The figure brings my mind down from the clouds and squarely into the moment. I look at him incredulously.

"What? How?"

"The gods are smiling down on us Marcus."

I grin widely and he grins back and winks at me.

He closes the joint and lights it. I grab a stool from the kitchen and sit in the usual spot.

"It was incredible today Marcus. Spin after spin coming off red. I never had to place more than three bets before I won."

I smile, making an effort to readjust my headspace and focus on what Franz is telling me. We have turned three thousand into about seventeen in just two days. Franz starts up again, always very chatty in his good moods:

"Marcus, look at that painting just above me and tell me what you see."

There is so much so suddenly flooding my mind and I can't really focus, but I try to do as I am told. I look above him at the hanging watercolor Aphrodite in the middle of the ocean and ponder it a while, struggling to push the dancing dollar signs from the foreground of my consciousness. I finally answer:

"I don't know Franz. Isolated beauty."

He nods his head with raised eyebrows and passes me the joint.

"Wow, that's beautiful Marcus. Very profound."

He squints, still nodding:

"You know what I see? I see my ex-wife."

I look at him with narrowed eyes waiting for him to continue. He looks over his shoulder at the painting, then grins at me again and leans back on the couch.

"Isn't that something? How we can both look at the exact same thing and see something entirely different?"

I pass him the joint and remain silent.

"When we make enough, when things get back to the way they used to be, I'm going to look her up Marcus, and I'm going to make her mine again. That elusive angel, I know I will find her.

She's all I was thinking about at the tables today. I truly believe she's the reason we're going to win. She's watching over me. This is my shot at redemption."

For whatever reason, Franz's confidence irks me.

"How do you know we're going to make it big Franz? Isn't it bad karma to talk about these things before the fact?"

I force a grin, but Franz's face goes serious. He sits up, staring out the patio door.

"I know. I just know. I've only had this feeling once before. It's a feeling like nothing else, Marcus. I can't explain it, but I recognize it. We're on the way up. I can feel it."

He inhales the smoke and leans back on the couch, still looking out the window at the starless sky. I look at him indifferently, happy that we won money today but still unable to fully comprehend the meaning of it. For now, it is just a bigger bank, more plastic chips to play with, and more of the same tomorrow.

"But don't worry Marcus. Experience has made me wiser, and I will not squander the opportunity this time around. When we get up to a few hundred thousand, I'm going to invest it all in real estate. It's a safer bet. The wheel is just a means to an end. I'm going to set myself up properly this time. Age and wisdom have made me modest."

I light a cigarette and check my watch. It's about ten o'clock.

"When Mina and I were living in the condo, high up on the strip, I felt as if, I don't know, being perched up there above the city and the people hustling to climb, I felt important. I felt above the others. I felt *entitled*. I didn't feel equal. I felt better."

Franz's eyes are shining with a stifled passion and lust for life itching to be unleashed. In the moment, I think to myself that everyone must *want* things; everyone must *want* to be more than they are, regardless of circumstance. But to admit to oneself that one wants is to admit that there is a lack that may never be filled. But, to be human must mean to strive...

"What do you think Marcus, do you think it's bad to feel better? Do you think I'm a hypocrite for wanting Mina back? Do you think I deserve her?"

I look at Franz's searching face with narrowed eyes, and then I look down at my hands, which are dry and brittle from the sharp sting of the cold outside, and then I look at Aphrodite floating all alone in the ocean. And I answer his question truthfully, as truthfully as I can:

"I have no idea, Franz."

He narrows his eyes at me before undoing a few buttons of his silly shirt, revealing his white chest hair and leather skin. He runs a hand through his hair and sighs audibly, before turning his attention back to me:

"What did you do today Marcus?"

He looks at me distractedly as he passes the joint. I turn it down and he puts it out in the ashtray.

"I stewed in self-pity."

Franz looks at me and raises an eyebrow before erupting into laughter. He settles down and takes his shirt off, hanging it up with care on one of the broken cupboards.

"You and your nerves kid."

I move to my room without answering, and Franz sprawls out on the couch. He dozes off within minutes. I jump in the shower and give myself a good scrub before getting to bed. I think about the money as I stare at the spackle drip ceiling, and it takes me a while to fall asleep.

My eyes are heavy, though my heart is fast.

I feel that tomorrow is going to be a very big day.

***

Franz and I head to the casino in the late afternoon. There is a blanket of snow on the ground and the sun is extremely strong today, blindingly so as it reflects off of the smooth ice and hardened snow. The icy pavement and rooftops shimmer in the light, as do the hoods of cars and windows. The glare hurts my eyes and makes the long drive to the casino unpleasant. It is so bright that I have to shield my eyes, at times unable to see a few car lengths ahead of me. We listen to one of Franz's old Iggy Pop discs on the way over; though Franz speaks the entire time about how today is going to be a big day.

I light a cigarette and check my watch. It's about three o'clock as we pull into the parking lot.

"Remember what I was telling you yesterday? About Mina and how I felt elevated in that condo… Do you believe it?"

"Believe what Franz?"

Franz shields his eyes too, as he looks upward into the sky. The brightness and glare are slowly blocked off by the cool shade of the concrete as we move into the garage.

"That there are extraordinary men out there, of a higher class say, who have the right to overstep the laws and limitations of the average man? To do whatever they know to be right, regardless of society and its conventions?"

We enter the parking garage and I flick the cigarette, turning to Franz:

"You doubting yourself, Franz?"

"No, of course not! It's just… sometimes, very rarely but sometimes I think it's almost unethical to think entirely for myself."

I turn to look at him and Franz looks back at me blankly.

"Franz, I think that any man capable of seeing things in a new way, a way that goes against the grain, and that he himself knows to be true, is a visionary. A visionary will often lead a solitary life, but he must fulfill his vision. It is his purpose."

"So is that a yes? You and I are outside of the rules, Marcus?"

"If you have the capacity to do something, what holds you but fear?"

Franz's lips curl into a pompous smile.

"I've taught you well."

We park in the regular spot, walk through the plaster and rubber smelling garage into the casino without a word, pass the doorman *Howdy, partner!* and climb up to the roulette tables. I stay with Franz for a few bets, which he splits, before he gets restless and accuses me of jinxing him. Franz asks to be left alone to work. I shrug it off and go change the one hundred and fifty dollars I won in blackjack a couple days ago back into chips.

I walk back down the glass staircase to the red-carpeted blackjack area and sit at the very same table. The croupier is not the same, as they switch tables periodically, and the players are all different except for the oriental man, who is seated in the same place again. He does not recognize me, or does not seem to, and this time he sits in a gray wool suit that looks very hot. He has sweat on his brow and about a thousand dollars in chips in front of him. He's nagging the dealer again- this time it is about the pace at which the cards are being dealt. There are two Jewish men also at the table, one gray-haired and the other younger, wearing black velvet Kippahs and simple black blazers over jeans. The only other player is an older French-Canadian gentleman with gold-rimmed glasses, wearing a white shirt and worn, rust-colored corduroys.

I again place all of my chips into the bet zone, and the dealer nods at me before dealing out the cards. I am dealt a twenty and the dealer shows a king. The two Jewish men are playing one set of cards and bust, as does the oriental man, though the French-Canadian stands at eighteen and I at twenty. The dealer turns over a seven to go with his king and pays the older gentleman and me.

I take back my chips and decide to settle in, having 'set the mood'. I change my bet to the table minimum of twenty dollars. The dealer passes out a new hand, and I can't help but overhear the Jewish men speaking loudly. They are in the middle of a heated conversation:

"Yes, but it's disrespectful. One believes in God his whole life and goes to synagogue every week, and then this, this *shmuck* on the Internet denounces it and basically insists it's all a waste of time. Wouldn't that infuriate you?"

The dealer deals me a fifteen and I hit, receiving a nine and busting.

"I don't know. Personally, I don't see the reason to take offence. It is an Internet comment. Don't you think it a little silly? People will follow the word of God if they wish to, and only if they wish to Rabbi."

The word 'rabbi' takes me by surprise. By my understanding, rabbis generally have dim views on gambling.

I size up the table. The oriental man seems to be breaking even, and continues to find reasons to complain to the dealer. The old man sits patiently and looks entirely indifferent to the turn of the cards. The Jewish men have lost three bets in a row and are running low on chips, with just about forty dollars left by my count. They play their bets standing, always the minimum, and continue arguing loudly.

"You are right, of course, but I cannot help but be bothered. The man is very intelligent but he thinks if you don't agree with him then you're simply wrong."

I bet fifty on the new deal and receive a sixteen with the dealer showing a two and I decide to stay. The dealer busts and everyone win but the Jewish men, having busted on a hit fifteen. I pull my winnings in across the soft green felt.

"So just exercise your reason and comment back calmly and be done with it. There's really no need to see it as an attack on the Jewish faith."

The Jewish men place their final four red chips into the bet zone and I impulsively decide to follow them. I place all of my chips, four hundred dollars worth, into the bet zone before me. The oriental man looks over, surprised by my bet, and soon the rest of the table is staring my way. The dealer looks at me and asks:

"Sir, you are betting four hundred dollars, are you sure you want to do that?"

I look over at the Jewish men with a blank face, and reply loud enough for them to hear:

"Yes, I feel I've got God on my side today."

The dealer nods and the Jewish men whisper to each other as the cards are dealt. The dealer turns up a six for the Jewish men, a seven for the Oriental man, a king for the old man and an ace for me before dealing his card face down. The second card comes a jack for the Jewish men, a second seven for the Oriental man, a nine for the old man, and a queen for me, giving me blackjack and an automatic three to two payout. I leap up out of my chair in excitement and the dealer immediately pays me my winnings. The dealer shows a king and the Jewish men stay their sixteen, the oriental man hits and busts with a nine, and the old man stays his nineteen. The dealer turns over a ten and cleans the table with a winning twenty. I count my chips and realize I have one thousand dollars on the table, so I decide to call it. I pocket my winnings and bid the dealer a good evening.

The Jewish men mutter to themselves and walk away from the table. I chase after them. I tap the taller and elder of the two, the supposed rabbi, on the shoulder, and hand him a hundred dollar chip.

He looks at me quizzically and I tell him defiantly:

"God granted me good fortune, but it is *I* who has chosen to share it with you rabbi."

The two men look at each other, confused.

"Ah, you overheard our conversation. Are you of the Jewish faith?"

"No. In fact, I'm not really religious at all."

The rabbi raises his eyebrows in surprise, and his friend folds his arms and rubs his chin.

"Then how am I to interpret your action?"

I look at the rabbi's old sagging face and into his blue eyes and I am at a loss.

"I don't know."

He looks more puzzled than before, and extends his hand to return the chip.

"I cannot accept this chip young man. It would not be right of me."

I look at the chip, lying in the old man's open palm and back the old man's blue eyes and *I* am suddenly confused. I've caught myself at the end of my momentum, and I suddenly realize I have given a stranger one hundred dollars without any real reason. A little embarrassed, I step back and shake my head.

"No, no. You keep it. It is entirely my will that you have it. God has nothing to do with it. But consider it a donation for the synagogue, if you wish. I... there's just one thing I want you to do for me. You seem a learned man, rabbi. Tell me something. Tell me something you've learned after a lifetime in the service of God. You must be a wise man. Tell me... something *true*. Please."

The rabbi's face is painted with extreme skepticism but the young man beside him whispers something into his ear, and the rabbi nods. His face softens and he clasps my arm. He says:

"My son, it is truly my belief that a man is merely the sum of his actions. And this is a very kind one. I will make mention of you tomorrow at the service."

And with that he and his friend smile, and turn to walk away.

I stand there watching them a while, letting the rabbi's words sink in before deciding to get some air.

I don't really have a lot of stamina when it comes to gambling, whether I am winning or losing. Just a few bets are all

I can stand. These games remind me too much of cycles, of ups and downs, and of futility. I think for that reason I may even enjoy losing more than winning, much in the way that one enjoys the slow melt of the spring more than the full bloom of the summer because the anticipation of the rise always promises more than the enjoyment of its arrival.

I walk away from the table, which is one of the outermost in a large cluster of tables on the floor just before the isolated poker room. There are maybe twenty tables, housing blackjack, war, and variations of poker that can be played against a dealer.

My heart is aching as I continue to think of the Rabbi's words. Not for any of the people around me, not for the losers, nor for the mindless vice of the casino, but because of the futility of it all. Whether I won or lost, it would not fill the void in my life. And knowing this, or acknowledging it in this moment, really lowers my spirits. So, with the nine hundred dollars in chips safely tucked away in my pocket, I walk aimlessly through the casino for a little while.

I look up at the ceilings of the atrium, and see the purple glow of the third-floor lounge. I think I can hear subtle sounds of laughter and merriment for an instant before they're lost in the clamor of the slots.

It is getting late in the evening and I can see through the atrium windows that the sun has set.

The floormen scattered around the casino in black suits walk around just as aimlessly as I do. I get the feeling that after someone wins, the managers tail behind for a while. For what reason I'm not sure, perhaps to scare the winners, to dissuade them from attempting to do something so foolish as winning money from the casino again. I walk for a few minutes, feeling the presence of a black suited man behind me, and I think to myself what a horrible life it must be, roaming the casino floors day in and day out, making a living off of the inevitable misfortunes of others. 'Patrons' as they call them, being led calmly like smiling sheep to the slaughterhouse. And I let that image contrast the rabbi's words of wisdom as I wander into a bathroom off to my left, daring the suited man to follow me.

He doesn't.

I take a look in the mirror and splash some water in my face. The scintillating glass backsplash fills my mind with notions of willing naiveté, and the necessity of other false promises. I think back to a grade school dance, then looking into the mirror and deliberately positioning my hair. It is the first time I can remember being overtaken by vanity. We are four boys in the washroom, chipped teal paint lining the walls and rust coloring the lip of the sink, just beneath the tap. The school is over one hundred years old and gives us a great, spooky haunted house feel. In fact, there are rumors among the children, and stories floating around that there is a ghost roaming the halls... And the mirror and that damned mirror and the first time I look in the mirror and search and know that there will be girls to impress, and I think so hideously that my happiness hinges on my hair being just right.

Oh women, what angels of love!

Sandy is in the gymnasium, and waiting to rebuff my innocent desire to dance with her. The realization comes eventually, perhaps not in that moment, but maybe it is the first time I open the door. The realization: that all virtue is but an arrow of longing unwillingly flung, plunging pointedly ever deeper into the heart of man. Delusion is objective because suffering is always subjective...

And then looking into the mirror, the mirror then and the mirror now, and asking myself:

Who do you think you are?

Merely a man lacking the humility to crumble beneath the pressures of mediocrity, and acceptance.

Who do you think you are?

A man with free will.

Who do you think you are?

God.

The image in the mirror flickers, though I do not blink. And my life flashes like images through a flipbook narrowing to nothing and disappearing. I refuse to acknowledge it, but then maybe I cannot help it. There is a fire fiercely burning, eating me up inside. I throw some water in my face again and dry myself with the paper towels dispensed by the wall. The paper is rigid, and real. I look once more in the mirror and I see myself cold, and old, and it is almost too much to bear and I want so badly to scream out.

But I don't.

I just wallow in the void.

And what exactly the void is I can't even begin to explain: a broken relationship with my parents, and all those around me? The foundation-shaking realization that I have never, not once in my life opened up to another human being in a raw, organic, unperturbed way? Exposure like a skinned cadaver in a sandstorm. And that disturbance, that inability to open myself to beauty, not the beauty of billboards, or the beauty of lust, but the beauty of unfiltered satisfaction and peace of mind. Having mind and heart at ease, trusting those around me, and my environment, and no longer needing to sport that sickly alabaster smile that, for a sick man just makes things just flow easier. Broken? It is an ugly word when applied to a vase, hideous when thinking of a human soul. And something about being in this casino brings all that ugliness out of me and into plain sight. The mirror is an abyss, and the glass scintillating backsplash is the straw that breaks the camel's back.

You don't understand my pain because you don't understand my pain because you *can't* understand my pain because it's *my* pain. The wonderful circular logic that keeps everyone at bay, and keeps me locked in my little bubble of dull, throbbing, manageable desperation.

I am not well.

I walk out of the bathroom, composed but my chest heavy, and I feel for the deck of cigarettes in my pocket. I have a few rolled up joints in the carton, and I decide to head down the stairs through the atrium, and then down to the designated smoking area.

The night air and the smoke in my lungs will calm me down. It always does.

The smoking area is an open space under the concrete beams holding up the main pavilion of the casino, and caged in with fencing. It is heated for winter usage with the help of high-powered heat lamps. There are ashtrays scattered about, and a temperature gauge on the bare concrete wall that controls the lamps.

There is no one here but an older woman who looks approximately fifty years old. She has thin jet-black hair and is heavily painted. She's wearing a thick black sweater over jeans. She leans against the wall, sizing me up with a cigarette in hand. She smokes the cigarette leisurely below one of the heat lamps, impervious to the cold in her position.

I light a joint and sit on one of the benches beneath a heat lamp of my own.

"I don't think you're supposed to be smoking that here."

She speaks dryly and with a nasty, mocking smile.

"So let them throw me out then."

She approaches and smiles at me. Her teeth are yellow, and black, and disgusting. Her nails are plastic and her face is wrinkled, though the skin is pulled back and artificially tightened- vanity fighting, but ultimately losing its eternal battle with decay.

"How much did you lose, kid?"

"I didn't lose."

I answer sharply. She scrunches her face in a confused frown. She moves a little closer and I notice her eyes are brown, though darkened and concealed by mascara and eye shadow. Her voice is raspy and strained.

"So why the long face? You're winning at the casino, isn't that the point?"

I mull on that a while, twirling the joint with my forefinger and thumb.

"I don't know. I just feel as though it's all… pointless. This place makes me feel like I'm running on a wheel."

"Honey, of course you're running on a wheel. We're all running on a wheel."

She smiles again, that same yellow repulsive smile.

"Yeah, sure. How much did you lose?"

"Oh I don't play the games, my husband does. My husband is a professional, sweetheart. He plays poker. We're here four or five days a week."

She winks at me and pulls on her cigarette. She's inching closer and I squirm a little, trying to keep some distance between us.

"Oh yeah? How's that?"

She sighs.

"Oh, exciting I guess."

Her words are spoken in a soft, languid cadence, but her eyes pulse with plastic seduction. She has an awful grin on her face, as though she acknowledges the exaggeration and object of her words. Her hands and eyes move in a slow synchronized linger.

"When he does really well, we get to go to Cabo. When he doesn't do so well, I don't mind resorting to other things to help make ends meet..."

"Other things?"

She leans forward to flick the ashes of her cigarette into the ashtray beside me, but mostly to brush her breasts against my arm.

"Nothing you'd want to hear about, honey, unless you want to be spending all of that scratch you just won."

There is a moment of silence as she smiles her crooked smile at me and I just sit there smoking, trying to look aloof. Despite the smoke and the open space, I can smell her heavy perfume. The smoking area is a platform on the exterior of the structure, in the back of the casino building, and isolated. The silence when no one is speaking is profound. All that can be heard is the gentle hum of the lamps and the battering wind whipping against the concrete.

The woman finishes her cigarette and tosses the butt to the

floor. I watch the exhaled smoke rise and dissipate in the dry, cold night air. My joint is small, just enough to last a few hauls, and is nearly done.

"What's the matter, kid? You got a girlfriend or something?"

"No."

"I'm surprised, what with a pretty face like yours."

Silence.

"You gamble a lot?"

"No."

"You got a job then?"

"No."

She snorts and smiles.

"A real contributor, aren't ya?"

She's annoying me now, and I make to get up and leave.

"You know, you remind me a lot of me when I was your age."

She sizes me up with her arms folded. Her tone changes, and speeds up, as she tries to recapture my attention. The contours of her face drop the act, and soften with her change of attitude:

"I was really idealistic too once upon a time, believe it or not. It got me down a lot. I used to think the things you think, probably. Making money is inherently immoral. All profit is derived from exploitation. Life is an ever-bobbing seesaw. So what's the point? Right? I used to think all of North America was a hopeless trap. Everyone here works a fake job, pushing paper, crunching numbers they don't even really understand and passing them up the pyramid."

I sigh.

"And now?"

"Well, now I guess I simply don't care. Why is a desk job more noble than what we do? All these suits close their eyes and contribute to the fact that there's a third world. Commerce, consumerism, mass production, it all hinges on having someone to exploit. For one side of the seesaw to go up, the other must come down. You cannot create matter, only move it. Money is very much the same, sweetheart. And the pawns that sit unquestioningly in their cubicles are just the bookkeepers for the racket. The lot of them. They don't care about anything, really. They're not good people."

She smiles that disgusting smile and unfolds her arms.

"Saying something like this, just acknowledging the inconsistencies in things makes you an outcast. Society shuns you because you refuse to be silenced. Whether they're financiers, or insurers, or salesmen, they're all gamblers and money counters and crooks. That's exactly what we are, as *actual* gamblers, minus the bureaucracy and self-importance that comes with wearing a suit to the office."

I finish the joint, watching her intently. Her face becomes flushed with frustration as she speaks. I try to remain indifferent to this stranger's words, but her passion compels me. She rambles like an insane person, but some of the things she is saying, I have to admit, have crossed my mind before. She's not entirely wrong.

I toss the butt, and she invites me inside with a shake of the head.

"Cmon' honey. Let's hit the lounge and have a drink."

She opens the door and I follow her up the stairs toward the lounge. She goes on rambling:

"You know, my friend works for a bank and the other day he has to call in sick. The bank insists he get up at six in the morning, so he can call in and tell them he doesn't feel well and won't be reporting to work. He emails them the night before, and they tell him that's unacceptable. Company policy. He has to call at six in the morning or they will consider his absence a refusal to work, which will result in termination. Company policy, do you believe that? You can't get a good night's sleep on the company's watch. Company policy. It sickens how people sacrifice all of their freedom for a mediocre pay and a false sense of stability."

She coughs a hacking cough and plays with her thin black hair. Her fake nails are decked with rhinestones.

Passing through the rows of slots, I notice a man playing 'Butterfly Sevens' who looks a lot like Steve. We make eye contact for a moment, but the woman pushes me forward so I move on. I look back, wondering what would Steve be doing here, but his head is turned. It probably isn't him; I mean what would Steve be doing here alone?

We reach the third floor and the purple lighting of the lounge, and take a seat. The tables are slick black vinyl, clean, and modern, and the chairs are a padded upholstered black. There are hollows in the walls, candlelit and back dropped with artificial purple light. The bar is glass, and the purple neon illuminates the large bottle display behind the glass counter. Smooth jazz is playing at a subdued volume, and there are black upholstered couches around a slick glass coffee table, where a large group of young women sit and talk.

The group laughs and I turn to have a look at them. They

seem entirely carefree.

A waitress promptly interrupts my reverie. She asks what we'd like, and I tell her we'll have two of whatever the lady likes as I place a green chip on the table. The woman orders two vodka martinis, and I look anxiously back over at the group of young women.

I catch sight of a milky nape and run my eyes up a beautiful smooth neck to an all too familiar chocolate brown hairline, done up in a ponytail. Her head is turned but I'm certain I recognize her. I excuse myself as the woman makes raspy small talk with the waitress, and I walk over to the couches.

"Joanie?"

She turns and flashes that familiar smile that heats my blood. She's wearing a red turtleneck over jeans, and sneakers. Her makeup isn't done. This is the most casual I have ever seen her. She is beautiful.

"Wow, Marcus. I didn't expect to see you here."

She smiles at me, waiting for me to lead the conversation. I notice she no longer has a cast on her arm. She catches the direction of my eyes:

"I got it off last week. All back to normal."

She smiles again and moves her arm up and down, laughing to break the tension. Her welcoming disposition makes me feel at ease.

After our last encounter, I felt as though I would never see this girl again, let alone ever have another chance at conversation with her. But her demeanor is inviting, which surprises and delights me, so I jump on the opportunity.

"I... I'm glad to see that. I was trying to have a conversation over there with my new friend, but the sight of you was too distracting."

Joanie looks over at the dark woman at the table and raises an eyebrow at me.

"Interesting choice in friends, Marcus. What was I doing that was so distracting?"

I smile timidly.

"I guess I just think you're so pretty, even the back of your head is distracting."

She erupts into laughter.

"Wow, that was awful."

I stand there feeling stupid for a second, but she again breaks the tension and introduces me to her friends. She's with four or five dim-looking women I don't pay much attention to, and I greet them with an unenthused collective wave. Joanie edges over and I sit down beside her on the couch.

"What was so awful about it?"

I ask her with a coy smile, enjoying very much her presence beside me. She looks at me with exaggerated exasperation, and exhales letting her shoulders droop.

"You really do think you're God's gift to women, don't you?"

Her eyes widen sarcastically as she says this.

I smile.

"Do you always feel contempt towards those who compliment you?"

She smiles back.

"Only when the compliment is delivered by a derelict."

"Let me buy you a drink."

"And why would I let you do that?"

"Because I just won some money and I want you to help me celebrate."

"Hmm. I don't think that's a good reason."

"Because I'm sorry and I like you and you like me."

She sighs.

"Because I'm sorry and I like you and I want you to like me?"

"I'm with my friends, I can't."

"Five minutes."

She fidgets a little, looks around the bar nervously.

"No. Not now. Another time. Call me."

"Okay, I will."

I smile and kiss her on the hand. I get up to leave and wave her dim-looking friends goodbye, ignoring the woman from the smoking room who still has her eyes fixed on me. As I leave the bar I do cast a parting glance and the dark woman raises a glass in toast, sitting alone at the table with her two vodka martinis.

Feeling excited, and thrilled with my encounter with Joanie, I decide to go check up on Franz. I walk down the glass staircase to the red carpet roulette area, and I see Franz in the distance, an unmistakable smile etched on his face. He looks really animated and plays a packed table. I approach and he throws his arms into the air, as the ball lands on red. I glance at the table and notice a yellow thousand dollar chip in play and a stack of what looks like about forty of them sitting in front of Franz. I tap him on the shoulder and he seems startled to see me.

"Franz, what's going on?"

"Hey, hey! Marcus! I'm absolutely killing that's what's going on!"

He grabs me by the shoulders and shakes me, smiling ear to ear.

"Here, go have a drink on me big guy!"

Franz hands me a green chip and takes a sip from his own drink, sitting in the table's golden cup holder. He turns his back to me, returning his attention to the table but I tap him once again on the shoulder.

"Franz, how come you're betting so much?"

He turns back toward me with a hint of impatience on his face.

"Don't worry about it kid, I have things under control."

I can smell whiskey on his breath.

"C'mon Franz, this is my money too. Why are you betting so much? And are you drunk?"

He sighs and puts an arm around my shoulder, leading me away from the crowd and the table.

"Marc, are you familiar with the bible?"

In a good mood from having seen Joanie, I can't help but laugh.

"The bible? No, I wouldn't say I'm that familiar with the bible. Why, does Jesus lay out his roulette strategy in there?"

Franz chuckles and jabs my arm playfully.

"Matthew 25:29: 'For whoever has will be given more, and they will have an abundance. Whoever does not have, even what they have will be taken from them.'"

I laugh again.

"You laugh but Matthew was right! When things go well, bet big! When things go poorly, run!"

I laugh even louder and Franz joins me. I show him the thousand dollars I won in blackjack and he laughs even louder still. We return to the table all smiles and Franz tells me he will place two more bets and then we can leave. He places a yellow chip on the red bet zone and I watch with extreme adrenaline pumping through my veins as the ball spins and spins around the wheel. The spin lands red, and we celebrate. The rush of adrenaline courses through me and makes me feel light as air. A thousand dollars materializes from the grace of God.

Franz takes the yellow chip we just won and adds it to the pile, leaving our original thousand-dollar wager in play. We watch the croupier spin the second spin, and we eye the plastic ball as it goes round and round and round and lands on black. The loss is so sudden that I am taken aback. But Franz has been here all day, and he slaps me on the back.

"Can't win em' all Marcus."

And he shrugs as the dealer scoops our thousand-dollar piece of plastic, along with all the other losing bets, into the hole at the back of the table.

I forget about that spin quickly, though, as we leave the casino smiling uncontrollably, up over thirty thousand dollars.

***

That night, Franz and I smoked on the way home and went straight to bed. That day was our longest session at the casino, and we were exhausted.

That night I had a dream, an insane dream that still haunts me. My mind was a whirl that whole day- it was a roller coaster of a day- and my head was not ready and settled when sleep came. I remember vividly the pangs of vibration than shot through my body, and I remember waking up in a shiver, and muttering to myself while blinking over and over in the darkness, uncertain whether everything was flickering or all was black.

***

I am wearing a trench coat. It is a beige one, timeless, with a black suede bowler hat on. I'm dressed like a European, like some sort of private detective roaming the streets. I have a recollection of an immense amount of money in cash. I reach for my breast, and I can feel it nestled safely inside the trench coat where no one can see it. It is an undisclosed sum, though enough to kill for. I feel it in my bones.

The street is cobblestone, bumpy, and hurts the arches of my feet. It feels as though I have been walking for long, in tightly fitting leather shoes that are at the height of fashion. There is a wet smell in the air, as though it has recently rained, though the streets are dry. The passersby walk and mingle, confident in the maintained clarity of the night sky. There are several kiosks around making a busy market of the open square. Some sort of popup bazaar, it seems.

I look up and see the starry sky, and a clear crescent-shaped moon against a mute, deep navy that stretches beyond the imaginable horizon. The streetlights hang like sunken stars, hollow in the dim of the calm, humid square.

I am being followed, though I walk at a casual pace. My cool exterior conceals my heart-racing interior. The train station is close by.

I can hear the clack of my steps against the cobblestone, even above the light bustle of the bazaar. They have been behind me for a while, though I feel no sense of rush. They are waiting for the right moment, as am I. They haven't pounced yet. I suppose I am not yet at my most vulnerable.

I am meeting someone- a woman, my woman- and going somewhere, though I can't remember why. I don't think they know either. Maybe they do. Something unspeakably significant hinges on my encounter, with *her*.

I want a new beginning. I want a fresh start.

I stop in front of the train station to smoke a cigarette and I look around, knowing now that this must be it. Confrontation is inevitable. I hold the flame to the cigarette, but the cigarette will not light. I check my watch; it is a few minutes to midnight.

I look around again. The architecture of the square is tall, gothic, and sinister. The hoards of people smile, though, and lessen the urgency of the moment.

A glimmer of light to my left and the shuffle of determined steps to my right confirm that I am surrounded. I don't know how many they are, but they've come for my money. They've come to take my freedom away.

The first one lurches at me awkwardly, and I jam the end of my cigarette into his face. The cigarette isn't lit, but he screams in agony and dissipates into wisps of warm smoke as his body hits the ground. The others rush to his aid, providing me a moment of distraction, which I use to slip away through a crowd of people now heading into the train station. In the terminus, before the giant screen ticking and turning with the various destinations and departures and arrivals, I spot her and take hold of her delicate hand. I lead her quickly through the crowd to our train on the platform across the way. The conductor waves us aboard but I turn to her, needing to have a look before we escape forever to perpetual bliss. She wears a headscarf and the contours of her face are obscure, but I can make out dark features.

I reach for her hand, again, though she moves hers away.

I say, desperate:

"If I could roll the universe into a ball, I would lay it at your feet."

She replies, apathetic:

"If you could roll the universe into a ball, you would sit and devour it alone."

She turns and boards the train as I fall to my knees, knowing that it is all over and screaming that it is all her fault. The screeching rails drown out my cries. The screech is the requiem for all my hopes and dreams, and slips into the fade as the train slowly pulls away.

***

I wake up a little jittery on Saturday, though ready to pick up where we left off.

Although it is an ugly day, Franz and I wake up in good moods. I had a night of sporadic sleep, but it's difficult not to be smiling given the circumstances.

It's unseasonably warm today, above zero, though gloomy

outside. It's raining, and the mixture of the rain and the warm weather is melting some of the snow and making the streets slushy, slippery, and difficult to navigate.

Franz is more excited than I have ever seen him, and his agitation shines through in the way he is picking compulsively at his fingers. He's wearing the same tacky shirt, though I have elected not to wear the same shirt for the fourth day straight. I'm dressed in a simple white t-shirt and jeans instead. This clearly annoys Franz, though his preoccupation with the seriousness of the day's proceedings keeps him from voicing his dissatisfaction. He shoots me the occasional dirty look before he returns his focus beyond the glass of his passenger side window to the dark and somber sky.

We park in the regular spot, P4, and walk out through the plaster and rubber and drywall and wet pavement of the parking garage. The electric glass doors open to the casino floor, and we climb the stairs into the atrium, and up another set of glass stairs to the red carpeting until we arrive at the teal-rimmed roulette tables.

The tables are bustling, packed, and radiating with the excitement that can only be generated on a Saturday at the casino. There are more people playing today than I have seen in the three days prior combined, and it is only about five o'clock. I can't imagine the staggering amounts of money being put at risk at any given moment. Almost all of the tables are open, and being played. The casino is alive with the sounds of the slots, the murmur of the crowds, and with laughter, excitement, and disappointment, all evoked by the twists and turns of chance.

Franz did warn me that Saturday nights at the casino are not like other nights. I quickly realize what he means. Each of the four roulette tables in the regular cluster of tables we play is being bet on by at least six people, most of whom are dressed nicely. There is a greater sense of urgency in the place, coupled with a greater sense of potential. I look over at Franz and I see him feeling into his pocket for our bank. The stack is now substantial. It makes me feel a little bit uncomfortable.

Franz counted it on the way over, one brown bill at a time. It is now held together in bands of ten thousand apiece. It totals thirty seven thousand four hundred dollars in physical, countable cash.

"We're making our move today."

I can barely hear Franz over the noises of croupiers calling out bets, chips shuffling about on felt, and plastic balls clacking against rosewood wheels. Screams shoot out from the crowd every so often. Some are positive, some frustrated. Franz keeps his voice low, so I inch closer:

"Five bets kid. Twelve hundred, twenty four hundred, forty eight hundred, ninety six hundred, and nineteen thousand two hundred. We leave here rich."

Franz's face is serene. I expected that the gravity of this moment, even in a man experienced in the way Franz is, would make for a flushed, agitated, or tense disposition. But Franz's face is serene, and the calmness in his face calms my own nerves. Franz's body language says it all: there is *nothing* to fear.

Fear? Fear what? Change? The unknown? Death slowly approaching us every passing second...

And the real potential for change flashes like lightning through my mind. I imagine it has flashed through Franz's mind all too many times, so many times in fact, that he has learned to control it better than I.

Franz's face is serene.

And I understand the game with two hearts.

The reason and math are real, but can only get you so far. The other side of the coin is emotion, and the desire that propels you to place the bet.

It is exactly this emotion and desire that lights Franz's face. He is fully in control of his fate. Of *our* fate.

He has somehow learned to bottle the emotion, to keep it ready at hand, to consume it as needed- in small, measured sips.

As if Franz can read my mind, as if he feels, as I feel, that we are connected in this moment, that our fates are connected in the same spins of the same wheel, he turns to me and with a nod of the head says:

"Humble yourself, kid."

He jabs me playfully on the shoulder with a confident smile and walks slowly toward the roulette wheel.

I follow close behind, enveloped in the same musky smell of the days before, and I am calmed by it. We are in this together and I have decided: I have faith in Franz.

The croupier greets us as we step up to the table. Franz pulls the absurd wad out, and spreads the bills on the table. The sight of all that money causes a small uproar in the crowd around the table. The most anyone else has in chips is five thousand. We are changing just over thirty-seven. I keep my hands in my pockets and try to stay out of the way. The plump dealer, whose nametag reads 'Gus', and whose nimble fingers will decide our fate, looks at the money with widened eyes and calls over a floor manager. A black suited man materializes lickety-split, and whispers something in the croupier's ear before smiling widely and approaching Franz.

"Follow me, sir."

He says this politely, and with a servile smile.

We are wagering too much for the outside tables, evidently, and are being moved to a separate room set aside for higher stakes. Franz nods without a trace of surprise or confusion, and skillfully ties all the money back into the rubber bands. We follow the black suited man up a staircase, and through a large black linoleum doorway being guarded by another, bigger black-suited man with an earpiece.

The room is fitted with a craps table played by seven or eight suited gentlemen, a blackjack table played by six men and a woman, also very well dressed, a vacant poker table, and a vacant roulette wheel.

There are black-suited men standing by the walls in every corner of the room.

The room smells of rich perfumes and colognes, and the men all wear expensive watches and have their hair styled. The lone woman in the room wears a sequent dress and extravagant jewels.

Another croupier is assigned to the table to accommodate us, though I don't like the look of him, and promptly tell Franz. Considering how much money we are bringing to the table, I think it is our privilege to decide on the croupier. Franz agrees with me and whispers something to our black suited escort. He nods, and leaves the room for a few moments.

The wheel in this room is slightly different to those on the floor. The colors of the wheel are more vibrant, and the leather armrest is red. The playing surface is cleaner, though the betting area has the same graphics. There is no digital screen delineating the prior winners.

The black-suited man returns followed by 'Gus', the croupier tending our regular table downstairs. The black-suited man smiles at us, as does 'Gus', who settles in behind the wheel. Upon seeing the wheel being opened for us, the woman from the blackjack table and a man from the craps table move over, nodding as they join us.

The escort leaves the room, and the doors close behind him.

The room falls quiet.

Well, it still resonates with the sounds of the tables and an occasional subdued cry of exhilaration, but compared to the casino floor it is quiet. We are sealed inside a vacuum.

The walls of the room are tiled halfway up, in a modern black and gold pattern of irregular interval, and are wallpapered the rest of the way to the ceiling. The ceiling is also wallpapered in a vertically striped gold and white alternation. The walls are bare on three sides though the wall at the back of the room, just behind the roulette table, is decorated with a pointillist painting of a potted plant and a gold-rimmed gold-faced clock ticking audibly just beside the painting.

There are lamps scattered about, glowing dimly, and a crystal chandelier hangs in the center of the room. The ceilings are about fifteen feet high, and there are white satin sofas and armchairs clustered in one corner of the room, by a tended bar.

Franz doesn't notice any of this, though. He just pulls the money out and spreads it on the table. The man and woman look on keenly as the dealer changes the sum into chips. We all wait patiently for the new game to begin. Each of them is playing about twenty thousand in chips. They do not bat an eye at our thirty seven thousand. The table minimum is one thousand per spin on the outside.

I stand behind Franz, absolutely silent, and every muscle in my body clenches as he places the first bet. 'Gus' smiles at us and wishes the table *bonne chance* as he puts the first ball into orbit. The ball spins around and round and lands indifferently in the nineteen red square.

Franz and I don't celebrate. In fact, neither of us move as Franz decides to let it ride. We are in it for the big score.

We stay in that room for nearly three hours. The room is quiet throughout, and hardly changes. A few new people shuffle in, well dressed and perfumed, and a few people shuffle out. The noises from the tables are consistent, and the tick of the gold-faced clock fills the dead air between spins. We bobble up and down, and our bank climbs as high as sixty thousand for a time. We bobble up and down, and plummet back down to as low as twenty.

I sweat profusely, though I hardly move an inch. The adrenaline surging through my veins is unprecedented.

I can barely think straight.

Franz keeps his composure though, throughout. He speaks to the dealer from time to time, makes small talk with the other gamblers, and even chuckles at lame gambling puns and clichés. It is remarkable how comfortable he seems with everything on the line, and absolutely everything outside of his control. It is of a strange kind, but it is faith. Franz has faith in the grand design, in his own destiny, and I am beginning to think I do too.

But then chance brings us to an impasse.

Four consecutive black spins bring us plummeting down to sixteen thousand in chips. Franz has been calm the entire night up until this point. And suddenly, everything unravels.

Franz turns swiftly toward me, his face overwrought with desperation, and says:

"You have to place this bet kid."

I am taken aback. I have hardly moved, or spoken a word in the last three hours.

"No, I cant Franz. You're better at this stuff than I am. I think you should do it. I'm not good with this stuff."

He is asking me to place a sixteen thousand dollar bet.

"Good? What the hell is good? You think if you're good, you win? Wrong. If you're lucky you win. If you're good you put yourself in a spot where it's easier to be lucky."

I can't even process his words. He's rambling, and I'm exhausted. I just want to get out of here.

Tomorrow is another day.

"I don't want to do it, Franz. Why don't you just split the money? We can restart the system from a lower initial bet. Let's just bet a thousand. What's the rush?"

He doesn't hear me. His eyes are wide and there is sweat on his brow. I thought that his patience and composure were inhuman, and I am beginning to see that I was right. Franz is cracking. The pressure is getting to him.

"Think about it. How do you win? What is winning? Winning is luck! It's good fortune; it's desires being met. It's not being good. Being good is handling variables well. Winning, having these variables favor you, is being lucky."

"I don't want to do it, Franz."

There is a crazed look in his eyes and they are darting madly around the room in calculation.

"And today, I have not been lucky. That's evident. Four black spins in a row. I haven't seen that in the past three days. I just don't have it today. That's just what it is. It's not meant to be. To be good, is to know when you need to shuffle things up, change the variables. I lost four bets in a row. I can't change the wheel, but I *can* change *me*. You need to place the bet, Marcus."

I'm sweating like a pig, and with the beginnings of a headache. I do not want to play that much money on a single spin of the wheel.

"I don't want to do it, Franz."

"Yes. Of course, it makes sense. You have to place the bet. It's the only way. If we win this bet we're back on track. And we will win this bet. I feel it. Trust me. Place the bet, Marcus."

He squeezes my arm vigorously, with a forced smile on his lips. The look on his face is surreal.

I look away from him and stare at the gold-faced clock hanging on the wall. The hands of the clock are running around its golden face deliberately, time delineated by golden Roman numerals at the three, six, nine, twelve. I look at the clock very intently and hear its subtle tick, even above the din of the room somehow. I watch the golden needle move from second to second- measured, steady, constant. Rebellious in its consistency! It is unstoppable. I measure the needle's movement, double-checking time until I feel certain that every second is indeed equal.

"Let's just come back tomorrow Franz."

Without taking my eyes off the clock, I hear the croupier put the ball in play. I listen to the first two spins around the wheel, and translate them into three seconds of the golden needle's tick.

Franz has his body turned away from the table, though he's

still squeezing my arm and repeating:

"Place the bet Marcus, place the bet Marcus"

I can feel the crazed agitation in his voice as he awaits the results of the spin. The croupier's glazed eyes droop in the direction of the clock, as he counts down the seconds to the end of his shift, to his freedom. I look at our chips, the sixteen stacked little yellow pieces of plastic that somehow in this moment personify my livelihood, and Franz's, and I think of the golden needle still trucking on and the last four spins coming out black. *Consistency.* I move the stack, instinctively, into the black bet zone, just as the croupier announces no more bets. The ball spins once, twice, three more times, and Franz still echoes his mantra squeezing my arm:

"Place the bet Marcus, place the bet, Marcus."

And then the ball hits the stopper, bounces three times, and lands comfortably in the pocket of the lucky red seven.

"Seven Red."

I feel the thud of absolute dejection.

The croupier's announcement sends Franz into a frenzy. He leaps up with a yelp and turns to take me into his arms, smiling with the ecstasy of release, as I watch the croupier's glazed eyes over Franz's shoulder. The croupier's steady arm indifferently shovels our sixteen little chips into the gaping hole at the back of the table.

Franz puts me down, still slapping me with congratulations, and turns to the table.

"Minimum bet is one thousand sir, would you like to buy some more chips?"

The croupier's glazed eyes are met by confusion quickly

turning.

"Where's my money?"

Franz leans into the table with both hands on the armrest and his face inching closer to the dealer's. The black suited man tending the door picks up on the hint of aggravation and urgency in Franz's voice. He unfolds his arms, and looks more intently in our direction.

"I'm sorry sir, you lost the last bet. Unfortunately, it came out red."

The other players begin to fidget uneasily and back away from the table, foreseeing a confrontation. Franz looks over his shoulder at me searchingly but I do not move. And then he turns back to the dealer with even more agitation:

"What the hell are you talking about you lowlife prick? We bet red. We always bet red. Now I ask you again, where is my money?"

The croupier's eyes widen, and he opens his arms pleadingly. The man in the suit whispers something into a black walkie-talkie and approaches, ready to intervene. Franz sees this, and grabs the croupier by the collar, bringing his forehead up against his own.

"WHERE THE FUCK IS MY MONEY?"

He screams so that the whole room hears, and the suited man lunges forward to separate Franz from the dealer. He calmly but firmly tells Franz it is time to go. The other suited men in the room converge on Franz, and two more suited men arrive at the door and stand there vigilant. I look at Franz's face and see the intensity in his eyes slacken with the realization that there is nowhere to go, and nothing to do. I just stand there, my head floating and my body anchored to the floor, waiting for the inevitable. Franz looks around the room one last time, as though calculating his options, before straightening himself out and smoothing his hair.

The golden needle ticks on all the same.

"No problem. I can use some air, I think."

The man in the black suit nods, and escorts Franz and I out of the room, down the glass staircase, through the red carpets, back through the atrium, and out of the casino. Franz does not look at me once, or even say a word. At the exit, the escort politely bids us good night and returns to his post.

We walk out, down the stairs to the P4 area of the parking garage and through the glass doors still without a word. I don't look at Franz, as I deal with my own realization of what just happened. I know, however, that he is going through his own inner turmoil. He is likely blaming me. The familiar smells of plaster and rubber enter my nostrils as we walk into the garage. I light a cigarette and turn to offer Franz one.

"Who in God's name do you think you are?"

His face is flushed with anger bubbling over and his upper lip is quivering, demanding confrontation. I remain motionless, with my arm extended and the pack of cigarettes open. I hold Franz's glare eye-to-eye, waiting for his next move.

"I said who the hell do you think you are?"

He slaps the cigarettes to the floor and steps closer. I look at the ground and sigh, hoping to avoid what I know deep down is inevitable. Franz shoves me and the cigarette in my mouth falls to the ground. He moves in and punches me square in the gut, knocking the air out of me. I collapse to my knees, gasping, but he hovers over me, not quite done.

"Did you think we were just going to smoke a cigarette and

forget about it? You selfish son of a bitch."

He bends over and delivers a right to my cheekbone, rattling my jaw and toppling me over. Franz punches me harder than I have ever been punched. My ears are ringing as I lay facedown on the ground.

"You cost me everything. Do you realize that?"

He's screaming now and I have a vague hope that a security guard, or a passerby, or someone will come and intervene. But then I know that no one intervenes when fights break out in parking lots like this one.

I try to get up, using my arms to lift myself to my knees. Franz moves in again and kicks me in the ribs, gassing me once more, and I sprawl out on my back gasping for air. He steps over me, so he can look me in the eye. The crazed look on his face makes me genuinely think he will kill me right there.

And I bow out. Like a complete coward, I bow out. I think that maybe this is it. Maybe the sum of my actions has led me here, to a plaster-and-rubber smelling demise, staring at the gray crumbling ceiling of an old parking garage.

"Who told you to bet black? We always bet red! Always!"

He runs his hands through his hair frantically and I grab at his feet, trying to lift myself up. Franz kicks my hands away and crouches over me, grabbing my hair to lift my head off the ground. He stares at me for a second or two, hatefully, and then punches me square in the nose. The pain is unlike any pain I have ever felt before. Franz shatters my nose with a single blow and for a moment, everything goes black. All I can hear is an echoing ring, like a pin falling in otherwise absolute silence.

I open my eyes and my vision is fuzzy. Blood is gushing out of my nose, into my eyes and all over my clothes. I want to scream out but I can't find the air.

"I'll never get to see her again! I'm going to be trapped in that apartment for the rest of my life!"

He howls in rage as he punches the wall. The punch bloodies his knuckles, and seems to calm him. He rubs his face. I see flickering images of him pacing around for I don't know how long. He mutters to himself. I can't hear what he mutters, but he finally sighs, lets his shoulders hang, and comes over to help me up. I lean against the car, clutching my ribs and doing my best to catch my breath. Franz pulls out his deck of cigarettes, puts one between my cut up lips and lights it, then lights one for himself.

He looks at me calmly, tilts his head back to exhale, and asks:

"Why did you bet black, Marcus?"

The cigarette hangs in my mouth more thanks to the sticky blood than the effort of my lips, and I can hardly pull on it. He slaps me softly in the face once or twice.

"Answer the question, Marcus."

He says this with a calmness that frightens me, and I gasp:

"I don't know."

Franz sighs and looks me dead in the eyes with the icy cool of a madman.

"I'll tell you why you bet black."

He slaps me in the face again.

"You ready? You bet black because humans don't run on systems or algorithms, kid, they run on hormones and sensations and spontaneous thoughts. And above all else, they run on emotion."

I stare at him as he leans on the support beam, the second to the left of the entrance, and I watch him smoke his cigarette. I feel that I'll black out from the pain in my nose any minute, but something in Franz's stare forbids it. He looks me in the face, angry but calculating, dejected but accepting of his fate, and his eyes narrow as he hatches an idea.

"Three hours in there and you go and bet black. Jesus."

He screams out into the empty echoing garage and I wince, anticipating more pain.

"But you and I will make this right. You and I", he pauses, pointing at me threateningly, "will make this right."

I cough up some blood into my hand.

"You and I will make this right, understood?"

I nod meekly.

"I said understood?"

He grabs me by the collar. I gasp, desperate not to be hit again.

"Yes."

"The gravy train comes by but every once in a little while, Marcus. Til it swings by again, it'll be the quiet desperation and suffering as usual. Now buck up, you need to drive us home."

He smiles and casually puts out his cigarette against the concrete beam. He walks back over toward me with a smile and slaps me in the face again, before opening the passenger side door and getting in the car. Franz's sudden change in demeanor might have worried me more if I wasn't so preoccupied with the agonizing pain shooting through my face and torso. I lean on the car and take a long haul of the cigarette to regain some composure. I'm intent on finishing the rest of the cigarette to calm myself and steady my shaking hands enough to drive. Franz, however, begins honking the car horn impatiently, so I put it out and get in the car. My eyes are smarting and the blood all over my face is drying, making it incredibly difficult for me to see.

"Take your shirt off and clean some of that blood up."

I pull out of the parking garage and get onto the one-lane bridge off Île Notre Dame. I'm going about half the speed limit, driving cautiously. My mind is in a whirl, but I cram all my thoughts to the periphery and focus simply on the road just in front of me. My vision is still fuzzy from the involuntary tears sprinkling from my eyes and tickling my cheek in a slow trickle mingled with blood.

There is the boatyard to my right. In the distance I see a scraggly barren tree on the side of the road, casting nightshade by a snowcapped three window gray vinyl shed, and I think to myself that all that is missing from this scene are feminine screams of agony.

"Speed up a little, would you?"

Franz's complaint snaps me back and I realize, looking through the rearview mirror, that there are three or four cars behind me honking for me to accelerate to the speed limit. I try to open my window to flip them off but the button doesn't work.

The button not working and my shitty old car infuriate me and I click the button compulsively, click the button and click the button and the futility reminds me, keeps me thinking about the lost money, and what it would have meant and all the potential I have squandered and all the possibility and I could have left the city and I could have made something of myself and I could have maybe just maybe been happy? Franz is silent, thinking, smoking a cigarette with his window open and with that angry look still on his face and I hate him in this moment and I wish I could slit his throat who the does he think he is attacking me like that and the button still won't open the bloody window and I'm going to lose my mind if those motherfuckers behind me don't stop fucking honking and my jaw aches and I think a tooth is loose and to hell with Franz I want to hit him in that ugly mug of his I want to see his blood and I could have shown them all with that money my mother and my father and all those idiots and it's stuffy in this damn car and I need to crack a window and now it's snowing and if this honking doesn't stop I swear to God...

Everything goes black as I slam the brakes in the middle of the street, causing the car behind me to rear-end me. Franz drops his cigarette and swears. He burns his leg as he is jerked forward.

"What the hell is wrong with you?"

A sudden burst of energy numbs the pain. I get out of the car and the guy behind me screams through his driver's window:

"Are you insane, you idiot?"

He says this before he catches sight of the crazed look in my face and the blood all over me. I rush his car, shirtless in the snowfall, and start kicking it and slapping his windshield. He closes his window with a frightened look on his face and I go back to my car to get the shovel in the back seat. Franz gets out of the car and screams at me:

"Marcus, what the hell are you doing? Get back in the car!"

I bring the shovel down with full force on the windshield and again and again and again until it cracks. The guy in the car starts honking again and my anger reaches a new level. I pull the switchblade out from my back pocket stick it in his driver's side tire, flattening it. He puts his car in reverse and floors it, with my switchblade still plunged in the tire, smashing the car behind him, and all of them suddenly circumventing my car with the opposite direction lane and driving away in a maddened hurry. Franz is running his hands through his hair and screaming at me:

"Are you insane? Are you insane?"

I exhale all of my angry demons and turn to look at Franz with a calm, patient smile.

And there are sirens eventually, but by then the cold really numbs the pain.

And yes, yes, I know there will be consequences, but I simply do not care.

'Marcus the Destroyer'

Franz was an extreme man. He lived an extreme life, and never found balance. His entire life unfolded like an adrenaline-fuelled roller-coaster ride seesawing between extreme highs and extreme lows. The deepest valley is measured only in contrast to the highest peak, and Franz knew how thin the air was up high, and how thick down low. He had fallen from life changing heights. Perhaps I am making excuses for him, I don't know. He was remarkable in that way. It struck me as remarkable that this man was still alive. It struck me as remarkable that this man was still striving after such staggering abject failure.

But things must eventually take their toll.

No man can escape the burden of his past, no matter how desperately he runs.

This became evident to me in the way Franz's emotions oscillated after the casino business. I imagined that throughout his life his emotions had oscillated as violently as his finances. But then, I don't think he was remarkable in that regard.

Money keeps a man level.

Franz had possessed it. He had lived the leisurely whimsical life of the rich.

And he had lost it. He had fallen from those heights to the mundane struggle of the poor.

He lingered there, perhaps in guilt, perhaps in repentance, perhaps simply paralyzed by circumstance. But his desire had yet been dormant, not destroyed.

He wanted.

He wanted very deeply, as it turned out. He admitted this to himself wholeheartedly while we were at the casino. He was alive again, as he put it, striving. That realization, the acceptance of the fact, the admission of desire reopened a door he could not close. Not again. 'There is no nobility in poverty, there is only desperation', or so he would say. Our loss was the straw that broke the camel's back. All that stuff we had discussed, about the chosen ones, about the wheel of fate selecting its winners, about abundance coming to the abundant, it had all proved to be false, or then, Franz and I simply didn't turn out to be the chosen ones we thought we were, or ought to be.

It's painful recollecting that day, sure. But that, too, is a crucial part of the healing process. Or so the doctors say. Admitting and coming to terms with the violence and injustice of the world is part of the healing process. Seeing things as they are, no matter how painful. Accepting things as they are, though always shining a positive light. Find the silver lining, despite everything.

I struggled with that last part.

Acceptance and repentance are necessary to bring clarity and peace of mind.

Fine.

I accept, but I do not know that I repent.

I still struggle to locate the silver lining in what happened to Franz.

***

The road rage incident after the casino washes over pretty quickly. Franz and I are taken in and held at the police station overnight. They ask me a lot of questions about my bloody face, and I think they understand that Franz has inflicted the damage. It may show on his knuckles. The context seems pretty obvious to me.

I tell the truth.

A very serious looking detective with a dark complexion and a shining bald crane questions me. He has a notepad out and everything. I tell him we suffered a loss at the casino that led to a little scuffle, and no I most certainly do not want to press charges. It ends there.

The driver whose tire I flattened does not want to press charges either. He called the police, but didn't leave any personal information, and didn't show up at the station. I suppose the crazed look in my eye dissuaded him. We are processed and released within the day.

And so we move on.

Neither of us really wants to talk about it, so we don't. Besides, there isn't really much to say. I don't expect Franz to apologize, and I don't want Franz to apologize. And as for myself, I have nothing to apologize·for. We just drop it and act as if nothing happened.

Alas, I am jobless, and despite Franz's government cheques, we don't have much wiggle room financially. As things stand, we receive just enough for cigarettes, a couple cheap meals a day, and rent.

For the entire month after the altercation in the casino parking lot, I acquiesce to most everything Franz tells me to do. Not so much because I fear him, though I admit that I do, but also because I feel that beneath the fury of his punches I was made to understand just how much my irresponsibility had really cost him. I squandered what was probably his last chance. All I had to do was follow the system and we wouldn't be in this mess. All I had to do was bet red.

Franz is no longer a young man.

It's not like I'm not angry myself- I can't breathe through my nose for an entire month. I think several times about ambushing Franz, about cutting him with my blade in revenge, about drawing his blood. But every time I think better of it, because deep down I do believe him when he says that we still have a chance. I am angry, but I still trust Franz's intuition. I hate him, but he is crafty and he is going to get us out of this jam. We're still in the same car, though it has taken quite a bit of damage. We can still salvage things.

I smoke a lot these days, somehow even more than usual. I need help to keep myself level, to keep myself from exploding at Franz. I need to keep myself from going off the deep end.

And still, I feel I owe him a vague debt for having somehow altered his fate. I have driven him back into this all too familiar frenzy, and madness, and desperation. If I only listened, we wouldn't be in this mess. It's my fault we are poor. I drove us off the cliff. Or, at least to the precipice. It is my fault we were pushed to what we did next.

It is my fault.

Our only scrap of hope for the whole month after the casino is this: Franz has a plan.

I hear about the plan piecemeal. The first piece comes very shortly after we're released. Maybe two weeks later.

It's a warm March this year; every day is a few degrees above freezing. We are living in pretty extreme poverty. The desperation is becoming too much to bear, and I am on the verge of giving up, and just getting a job. But then, Franz's plan convinces me not to.

One day, Franz approaches me. He approaches me as a general might approach a subordinate, and he lays down the rules. After a couple of motionless weeks on the couch, the twinkle in his eye has returned. It is time. He is calling on me to undo my wrong. He knows the way to get us back on track. The first detail he insists on strikes me as arbitrary. He is insistent that we need suits for the job. It is his reasoning that suits will give us a more clinical and professional look, and thus we will be more intimidating. This will help us to receive greater cooperation from the bystanders, and reduce the negotiating time with the clerks. I suppose that reasoning makes sense. The way he sees it, we need to be in and out in less than ten minutes if we have any chance of success.

Next, he tells me about the place. The place he chooses is the LCBO in Hawkesbury. The LCBO is the Liquor Control Board of Ontario, the crown corporation responsible for the sale of alcohol in the province of Ontario. It is the equivalent of the Société des Alcools du Québec, or the SAQ, the governmental body that runs liquor stores in the province of Québec. Franz says our odds are better over provincial lines though- something about jurisdictions and a buffer zone. He tells me I just need to trust him in these matters. So it is the LCBO.

He speaks of the details of the plan as though he has already worked everything out. He lays out precision details as though he has already executed a plan of this kind, perhaps this exact plan in the past. He has descriptions, numbers, addresses that are startlingly precise. I do not ask questions that I feel Franz does not want to answer. I do not ask questions that I feel are irrelevant.

His plan strikes me as slightly foolish, but then so did the gambling, and it nearly worked. His confidence is imperative, and his temperament is the same ice cold it was in the casino.

I've seen what he can do when he puts his mind to it. His temperament when he explains the elements of the plan, the coolness in his eyes, the steadiness of his jaw, the crispness of his words, the power of his stance… they all silence my doubts and make me feel that we can pull it off. The plan is plausible, though barely.

The most important thing, and Franz stresses this over and over again, is to *remain calm and composed throughout.*

We will wear pantyhose over our faces to prevent identification. We will bleach our hair with peroxide. We will raise our guns, and scream out: "This is a heist!"

I am to calmly round the clientele into a corner of the liquor store. Franz will handle the cash registers. We will walk in with an empty duffel bag, and we will walk out with a full duffel bag and be on our way. In and out in less than ten minutes.

Franz supplies everything.

I try to stay out of the way.

It takes Franz a couple weeks to get his hands on everything we need. I think he began putting the wheels in motion the very afternoon we were released from holding. The whole thing comes together astonishingly fast.

Those two weeks he was lying on the couch smoking cigarettes, staring out the patio door, I thought he was brooding. I thought he was coming to terms with things. It turns out he was scheming. I overheard a few strange phone calls but didn't think anything of them at the time. By the time I was in the know, the plan was already in motion.

Then one day, Franz says everything is finally worked out. We've got the outfits, a getaway car, and a driver. The location has been staked, and Franz has selected the day and time we will do it. He makes it all sound so simple. His certainty is very convincing.

The Hawkesbury LCBO is the best location because Franz is allegedly familiar with the surroundings. Also, it is far enough away that we will be able to escape the breadth of the investigation as we cross provincial lines. He picks a Tuesday afternoon just around dusk because he thinks it will be late enough in the day so that the cashes might be full, but that the store will be mostly empty at an off-peak hour. We will probably make out with less money than if we'd come in just before closing, but the risk of things going wrong will be greatly reduced. Or so Franz claims. Franz has calculated that we will score between three and eight thousand dollars emptying the cash registers. The math behind that calculation he does not reveal. I do not ask any questions he does not want to answer, or that I deem irrelevant.

He says he knows eight thousand isn't enough to live, but that it will be another bankroll, and provide another opportunity to win big. 'Capital breeds capital', and this time he's sure to make it big because he will make sure that I don't ruin things for him.

I nod and smile in agreement, though I notice the barely contained, crazed urgency sounding through Franz's words. His excitement gushes through as he explains his designs, despite his best attempts to keep it drawn.

He is insane.

I see it in his eyes.

And I follow him without a word.

The day before the job, I wait at the apartment while he goes out to get the supplies. There is a lot going on out of sight, but again, I do not ask questions. I just hang around the apartment waiting, mostly. He leaves in the morning and returns the very night with two duffel bags. One has my supplies in it, and the other has his.

The sight of the duffel bags makes everything suddenly real to me, and I feel a surge of adrenaline as we unzip the bags.

We open them up on the coffee table, smoking cigarettes as we discuss the details of the job for the umpteenth time. The first thing I pull out of the bag is the suit. Franz's suit is gray-checkered flannel and mine is navy with a white pinstripe. I don't understand the need for such garish attire, but I keep quiet. Franz says we will wear sneakers with the suits, so that we don't risk tripping in dress shoes. This little detail makes sense to me. It seems to me a trick of experience, and reassures me that Franz knows what he is doing.

The next things we pull from the bags are the stockings for our faces, and the peroxide to bleach our hair.

At the bottom of the bag, I feel the cold touch of a steel barrel. I lift the gun from the bag to have a look at it, and I point it at Franz.

"Hey! Don't fool around with that thing, it's loaded!"

Franz pulls the gun from my hand and puts it in his own bag.

Again, I don't ask any questions. Franz has a connection, I'm sure, and I don't want to know any more. It is better for both of us if I don't.

"The guns I got us are black eight-millimeter pistols with a ten round cartridge. There's minimum recoil, so even a beginner can fire with relative ease. Just point decisively, and if you have to pull the trigger, you can be confident the gun will respond smoothly. The bullet will go exactly where you direct it."

I have never fired a gun before. I have never handled a

gun before. I have never seen a real gun before.

Franz assures me it is easy, handles the guns deftly.

"Just grip, point, and pull."

Franz repeats himself and mimes a demonstration, side faced and with an arm extended.

"The recoil on these small guns is minimal, trust me. Besides, we aren't going to be firing anyway, if all goes according to plan."

He winks and shows me the safety button.

"And it will go according to plan, Marcus. It'll be easy as pie, don't you worry."

Franz explains the getaway plan one more time. Franz has called in a friend who will drive us there and back for a ten percent stake in the job. Our getaway driver is Hector, Franz's burly Latino mechanic. He'll play the final role in the plan.

"Don't worry, I've done business with Hector before. He's trustworthy, and he can drive like a madman."

Franz is completely self-assured. He smiles at me and winks again, as he continues to play out the scene in the living room, waving his gun and laughing.

Hawkesbury is located on the border of Québec and Ontario, just across the Outaouais River. The LCBO is located on Main Street, just off Chenail Street, which turns into John Street, which turns into Maple Street as one crosses the *Rivière des Outaouais* back into Québec. The Ontario Provincial Police (OPP) has a station two blocks away from the LCBO, on Cartier Boulevard, and will be close at hand. There is no need to worry, though Franz stresses that *time is of the essence*.

IDLE HANDS

According to Franz, this particular LCBO is one of the older liquor stores in the province of Ontario and has not been fitted with a silent alarm trigger. I'm skeptical of this statement, but I am not asking questions. Franz seems incredibly sure of this. Besides, I have never been to Hawkesbury. What do I know?

This fact, that it has no silent alarm, means the only commotion we have to worry about is the outside world taking notice of us while we are working inside. According to Franz's calculations, we will have fifteen minutes inside the store before the police are certain to arrive. Franz says this gives us ample time to execute the heist. While the cashes are being emptied, in addition to rounding up the clientele and keeping them calm, I am to acquire a set of car keys from one of the patrons. Franz and I will then use these car keys to drive the stolen car a few blocks up Main Street to our rendezvous point with Hector behind the local hardware store- *Matériaux Laperrière*. When we get there, we will dump everything but the money into a dumpster. Then, we will douse the dumpster in gasoline, light it on fire, change into street clothes, and be off scot-free in Hector's innocuous eggplant minivan. Simple.

The day of the heist is Tuesday, March fifteenth.

We hit the road about two in the afternoon. It is about a forty-five minute drive to Hawkesbury.

Hector picks us up at the apartment. Hector doesn't speak much English, and keeps his eyes on the road ahead. He is plump and has a beard as thick as his Latino accent. He wears a plaid shirt with a trucker cap.

Franz and I bring our suits in the duffel bags. We change on the way over. I sit in the back seat of the minivan, and Hector drives with Franz in the passenger seat. The minivan is old and dusty- Hector uses it for moving materials and car pieces. There is a large white cross hanging from the rearview mirror.

In the mirror, I can see my reflection. My face has healed in the month or so since my altercation with Franz, though my nose is still sensitive and somewhat swollen. I still see red every time I blow my nose.

Hector is playing a mix cd. A 'Sublime' song is scratching through the old minivan's speakers. The quality is terrible. There is a lot of static- shifting volumes, frequencies, and sounds. They come together to form music only for a few seconds at a time.

"So what do we do when we get there?"

I spark a cigarette and check my watch. It's about two forty, and we've been on the road about half an hour. The sun is still bright in the sky.

"Hector will park the van at our meeting point down Main Street and we will walk over to the liquor store."

Franz lights a cigarette of his own and pulls a bottle of whiskey from his duffel bag.

"In these suits?"

"Yes in these suits."

"Isn't that a little suspicious?"

He pops the top off the bottle, and turns to shoot me an annoyed look.

"You know what your problem is? You ask too many questions."

He takes a swig of whiskey and offers me the bottle. I shake my head no and he shrugs. I smoke my cigarette, watching the white-capped trees and the snow covered plains beyond the dusty car window.

"Marcus, are you familiar with the story of Faust?"

Franz starts up again, filling the dead air. The radio is off- we got fed up of the scratching noises. Franz cracks a window and the sound of air seeping in and blowing through my hair rouses me from introspection and worry.

"No, Franz, I can't say that I am."

Franz looks surprised.

"A well-read guy like you? Well, in Germany, it's common folklore. Allow me to bring you up to speed."

Franz turns in his seat so that he can face both Hector and myself; though I am certain Hector is not listening to him. I smoke my cigarette and let the nicotine calm my nerves. I am very anxious today, and the cigarette helps to steady me. The armrest in the back seat has been stripped of its protective coating, and the jagged ends of plastic dig uncomfortably into my arm.

"Legend has it that Dr. Faust was a scholar, with a thirst for knowledge that drove him to read thousands and thousands of books, hardly ever leaving his study. And yet, after all his reading, and questioning, and posturing, and reflection, Faust was left dissatisfied because he could not find *truth*."

Franz shakes the bottle and I watch the brown liquid swish around in the sunlight. Franz smirks, enjoying the attention:

"And so the devil, sensing Faust's melancholy, pounces on him in his vulnerable state. The devil appears to Faust in the form of a squire, Mephistopheles, who offers Faust unlimited earthly knowledge for a period of twenty four years, in exchange for his soul for the rest of eternity, once the twenty four years are complete."

I raise an eyebrow and contemplate Franz's face. His eyes are filled with an excitement that ignores the significance of the drive. He seems somehow unbothered by where we are going, and what we will do there. It eludes him that our lives will very shortly be in danger. His whimsy, or maybe it is the whiskey that enables him to stay squarely in the moment and maintain a light stress-free ease... Whatever it is, his lightheartedness is infectious.

"So what happens to him?"

Franz smiles his bleached white smile, now matching his bleached blonde thinning old man's hair:

"Well, Faust takes the deal of course. I don't know that it would be much of a story otherwise."

I look Franz in the face as he sits there smiling at me. Though I try very hard, I'm unable to ignore the fact that in less than an hour we are going to improvise a liquor store robbery.

"I don't know if we should walk up the street in these suits. It's suspicious. And when are we going to slip on the pantyhose?"

Franz shakes his head.

"You miss the point entirely."

I lean forward and put my cigarette butt through the crack in the passenger window.

"I don't think I do, Franz. I think you should be a little more prepared with answers to these questions."

"The only thing I can tell you is not to overthink things. Look at it as a game, Marcus. It's very simple. Just don't be neurotic."

Franz's nonchalance irritates me. His stupid face is relaxed and calm as if everything, no matter how insane, is routine.

"Neurotic and cerebral are synonyms, Franz. I still don't think it's wise for us to walk around town in these suits. It draws attention. Not to mention our stupid surfer-boy hair."

Franz is annoyed.

"You are unbelievable kid. Even with a broken nose, you can sniff out weaknesses like a bloodhound. You know, you would have made a good boxer. Find out where your opponent's weakness is, and bludgeon him. It's a mental exercise more than a physical one. Find the weak spot in a structure and take your sickle to it mercilessly until it all topples down. You love that, don't you kid? Wherever there's a weakness you're hovering with your sickle. Marcus the destroyer, hovering with his sickle."

Franz chuckles and slaps Hector in the arm. Hector laughs in chorus, though I'm sure he has no idea what we're talking about.

"Marcus! There will be weaknesses in every structure. Marcus! We are not gods Marcus, but *men*!"

Franz flexes his bicep, taking a swig of the bottle with the other arm.

"Instead of bringing everything man made crumbling down, instead of always hanging your head low, or raising that broken nose of yours to the folly of man, why don't you build something for once in your life? Why don't you *try*? Take a shot! Failure is not the worst thing that can happen to you, take it from me!"

He takes another swig of the bottle and tosses his cigarette, before shaking all over and slapping himself in the face a few times. Then, with eyes wide open, he holds his hand out, looking me straight in the eyes:

"Seize this opportunity with me, my son, and I shall fulfill all your wildest dreams."

Franz looks back at me with wide eyes and an outstretched arm. With a smirk, I reach for his hand and he smiles. He shakes it firmly. His hands are warm. I yank the bottle out of his lap and take a swig of my own, figuring I could use some loosening up.

Looking out the dusty window, my mind flitters to Joanie and the way she smiles and it somehow comforts me and makes me feel better. I hand Franz the bottle and he takes another swig.

"Easy on the juice Franz."

"Three swigs Marcus, that's the recipe for success! And one more for good measure!"

He takes another swig from the bottle and I yank it from his hands. Franz is smiling like a madman.

"I think I'm going to give that Joanie girl a call after we pull this off."

"Aghhh! Stay away from women Marcus. You're too young for that. Women, they'll just set your soul on fire. Men, we're all masochists and we think that fire is love, but it's not kid! It's just fire."

I laugh at Franz's slurred rant and he goes on:

"What's more kid, the past is better than the present! You know why? Because it's free! Mankind is a fool for novelty. The archives of information we already possess are endless. Like a needle in the groove of a record, the sheep get trapped in these notions of modern trends and cannot travel to a headspace beyond what is at the forefront of the public eye. It's sickening."

Franz waves his arms emphatically as he conducts his irrelevant rants. I laugh some more at Franz's misplaced passion, watching the trees go by outside the window, and the pastures of farmlands and far-off silos and wooden fences three feet high. I take a second and last swig of the bottle. The sky is blue and there is scarcely a cloud in the sky and I feel fantastic and confident, and ready to redeem myself and move forward into the unknown.

"Five minutes."

Hector speaks up over the radio, now spitting some syncopated Hispanic dance music.

The wind still seeping in through the window is mild. The howling winds of winter have gone, and have been replaced with the soft cleansing winds of spring. The winds of spring are the winds of growth, of *renouvellement*.

We passed the provincial lines a while back, and are now crossing the bridge into Hawkesbury. The sky is a beautiful blue and the sun is full, and strong, and shines down, shimmering on the melting ice and flowing water of the Outaouais River.

There are craggy barren trees and resilient pines on both sides of us as we pass a cluster of small houses in the wooded area on the outskirts of the town. Hector drives on quietly, past the 'warm welcome' of the Hawkesbury town limits, population ten thousand eight hundred and seventy. There are tool warehouses, and used car lots, and a man driving an old convertible though the weather hovers but a few degrees above freezing.

I see an old barbershop, 'Barbier Simon', with one of those red and blue perpetually spinning poles, and a run down radio station, 'The Jewel', beside a puppy mill. And as we pass the center of the town I see the green patina of a gray stone church, and the town's catholic high school with its giant wooden cross jutting from the lawn just adjacent. Hector drives on, and I take in the sights of the town's Main Street, sprinkled on both sides with various mom and pop businesses that embody the heart and soul of the little town.

Up Main Street, we pass the LCBO. I watch it come and go intently. It has a lit up green sign out front, back dropped by little purple grapevines, and looks to be pretty active. It is located in a strip mall, on a major intersection of Main Street. It has a large gravel parking lot out front, full of cars.

I light a cigarette and inhale long and hard, pressing down on the nausea and nerves rising from my stomach. I look in the rearview mirror once again at my broken face and bleached blonde hair, and I feel incredibly self-conscious of the way I look. The navy pinstripe suit is just the cherry on top. I check my watch and see that it is just past three in the afternoon.

"Franz, isn't it still too early? The place looks very busy."

My nerves betray me, and Franz laughs and slaps Hector's arm. Hector laughs on cue.

"Looks a little spiffier than the last time, doesn't it Hector?"

He and Hector laugh again.

"But then, we look a little spiffier too."

Franz opens the passenger side mirror and plays with his hair, appraising the way he looks in his suit. He pulls his lapels and nods, liking what he sees. Then, addressing me:

"Yes little one, fret not. Hector's going to park at the spot and we're going to grab a bite to eat until the sun is about to set. I don't know about you but I am starving."

He looks back at me but I don't say a word.

"We eat. Then we make our move. *Capiche?*"

I nod.

I smoke my cigarette carefully, trying not to get any ash on my cheap suit as Hector parks in the gravel lot behind the hardware store. The hardware store is, by my estimation, about a fifteen-minute walk from the liquor store.

We step out and walk down Main Street, a burly Latino in plaid and two city slickers in over-the-top suits. We draw several strange looks and I feel absolutely ridiculous. Franz is even shamelessly wearing knock-off designer sunglasses. It's all too much.

There are several people riding bicycles, and I can overhear chatter in both English and French. I wonder about life in this town and the culture here. It is located just on the border of French-speaking and English-speaking provinces.

I can feel the gravel crunch beneath my sneakers and it makes me all the more aware that we stick out like sore thumbs. Little streams of water run through the street- the runoff from the slowly melting snow. A few kids are laughing and screaming, running around a slowly melting snowman. The snowman looks grotesque, as his head has melted to half the size it should be, and he's lost an eye in the process.

We continue to walk until we are about a block from the liquor store when Franz decides suddenly on a Chinese buffet.

We follow him up the stairs and a chime rings as we enter the restaurant. Franz sizes the place up before leading us to a table by the wall. It is a small restaurant, fitted with maybe twenty or so mahogany-stained tables. The place is empty but for a plump middle-aged Caucasian woman sitting behind the bar at the back of the restaurant, figuring some paperwork with a calculator. Hector and I follow Franz to the table he chooses, by the wood-paneled median separating the green-carpeted dining room from the steel-heated buffet line. The woman comes over and greets us in French, pouring us glasses of ice water and quickly wishing us *Bon Appétit* before returning to her paperwork.

The buffet looks as though it has just been laid out, and has all the regular North American 'Chinese' foods: doughy hydrogenated fried meats in sweet sugary sauces, fried potatoes, fried shrimp, fried rice, fried eggrolls. Franz and Hector fill their plates nearly to the brim, but my stomach is uneasy, and though I am hungry I decide on just a small portion of fried rice.

Franz and Hector stuff their faces and make dirty jokes in a coarse cross between English and Hispanic profanity.

The restaurant is decorated with long red plastic dragons hanging from the ceiling. The walls are painted a dated vintage yellow, with a mahogany wood paneling half the way up. There is a giant fan hanging on the restaurant's back wall, depicting a geisha coyly covering her face with a fan. The bar in the back is sheltered under a *faux toît chinois* protruding from the wall, under which hangs a rack of opaque water stained wine glasses. I imagine those glasses must have been here since the restaurant's opening. The proprietor looks up from her calculator every now and again, scrutinizing us as I scrutinize her restaurant, her only patrons in corny suits and bleached blonde hair.

"What do you think, Marcus?"

Franz's voice brings me back to the table, to my plate of rice, to the place mats depicting the various animals of the Chinese New Year.

"I think this restaurant looks like a front."

Franz erupts into laughter, revealing the doughy half-chewed General Tao in his mouth. Hector laughs too, imitating Franz. An aproned oriental man comes out of the kitchen and argues with the proprietor in a heavily accented English. He's screaming something about the proper water content of the

'Kaizen Soup'.

"Seriously though, you agree with me, don't you? This place is totally a hick town. Hector says he's seen worse, but this place is a total dump."

I start laughing myself, and Hector follows suit. Franz pulls a flask from his breast pocket and takes a swig, passing it over to me.

"I'm telling you, kid, this is one of those places you see on dateline every now and again. Messed up people live in this town."

I nearly spit out the whiskey. The three of us sit there laughing a while as the owner wraps up her discussion with the oriental chef. The door chimes ring, announcing the arrival of new diners, and the three of us turn to have a look.

A husky, stern, grizzled man in paint-stained denim overalls walks in, followed by a morbid-looking obese woman in a yellow sweater. They waddle over to a table by the door, and Franz exclaims:

"Taxi!"

The juvenile outburst creates raucous laughter at our table, though the other patrons pretend not to have heard. I turn to have a look at them and I notice the man in overalls staring menacingly at Franz, who amusedly stares back. And the contrast between the overalls and Franz's silly suit and over-the-top glasses makes me laugh even harder.

Franz and Hector fill their plates again, and Franz starts up again:

"What is it with the Chinese and their damn symbols? Why the hell does that culture get a monopoly on the symbol industry? What the hell makes them so wise? Monkey, pig, dragon. What gives?"

I laugh some more. Franz is really on a roll now.

"And fortune cookies, what a crock!"

I actually enjoy fortune cookies...

"Oh that reminds me, I want to grab a few before we go."

I get up and realize I'm a little woozy. I walk over to the buffet and grab a handful of cookies for the table. I pass beside the obese woman lifting heaps of food onto her plate. I return to the table and drop the cookies in the center, keeping three for myself.

"You're only supposed to get one fortune kid, or it doesn't come true."

Franz's cackling is the only sound but the muffled sounds of chewing, and the occasional cling of silverware.

I crack open the first cookie, and it reads: 'Keep your eyes open and take advantage of the unexpected'. I eat the cookie as Franz and Hector read their fortunes aloud. I crack another and it reads: 'Muddied are the waters of indecision'. I crack the third one and it's empty.

"Let's pay the bill and get on with it. I can't stand to be in this hick town any longer."

Franz is still staring down at the overall man, who doesn't back down.

"C'mon Franz, don't be so cynical. Don't generalize like that, it's not fair. You don't even know the guy."

"Generalities are intellectually necessary evils. And I hate hicks."

Franz puts enough money on the table to cover the bill. We rise to leave, and I watch with uninhibited disgust as the woman in the yellow sweater waddles to the buffet, already filling her third or fourth plate.

Outside in the fresh air, I light a cigarette and watch the clouds dissipate in the now mauve and cobalt sky. I check my watch and see that it is nearly five o'clock.

It dawns on me that the time to act is now.

Despite the light air in the restaurant, the three of us sense the seriousness of the moment and grow solemn. Franz and I shake hands with Hector and go opposite ways. We walk over to the liquor store in silence, through the gravel parking lot all the way up to the automatic glass doors before Franz stops. He puts down the duffel bag containing the guns and stockings. The parking area is a lot less crowded, and I can see through the glass doors that there aren't more than a dozen people inside.

"Don't forget: scream loud, make them feel the gravity in your voice. Project! And get a set of car keys nice and early. We'll be out of here in no time."

Franz burps and jabs me amicably in the arm. We slip on the pantyhose, and he hands me my gun.

"Ready?"

I catch a glimpse of my reflection in the display window and I think I am going to vomit.

"Marcus, you ready?"

I see my face, and everything now tinted black with the stocking on my head, and I wonder, for just a split second, how I got here.

"Yeah."

"Let's go."

Franz and I rush in through the glass doors and Franz pistol-whips the poor sap unlucky enough to be standing by the entrance. He crumples to the floor bleeding as Franz raises his gun to the sky, screaming:

"THIS IS A HOLDUP, EVERYONE ON THE GROUND. DON'T MAKE ME SAY IT TWICE."

Cries around the store as the patrons crouch to their knees and hide behind the aisles. The store is bright, and large, and has about twenty wooden aisles of assorted spirits. There are more people than I expected there to be, though most are now on the ground and seem ready to cooperate.

Franz rushes straight for the cash registers and begins yelling at the cashiers and I realize I am on my own. My ears are ringing and the adrenaline is astounding and I am standing there with both hands on the pistol, pointing at no one and nothing in particular.

"Everyone in the back, by the wine bottles, now."

I say this aloud but the ringing in my ears is so loud that I can't hear my own voice.

No one moves, and all keep their eyes on Franz. It's like I'm not even here. I can slip away quietly if I really want to…

"I SAID, EVERYONE IN THE BACK BY THE WINE BOTTLES. NOW!"

The patrons suddenly spring into motion, and I lead them with pointed gun to the back of the store. Every muscle in my body is clenched and I am sweating profusely beneath the stocking. The lights of the store blare down on me, and I feel exposed, though I know I am safe beneath the black tint of the stocking. The ticking seconds are slowed, and I can hear my own breathing.

"EVERYONE ON THEIR KNEES WITH THEIR HANDS WHERE I CAN SEE THEM. ANY MONKEY BUSINESS AND I WILL NOT HESITATE TO SHOOT."

The patrons whimper, but follow orders. There are about fifteen or so middle-aged townspeople innocently coming to restock the liquor cabinet after a hard day's work. I've lined them up by the Italian wines section, in an alcove at the back of the store. Taking my bearings, I notice the exit sign nearby. The door leads to the storage area back store, and just beyond are the doors to the outside world.

The store has wood detailing and looks rustic, though it is evidently a modern store. It occurs to me that there likely *is* a silent alarm in here, and the realization sends a spurt of adrenaline out to my extremities. I can see the fear in the townspeople's' faces, though they mostly stare at the ground, not daring to look at me. I can hear Franz in the background, screaming even louder than I was, terrorizing the cashiers with constant threats.

"HOW WE COMING ALONG?"

"ALMOST THERE, DID YOU GET THE KEYS?"

Franz calls over to me and I realize I had forgotten the keys.

"YOU! YA YOU WITH THE GREEN SWEATER-VEST! GIVE ME YOUR CAR KEYS. NOW!"

I point the gun menacingly at an old man and he slowly reaches with trembling hands into his back pocket for the keys, and whimpers as he throws them over. I reach down, jumpy as all hell and with eyes staying squarely on the lot of them, and I feel for the keys, drop them, and pick them up again.

"GOT THEM."

"GOOD. THE BAG IS FULL. I'M TOSSING IT OVER TO YOU NOW, THEN WE HEAD OUT THE BACK DOOR."

I hear Franz toss the bag over to me, and feel it hit the heel of my foot. I know the job is nearly done, and my tightened muscles ease up just a little.

The front door chime goes off.

Everything tightens tenfold as I turn to look, and recognize the paint-stained overalls and giant yellow sweater from the restaurant. Franz pounces on them, pointing the gun and screaming at them to get on their knees.

"You son of a bitch!"

The old man is giving Franz a hard time. They have walked into a heist and given their physical state, they have no chance of turning and running away. My body turns to concrete as I watch the bearded laborer plead with Franz, with his hands raised, but Franz won't let them leave.

"My wife has a back condition, she needs to stay upright. We won't say a damn thing. Just let us go."

"DOWN! NOW!"

Franz's crazed voice resonates above the bawling and cries of the obese woman. Nearly everyone in the store is crying. The husband has eased up a bit, and now pleads with Franz.

"Please, you need to understand, she cannot get in that position, she has to keep her spine upright. Please."

"LISTEN TO ME YOU STUPID HICK, TELL YOUR WIFE TO GET DOWN NOW OR I'LL SHOOT THE BITCH."

"Okay, please, just stay calm, there's no reason."

The woman bawls louder as Franz's patience wears thin, and I just stand there, jerking back and forth, panic-stricken and dumb.

"THIS IS YOUR LAST CHANCE!"

The woman whimpers again and clutches her face, though neither of them gets on the ground. And then in a flash: a single bullet cracks from the barrel of Franz's gun.

The obese woman cries out, then crumples like a sack of potatoes clutching her stomach. The old man's face widens in shock, and terror, and...

"LET'S GO!"

Franz frantically turns in my direction and aggressively swings his arms toward the back of the store, indicating that we should go.

I can't really move, though.

Time slows as I take it all in.

I watch through the black tint as the lady clutches her stomach, and the blood just *pours* out of her onto the vinyl floor. It is the first time I have ever witnessed death. It is surprisingly matter of fact. She will die, I know. Her fluids are gushing from her. It looks like she'll be depleted very soon. How much blood can there be in a human being? Her yelps will stop soon. And then, silence.

Franz showed no mercy. He took her life on a whim.

And now she's gone to silence. Oblivion is opening its gaping mouth and swallowing her whole. I can see it happening, but nothing has changed.

I see her husband, all in a flash, with white-hot hatred in his eyes, perhaps a tear, he is a little too far to distinguish tear from sweat and blood, drawing from a concealed holster a shining silver revolver. Franz has his back turned to him and is moving toward me. The sound of the tiny, but powerful explosion resonates throughout the entire universe in that split second. Franz is mid-stride when the slug makes contact, and he topples face first to the ground.

He seems lifeless even before he hits the floor. I say this because of the way he falls. He falls like an inanimate lump of mass, and makes no effort to break the impact.

Franz's head ricochets off the floor, once, twice, and does not move again. All force just leaves his body. It just lays there, a motionless heap of matter that used to be Franz. The crimson pool forms quickly, as quickly as the woman's, and looks very much the same. I can't see his face, and it bothers me. I wonder if his face has slackened, or if his teeth were still grit in the moment of death.

The reflection is cut short by a projectile whizzing by me, just over my right shoulder, exploding a bottle of wine just behind me. The scarlet wine falls to the floor and mixes with the crimson blood, staining the tableau. I can't tell the difference between the blood and the wine. I look up to the sight of the old man still clenching his revolver. He's poised to fire again in my direction.

I grab the bag lying just by my foot and run mightily into the back store, and out the back door into the fading daylight. The back of the store has a gravel pathway about three feet wide that runs parallel with Main Street. And the gravel on the pavement feels the same as it did earlier beneath my shoe soles. I stand there a while, paralyzed by all I have just witnessed, seemingly unable to control my body. I don't know how long I stand there sweating, but I'm roused from my reverie by the loud crack of a gunshot, and shortly thereafter, the sound of sirens in the distance.

A sudden arm on my shoulder makes me jump:

"MARCUS!"

My eyes refocus and I turn to see Franz, still black tinted by the stocking on my head. He limped through the back door, followed by a trail of blood and clutching his abdomen.

The sirens are growing louder in their approach, and they sharpen my senses with the promise of long, long sentence if I don't get out of here now.

Franz pants, and gasps:

"Marcus, I killed the bastard. I can't walk, you need to carry me to the car."

And Franz stretches his arm out and it shakes and I can see his fatigue. It is the fatigue of the old and weary. It is the fatigue of the battered, beaten, and dejected. It is the fatigue of those who have lived too long, and accomplished too little.

"Quick, let me hop on your shoulders! Agh."

He groans and clutches his lower back, though he stands hunched over and blood still trickles down his coattails.

I look at the bag full of money, and then I look again at Franz.

Though I can't see his face, his body language is feeble. I realize that this is his most vulnerable moment. In fact, this is the only time I have ever seen Franz vulnerable at all. He leans on the open backdoor, waiting for me to help him to freedom.

He reaches out a hand again, and I can hear the sirens closer than ever. It sounds as though they will pull into the parking lot of the LCBO any second.

So I pull the switchblade from my back pocket. Franz has his head down, and with his breathing growing heavier I open the blade and plunge it deep into Franz's gunshot wound. I turn the blade inside, and open him up further until he is out of his misery.

His eyes open wide beneath the stocking. I can tell from the contours of his face up close. My free arm clutches his gun-wielding arm and escorts him gently to the ground. My eyes stay with his through the stockings, his escorts to the eternal slumber of the afterlife. He whimpers, and groans, and then silence. The last sound he makes is the thump of his limp body against the gravel. The blood continues to pour out of him from the open wound.

I wish I could stay here a while, but the sirens have arrived. I wish I could stay here a while, and see them find Franz. I wish I could see them bring Franz to the morgue and try to identify him. I wish I could know who they'd call, once they figured who Franz is, or was.

I wonder if they'd maybe call Mina.

I shed my clothing as I run, ears ringing, but I have the presence of mind to hold on to the gun and the blade. The run is swift, I believe, those few moments really are a blur, and I arrive at the car alone, in my underwear, with the heavy duffel bag in my left hand.

"GO, GO!"

Hector looks at me dumbly, but he's very relaxed.

"Franz?"

"MUERTE, GO!"

"Oh."

There is a little sadness in Hector's reception, just enough for

me to notice. He shifts the car calmly into gear and hits the
road.

The tires screech on the pavement and we are soon over
the bridge, though Hector follows the speed limits and falls into
line, once we are safe beyond a reasonable doubt.

'Sign Here'

Never mind the past. The beauty of youth is in the way it recovers more quickly than old age. Youth bounces back. Youth is firm and soft. It does not sag, droop, or linger. It does not fester, or chafe. It slips away unscathed, and it retains its novelty.

I'll stop thinking of him eventually.

There was nothing I could do. The choice was not mine. He put me in a situation that could not have yielded any other outcome. I still have a whole life yet to live. I am still young.

Franz clearly had a death wish. It does not mean that I must have a death wish.

I am still young. I want things. Maybe I will warm to the idea of a sweet girl, a suburban house, little tikes, and a dog. I am still young. Everything is still possible.

But then, what is youth?

Youth is infinite.

Youth cannot fathom time and space and has not yet been touched by the all-penetrating hand of decay.

Idealism blooms in this ideal state, where death is but an idea- not to be feared, but mocked.

Youth is not ignorance.

Youth is freedom from the shackles of cynicism we call wisdom, the quantification of life we call reason, and the foolish self-delusion of certainty we call knowledge. Youth is new and novel and sweet and unassuming! Only from this unassuming can one be open, and only in being open can one find love.

I can still find love.

Youth… must be… is… love…

Youth is forgetfulness.

My youth will help me to forget.

***

I call Joanie, after our encounter at the casino. We talk a long while over the phone, catch up, and she agrees to see me. I don't tell her anything about Franz. She thinks I work at a bank.

We set up a date for a Friday night. I pick out a bar with dim lighting. I'm counting on the alcohol to help us along, though not in copious amounts.

Everything in moderation!

It may be a slightly uncomfortable conversation. We haven't spoken face to face since…

We meet at the bar. It's an old-time bar with bogus bird heads hanging from the walls. There are several different exotic species of birds staring down at us as we sit.

It is dim in here, and there is a live band playing at the far end of the room, on a small, elevated stage. They're playing some poppy music that involves banjos. They're doing a cover of that song: *You can get addicted to a certain kind of sadness…*

We sit at a table made of wood. It's naked oak, to be exact.

Joanie orders white wine and I order a whiskey, neat.

I dress up real nice for the occasion. I'm wearing a nice button up shirt in a very neutral green, and my cleanest pair of blue jeans. These jeans don't have any holes in them.

I have a little bit of money now, for new clothes. It feels really, really good having money for clothes. Joanie wears a black cotton long sleeve sweater with a plunging neckline, though she covers up with a sophisticated red silk shawl.

We sit there for a while, and neither of us really speaks. I'm still a little on edge, to be perfectly honest. We make piecemeal small talk though, waiting for the liquor to arrive and loosen us up. We take in our surroundings, and the band playing. Careful smiles are etched on our lips.

The waiter brings the drinks.

Her lips are rouged, thin, soft looking. Her hair is straightened, glossy, sleek, sheen, long, and dangerous. She looks very mature. She looks very pretty. She looks young enough to be carefree, but old enough to have a sense of direction. She's finishing up her degree this spring- in a few weeks, as a matter of fact.

"So Marcus, I realize I've never asked you, what *are* your ambitions?"

She plays her part well, leading the conversation into the desert of adulthood. Something about her seems different, seems changed. Something inexplicable makes her seem so suddenly *engaged*.

She's starting to look ahead.

"I've decided to immerse myself in my job at the bank and climb the corporate ladder. Financial stability and the eventual reward of retirement are my primary ambitions."

I lie the cardboard lie monotonously. I want to sleep with her and to win the lottery.

Though perhaps a change *has* inevitably begun to take place in me. I want to forget the past. I want to live my life looking toward the future. I want to take steps forward.

I genuinely do *want to want* the things I *should want*.

She looks me in the eyes, searching them though I remain protected by the dim, and her expression softens. She loosens the shawl around her shoulders, revealing a small amount of cleavage, and leans forward. I can feel her energy drawing me in.

"I think those are excellent ambitions. You could do it, Marcus, I believe in you."

She smiles and touches my hand.

The touch sharpens my senses and fills my mind with a vague, unaccountable, overwhelming desire to satisfy her.

I want her to be proud of me. She could help me to forget.

I want her to smile the smile that she's smiling right now. I want her to smile that smile again and again. I want the smile of acceptance to shine down on me. I want to be uplifted by her acceptance. It can help me to forget.

I want to be *normal*. She can help me to be normal.

"Thanks, Joanie. What about you?"

She smiles her brilliant smile and I feel lighter in my chair. The room is dark but her smile brightens it a little. I stare into her brown irises and search for the contours. The band stops playing and the air is filled only with the sounds of muffled chatter, and glasses clinking. She moves her head forward in a downward motion and flips her hair forward, spreading it from a unified entity into individual strands, and then flips it back again and runs her slender fingers through it.

"I think when I finish school I want to teach little kids. Or work with them in some way…"

She smiles again and my buttocks lift entirely off the chair. I imagine that sleeping with her would be more than just duct taping a leak. Even in the darkness of the room, I think she can see the twinkle in my eye. I can feel her feeding on it.

For the first time in my life, I want very genuinely to give over the keys.

"It's crazy isn't it?"

She starts up again and I reach over across bare oak table and take her hand into mine.

"What's crazy?"

"How quickly things can change."

The drop of melancholy in her voice falls into the ocean of it inside me, and I enjoy the small ripples petering out at the very tips of my fingers.

I want to tell her about Franz, about everything that has happened to me. Not yet. I want her to see all that I have done, and to absolve me.

But I cannot.

And she cannot.

Not yet.

Perhaps not at all.

No, just, not yet.

"Yes, things do change very quickly, but I think change is often for the better, Joanie."

We exchange a smile.

"So why now Marcus?"

"What do you mean?"

She looks at me expectantly with pursed lips and narrowed eyes.

I sigh.

"I've been skipping rocks for too long."

She smiles at me and sips her wine without breaking eye contact.

"And now you've happened upon a stone too precious to throw?"

She puts a finger to her temple and smiles her crooked smile. Her lips are curved with skepticism. Her teeth are brilliant.

She wants to believe me. I am almost there.

"Yes. I want to pocket it."

She smiles again, the fantastic smile I have so long coveted.

I smile back.

"With a mouth like yours, you could run for office someday."

I look at her intensely. She holds my gaze and the smile fades from her face. She gives my hand a squeeze and I become conscious of her smell, and the softness of her skin. Without taking her eyes off of me, she asks:

"So then, you're done?"

I think of everything before this moment and a twinge runs up my spine, exploding in the center of my skull.

Am I done?

How can I be done?

I wince.

"Yes."

Her eyes reflect doubt.

"Yes?"

I anticipate the twinge this time and numb it with the whiskey.

"Yes."

I mean it.

Her eyes are glossy, though not as glossy as the first time we met. She always looks on the verge of tears.

"And how about you Joanie... are you done?"

She sips her wine carefully and replies thoughtfully, focused on my hand resting gently in hers:

"Yes."

We sit there hand in hand for a moment or two. When the waiter comes by, I ask for the cheque. Joanie takes her shawl off and the sight of pale bare skin excites me. I watch her intently as she struts over to the women's washroom.

I pay the bill while she's in there. When she returns to the table, we finish the last few drops of our drinks.

"Do you think we're really ready?"

She asks with a hint of concern.

"For what?"

The reassuring grin on my face helps to lighten her doubts.

"To get old?"

Her eyes glow with enthusiasm.

"Does that really happen overnight?"

She caresses my arm.

"No."

She looks up at me.

"But I do think it stems from a conscious decision."

I help Joanie get her jacket on, and I put my arms firmly on her shoulders. I slowly move them down around Joanie's waist. I lean around her and kiss her on the cheek, tasting the vulnerability of her soft delicate skin, and I hold her hand tenderly. With both of us looking forward, I answer:

"Well, in that case, yes. We're ready."

She turns to look at me over her shoulder and smiles, her eyes heavy with great hope. I put a hand to her soft face and lean in to kiss her, my eyes blissfully closed.

'Violet Overcome by White'

Hector drives directly to the apartment. I am sweating lavishly, heaving, still frantic forty-five minutes after the fact. Hector's impassive face calms me a little. It doesn't seem as though he suspects a thing. Death is a hazard of crime. Franz simply made a mistake, and that was that.

When we get there, I bring the bag up into the apartment. Hector asks for his share immediately, so I count up the bag. There is a little over seven thousand dollars in the bag, in random denominations. The bills aren't bound so it takes us a while to figure things out. I give Hector an even thousand, and he helps me move the furniture out of the apartment. I throw everything out. The CD's, the books, the vinyl- everything goes in the dumpster. Hector helps me move the ash-stained couch onto the curb, where I am certain it will be picked up. Even the Aphrodite has to go. I think very briefly about keeping it, but decide that's unwise. I need to cut all ties to this place. Anything that has my fingerprints has to go. Anything that suggests I've been here has to go. Anything that reminds me in the least of Franz, even the Aphrodite, has to go. I leave it on the curb with the couch.

There is no documentation linking me in any way to this apartment. Hardly anyone knew I was living here, maybe Jean Marie, maybe Jenna. My name is not on the lease.

Hector lets me stay on his couch for a few days afterwards. It takes me a few days to get back on my feet. The whole thing took a lot out of me. I can't focus. I hardly speak. I stew in self-imposed solitude, dwelling on this vague sense of guilt. I rationalize that I am not responsible, that Franz had it coming to him, that he put himself in that situation, that his big mouth sealed his fate. But my innards often disagree with me.

It's not even that Franz was that important to me, or that I needed him to get by- the truth is I am probably much better off without him. I decide that time and time again. I follow the logical train of thought that leads me to the fact that I am better off without him over and over, until I finally accept it.

It's not that I feel so much sentimental in a way that longs for Franz, or regrets deeply that Franz is gone. It's more of a paralyzing sensation of unprecedented numbness.

I don't cry or anything, in the apartment while we gut it, or even at Hector's. I think that maybe I should. I think I should let things out -vent- but I can't.

I don't leave Hector's apartment for a week. I don't even get up off the couch for the first two days. I just lie there and smoke cigarettes. I don't even bother to take my shoes off. The duffel bag sits in the entrance, and I watch it for a while every day. I half expect it to get up and leave. That bag is what Franz's life amounted to. He died for it.

Hector brings me food, taking money out of the bag to pay our meals, and I don't complain. He lets me smoke cigarettes on the couch. I don't know how he does it, but he doesn't skip a beat. The day after the heist, he goes back to work at the garage as if nothing has happened.

Really, though, nothing has.

It takes two weeks until I feel completely depleted and I absolutely have to go back out into the world again. For the most part, I have been sitting around staring at the walls, at the duffel bag, stewing in emotions I can't really describe.

After two weeks, I feel safer. I think I would have heard from the police by now.

Still, there is some bizarre mental block.

I wonder where he is, now that he's gone.

Heaven, hell, purgatory, nothingness?

The void?

I'll inevitably wind up there myself.

Then life sweeps me up again, and I have to forget about it and move on.

Dwelling, like worrying, is a waste of time.

I am still young.

I am too young to stop.

I work up the courage to spend the money.

I leave Hector's for good and move into a nice three and a half in the plateau, about ten minutes outside of the city center. I find a really great place, with an exposed brick wall and an island in the kitchen. It's very chic. Naturally, it is a lot more expensive. So I find a real job because I know that the cash I am sitting on will eventually dry up, and life cannot be lived without income.

I tell myself that life is shaped by the conscious decisions one makes. So I make the conscious decision to let life be simple. After all, life is very simple, if one is willing to let it be. At the end of the day, I am in control of the variables that enter my life. I am in control of my headspace. I am in control of what needs to be foregrounded and back grounded, and I need to exercise this control to get myself back on track. I am the architect of my own destiny, and I am going to work at building something worthwhile. I am ready.

It takes me just a week to find a real job. I pass the interview process with flying colors, with the help of convincingly expressed timeless banalities like: 'I am punctual, I love to work hard, I can see myself growing with the bank.' I also wear expensive cologne and a tie to the interview. They offer me a full-time position as a customer service representative.

It pays well, offers excellent benefits, and provides a stable mold. It is simple, and repetitive. The office is in the city center. I take the metro there every day.

I am placed in a cubicle by the office kitchenette. I can hear the blender go off every time an employee on a health kick makes a smoothie. I can also hear the murmurs of office gossip as the employees take their little coffee breaks.

The office is gray. The walls of my cubicle are gray. The carpeting on every floor is gray. The telephone I make calls with is gray. Most of the employees have gray hair.

My cubicle is equipped with a telephone, a computer, pens and paper, folders, and a few drawers full of paperclips and highlighters. The day's work is delivered every morning at eight in the form of a neat stack of folders, dossiers, and documents. I answer the phone and have mindless conversations all day. 'Yes sir, let me just pull up your account information'. 'Well, unfortunately, that's the best I can do for you today, sir.' The mail cart bumps into the back of my chair as it makes its rounds at about ten in the morning every day. The poor sap pushing it suffered a stroke, and the left half of his face is paralyzed. He looks as though half his face is melting, and the other half is molded into a permanent grimace. He wears a white shirt and a pocket protector. His shoes are scuffed.

I try hard, though, not to pay any mind to any of that. I sit next to the other suited nine-to-fivers, smile when appropriate, and nod politely when others speak to me. I laugh at the corny jokes the office squares make. 'See you later alligator'. 'In a while crocodile'. Wink and finger point. I am very civil with the clientele and keep my calm. I am very professional. Optimism. There is always more optimism. Someone shits on you because they missed a payment, and you come back with so much optimism that they can't help but have a good day.

It takes some practice, sure, but I eventually master what I thought I could never do- I learn to turn my brain off for eight hours a day. And funny enough, I find that I quite enjoy the silence.

When I get home from work, I do what the others do. I watch television. I watch whatever the majority of the office watches, so that I'll have something to contribute by the water cooler. The hot show right now is a sitcom about a dim-witted group of young professionals making their way in the big city. Many of the scenes take place in a bar. The jobs they work are almost irrelevant to the plot.

I buy cheap suits and iron them weekly.

I have one navy blue one- it is my favorite- that I wear every second day. I also have a charcoal suit, and a black suit.

My boss tells me that it isn't necessary to wear a suit every day, but I reply that I think it makes an impression. That answer makes him smile.

I open an investments portfolio. Oh, nothing too extravagant, just some low-risk mutual funds. Most of my investments are concentrated in low-risk low-yield bonds. I have a percentage of my earnings funneled into them bi-weekly. I hope that they will eventually grow enough so that I, or Joanie and I, can one day buy a house.

And yes, I get the girl!

In spite of, or perhaps thanks to my daily boredom, I get the girl.

Well, sort of.

Joanie and I go on a few nice dates and get to know each other better. A romance novel can easily be written about our first few weeks together. They are so rosy, and sweet. We have butterflies around each other, are both so nervous, and even stumble when we speak. My heart races when I'm with her, and honestly, life is fantastic. Things are beautiful behind the rose colored lens, really. I have money in my pockets. I'm not worrying about paying rent, or struggling to muster up the money I need to satisfy my wants. Everything is above board. And best of all, I'm not chasing meaningless sex anymore. I'm not really chasing anything anymore! I am stable, I am constant, and I am predictable.

I am happy!

For that little while, I taste something I never have before, and I truly do think it is happiness. For the first time in my life, I feel that my wheels are on a track. And that eases things for me. I am in cruise control. It gives me a great sense of direction, and an even greater sense of purpose.

Taking care of the bank's customers is a necessary task. And I execute this task. I am necessary. I execute a necessary task.

But things are going too well.

My legitimacy, and acceptance into society, and my happiness with Joanie all let my guard down, for the first time in a long while. I exhale and stop thinking. I let myself go for the first time in a long while. It feels as though a weight has been lifted from my shoulders, and my life really does take on a new meaning. It's like a cloud has been lifted, and I am emerging from a mist. I am resurfacing from muddled waters. I am a flower in bloom. All of the clichés apply.

I never, ever think of Franz, or of anything that is behind me. I just don't have the time. I am too busy. It isn't that difficult to keep busy, what with all the new responsibilities being thrown my way, occupying my time, and filling my headspace. I am not just coping- hell, I am thriving!

I am on cloud nine.

But I am flying too close to the sun.

It happened on a Friday afternoon in May. The exact date must be available somewhere in the papers. It's not important. I've been building to this moment. I've been trying to explain it.

I still don't know that I have.

But here goes.

It is Joanie's last week in school and her last day of classes before exams. She's graduating. And I am so proud of her. My heart is gushing with love for her. We are on our way.

She finishes class at three in the afternoon on this particular Friday. I decide to leave work at noon so that I can surprise her at school. Seeing as it is a Friday and I am a punctual and hard worker, the manager gives me the go ahead. I haven't taken a day off yet. I have been working the job for about a month or so. I want to surprise Joanie at school, to congratulate her, to hug and kiss her. I plan to take her to dinner, and pamper her. I really think she deserves it.

I drive over in my new Toyota. I financed a new Toyota when I started working at the bank. I think I deserved it. I used what was left of the duffel bag as a down payment. I had to get rid of it anyway. It was evidence. The car is modest and dependable. The rest of the money for the payments is taken directly out of my paycheque every month.

I park on Sherbrooke near Crescent, seeing as it is a nice

day. The sun is out and I want to walk over to the campus, and reminisce a little while enjoying the weather. So much has changed in the year since I have graduated. I know her class is in the Hill building on de Maisonneuve and finishes at three. It is maybe two forty when I park and pay the meter.

It is a crisp spring afternoon. I walk up Crescent Street by all the bars. Some of them are already bustling, full with students and professionals who have taken the afternoon off. The terraces are open. It is a comfortable afternoon; just warm enough to make jackets optional.

I am wearing my brown leather jacket, though. It's new, and was a gift from Joanie. I got her one of her own too, so we'd match. It is my favorite jacket. It reminds me of her. We wear them together because we are a team. A unit.

I walk down the street comfortable in casual Friday jeans. I light a cigarette and check my watch. It is two fifty two. I pick up my pace, not wanting to be late, hoping to catch Joanie just as she leaves the building, to surprise her, and light up her beautiful face. I really am excited, and the weather has me in such a great mood.

I walk up de Maisonneuve, still rushing, and I begin to feel pockets of perspiration forming inside the jacket. I get to the corner by the building just in time, two fifty eight, and lean on one of the pillars outside the building, waiting for her. The Hill building houses the arts faculties. The building is white and old, and I look it up and down smoking my cigarette, considering the fact that the arts building is old and decrepit, while the new business building up the street is state of the art.

There is no sign of Joanie, so I light another cigarette.

I smoke my cigarette a while, letting my heart-rate readjust itself, before checking my watch and noticing it's now ten past three, and there's still no sign of Joanie. I chuck my third or fourth cigarette into the street, watching the sparks fly and quickly die as the embers meet the pavement, and walk a little further up the street. I look up at the University's buildings and notice a whole lot of scaffolding. As I light another cigarette, beginning to worry, I think to myself that the fact that everything is always under constant construction drives me insane.

For some reason, I really contemplate the steel scaffolding. It's all along one side of a student apartment complex, and the street is shut down because of the hazard of falling objects. There are *pas de stationnement* signs everywhere. They're the orange kind that the city weighs down with heavy rubber platforms, so that the signs don't get blown away with the wind. I look up and see the sky is very clear today, and the sun is strong. And as I stroll up the street in front of the arts building, I'm struck straight in the eyes by a pupil-penetrating gleam of light that reflects off of the scaffolding.

I turn instinctively to shield my eyes, and I drop my cigarette.

This is the moment. This is the moment when my world implodes.

I catch sight of Joanie across the street, her back against a pillar of the library building, with her arms around Steve's neck. The two are lip locked.

My first reaction is simply one of awe.

It can't be.

No.

I rub my eyes.

She's wearing the leather jacket I bought her. Steve is running his hands all over her. They aren't holding back. She's lapping at his mouth and he's grabbing away at her backside.

And I'm just standing here with my mouth wide open and my chest turning to quicksand.

The street isn't that wide, and my eyesight is pretty good. It is undoubtedly they.

It's over.

This is it.

The final bubble is inevitably bursting.

And images of what could have been flash through my mind. For a while, everything was so damn beautiful. I'd look in her eyes and put a hand to her soft cheek, or behind her beautiful neck and I would kiss her with everything I had because our souls were connected. And touching something so raw was overwhelming but in a good way. She would help me forget. She would make it go away.

I have done everything right!

It isn't fair!

I have fallen into line!

And just like that, it is gone.

I watch Steve handle everything I have ever wanted like a throwaway plaything. His tongue slithers around inside my salvation, cheapening it to sin, eradicating any chance I ever had to see the light. Shattering my hopes of normality. And the scorching sap of betrayal seeps thick through the shock.

Once the awe wears off- it wears off pretty quick- the next sensation that sets in is one of a giant vice slowly tightening, pulverizing my chest cavity. I just stand there a while with my mouth open, short of breath, luxuriating in the very distinct agony only swift and fully penetrating heartbreak can provide.

The machinery in my mind is malfunctioning.

And they don't stop. Across the street, I mean. They start getting into it even heavier. I watch him slowly move his hands down her back and caress her soft, shapely backside.

Oh, Joanie! She always had the sweetest little backside! A perfect little peach! So ripe, so tempting! I am not ashamed to say, I would succumb to taking a little bite every now and then...

I think it is once the self-pitying stops- I can't really tell how long I stand there, time stands still from my perspective- that I snap.

I rush across the street, oblivious to traffic, with my fists clenched. Cars honk, and cyclists slam their brakes and scream obscenities at me.

In close, I can see that they both have their eyes closed and I stand there a little while, smelling the pollution in the air and taking in the sounds of the city back grounding the sickeningly amplified sounds of lips sinfully smacking.

I grab Steve by the shoulders and violently rip him off of Joanie.

His eyes widen in surprise and he exclaims:

"Holy shit Marc-"

My fist is already in flight as he processes the quick change from lost in lust to what I presume would be frozen in fear. And I hit him hard in the jaw just as the words leap from his tongue and he wavers, staggering backward several steps but not falling.

I raise my arm again in attack and Joanie steps in, frantically screaming:

"Marcus, no, stop!"

I can't see her face, which is probably best because I am already blind with rage. Joanie chooses to intervene by foolishly coiling herself around my raised arm, leaving me no choice but to slap her fiercely across the face, disorienting her and sending her to the ground.

I do regret hitting Joanie.

Steven composes himself and lunges toward me while I have my back turned, punching me in the back of the head. The impact of the punch sends me to the ground, dizzied, and he attempts to mount me to continue his attack. The weight of his body over mine pushes me into the pavement and the pain sharpens me. I feel him behind me and instinctually reach for the switchblade in my back pocket, which I swiftly open and thrust in his direction. I feel the steel meet flesh, and then ligament or perhaps bone, and I turn the blade hard before yanking it out.

Steven screams in agony and clutches his leg, falling to the floor. I seize the moment, raising myself from the pavement with the help of my bloodied palms, and mount Steven with the bloodied blade still in hand. He is clutching his thigh, which is bleeding profusely, forming a small puddle of blood on the pavement before the school.

I throw the blade, no longer having any need for it, and deliver a flurry of fifteen or sixteen punches to his face, shrewdly alternating fists so as not to break any knuckles.

And then as I sit above him, I stare down into his bloodied swollen face and just soak it all in. I feel something I have never felt before. I feel... I feel like a God, doling out punishment. The adrenaline surges, then lessens, and I'm overcome by dizziness.

This is where the machinery really starts malfunctioning.

My perception begins undulating between blurred colors and darkness, and I close my eyes.

I suddenly stand in a great, dark forest, on the precipice of an equally dark clearing. Will-o-wisps glow above a thick marsh, and figures move in the shadows. I watch the dark, animated waters flitter and dance as they beckon me to dive. The sounds of solemn incantations and the hazy smell of smoke take hold of my body and I think to myself that I must be hallucinating, but that is not enough to rouse me from the vision. I lean down and grab a handful of dirt, and I can feel the soil wet between my fingertips, and see a worm struggling to wriggle free.

I look deep into the marshy black waters and they call me ever more seductively, drawing me slowly closer. And with a release that elevates me above consciousness, I drop to my knees and let myself fall open armed. Just as I am about to be consumed, I open my eyes to the sky and am stricken by a sharp pain, as the sun above shines straight into my eyes.

I smell fresh blood and soon I hear Steven's awful cries. I look over and see Joanie stir, and feel Steven struggling to free himself from beneath my crushing weight. I can hardly comprehend what is happening. There are reverberations in my head trapping me in an emotional tremolo from which I cannot escape, and so I let out a scream, a primal scream louder and longer and more powerful than the culmination of everything I have ever done. And I look up to the clear azure sky, with marshmallow clouds carelessly drifting, and the sun still shining down upon us, same as it had forever before, same as it would forever after. And I look down at Steven's caved in bloodied face and I feel an unbelievable high.

I feel it.

I am superior, elevated, *entitled*.

I feel it.

I rise up off of Steven's prostrate body, now feeling quite serene, and notice my jacket is ripped around the arms. I remove it and toss it to the ground by Joanie. Joanie shuffles over to Steven, whimpering at the sight of what I have done. Steven looks at her and I think I see a hint of relief in his eyes.

So, with my solid leather boots on, I kick Steven on the side of the head.

Joanie screams, but his body stops stirring.

People are swarming now, and standing in a row, scared little sheep watching me, drawn by Joanie's feminine cries of agony.

I turn and try to look each and every one of them in the eyes, feeding on the fear and uncertainty and worry, and I lunge madly towards them to drive them back. They respond by jolting back with cries of fear that make me laugh out loud. I turn to see Joanie leaning over Steven and holding his hand. Steven doesn't move an inch. His chest is heaving though, so I know he is still alive.

I look down at my hands and contemplate my next move. It can't be more than a few seconds, though it feels much, much longer.

Time ticks slow.

I will it so.

And the idea to sever his head comes to me very strong, like a revelation rising from the depths of my soul to the tips of my fingers and I let the notion carry me, trusting my impulse.

I lift one of the *pas de stationnement* signs from its rubber bottom and stand before Steven's body. Joanie catches sight of my shadow and looks up at me, a beautiful fear like I have never seen further plumps her tear-swollen eyes and I ask her, softly, in my sweetest pillow talk voice:

"Would you move over sweetheart?"

I raise the sign atop my head, with no one to stop me, and bring it down with full force on Steven's neck. The impact is hard, but muffled, and gamey. Like trying to cut very thick nervy putty with a makeshift axe. And the first blow is not enough. The sign only penetrates about halfway.

I hear the gasps and screams of onlookers, though none of them does a thing but watch the blood spurt out from his neck, watching as much in horror as in entertainment as I execute an 'innocent' man. The distinct agony in Joanie's cries pierces through the other noise.

"Marcus please!"

She sounds far off in the distance. I can only focus on the stream of red flowing from the neck and the task I have to complete.

And I raise the sign once more, and bring it down with full force, muscles bulging with full exertion. This time I hear the thud of steel against the pavement.

But still, the head is not completely severed. There is one stubborn ligament, or nerve ending, I don't know I'm not a doctor and everything looks pretty much the same coated thickly in crimson, that holds the head to the body. The eyes are vacant, though.

I smile.

I shake my head and stare at the ligament for a sagging second, lamenting the imperfection of the universe. And then I summon all the energy I have left to bring the sign down one final time, rectifying this imperfection, and ending the uncertainty.

And then, I sit down.

The thought of running does not occur to me. Why should I run? It isn't too much longer before the sirens blare, but I don't run.

I sit down beside the body, and beside Joanie, stroking her beautiful hair with my bloody hands, and a sickly smile on my face. The adrenaline flowing through my veins numbs me all over. There is a standing ovation going off in my head, as I stare at Joanie's horrified face and watch her mouth screams of agony I cannot hear. I watch the rest of her face become contorted by horrible emotion. And I watch it as it gives up and goes catatonic. The ovation in my head, the screams, and the sirens melt into a really beautiful angelic echo ringing and ringing and ringing throughout infinity.

When the police pick me up, I don't resist. I know the drill. Though they rough me up a little bit more this time due, I think, to the heinousness of my crime.

***

I found out later that Joanie and Steve had been in contact since the party where we all met. They were together that time I saw her at the casino. She had been leading a double life.

It was all an illusion, Joanie and me. All of it was an illusion, really. Joanie is probably receiving her own psychiatric care somewhere, on the outside, though it comforts me to think that she probably still wakes up in a cold sweat from time to time. I can hear her scream in agony sometimes, in my sweetest dreams.

There are a few last details I should probably relay...

The trial went as expected. The trial was never the point,

though. They condemned me like simple-minded fools. I knew they wouldn't understand the beauty of what I had accomplished. How could they?

They assigned me a public defender for the trial, and he was an absolute buffoon.

I was certain to end up in jail.

So I took my fate into my own hands.

I acted absolutely insane. I slapped a glass of water off of the table while the prosecutor was speaking, broke out in fits of barking or violent screams, then went completely catatonic for an hour or two.

I began bawling in court at one point, and stood, screaming over the judge, and delivered an articulate speech about the soul needing to be cleansed through the eyes. 'For tears are the byproducts of the purge, and cleanse the soul of all bad breeding! But what of the man who summons sensation? When everything has become a trifle, flattened, so that he can pick sadness or redemption, fear or triumph from the shelf like produce? What are we to make of the man who cannot be left to himself, who must constantly seek change and novelty, for to face himself is to face emptiness, and feel the fall and have no feet on the ground? Bleak, your honor, are shallow waters, and the overwhelming desire to swim!'

And then I sat back down and began barking at the top of my lungs for ten minutes straight until the bailiff was forced to restrain me with a sedative. At one point, I was brought before the judge with a muzzle. I thrashed madly, refusing to sit still.

Eventually, I got what I wanted.

The judge deemed me unfit to stand trial.

And that, pretty much, is how I got here.

They call this place Riverside, though I can't say that I've ever seen the river.

I guess it's a comforting mental image though, to think that I'm by a river. Rivers flow, rivers renew, and rivers cleanse. *Renouvellement*. You can never step in the same river twice, so the saying goes. I think it is an apt metaphor for a deranged mind.

Life is best lived in the company of comforting mental images.

I haven't seen much of anything, really, while I've been here. Mostly just white rooms, and white tunics. The constant smell of antiseptic sterilizes the mind the same way its sting sterilizes the flesh.

I've had lots of time to think, though...

There are so many questions I wish I could answer.

Was I insane all along? Did I become insane? Was it a momentary thing? Was latent insanity brought out of me through circumstance? Was I predisposed to it genetically? Am I even insane?

The doctors here throw the word psychosis around like pop stars do the word love.

What even constitutes someone as a psychopath? Is it the ability to conjure catharsis at will? The ability to fake emotion? Is it maybe the ability to repress emotion until it can no longer be felt?

Please.

That wouldn't leave much room for sanity.

What *I* think, is that as humans, we are cast into the fray with nothing but an inborn propulsion to rise.

And our lives are lived reckoning the question: rise to what?

Power?

Control?

Omniscience?

I don't know. I'm too young to have this figured out.

Seeing as my arms are tied, I'm going to have to trust that this has all been transcribed as I've dictated it. The doctors here say coming to terms with what has led me here is the first step to my recovery. Though I'm not so sure recovery is the game plan.

Enlightenment comes at a price.

Besides, I like it here. It's calm. And I finally get to be alone.

I don't know if anyone would listen to a 'madman', but *I know* my experiences have made me wise.

So, to anyone out there who may be reading this, and who may not be certain of the path, I'd like to offer this consolation.

I have sought long and hard, and found but one *truth* thus far.

That *truth* is simple.

It is this: that freedom, *true* freedom, is a white-walled room of infinite canvas.